UNWELCOME GHOST

HAUNTED EVERLY AFTER MYSTERIES
BOOK ELEVEN

REGINA WELLING
ERIN LYNN

Willow Hill
BOOKS

CONTENTS

UNWELCOME GHOST

CHAPTER ONE

$\mathcal{I}$t had been four months, twelve days, and seven hours since I'd seen a ghost. That might not sound like much to you, but to me, it was the equivalent of being wined and dined by my favorite celebrity, buying a winning lottery ticket on the way home, then enjoying a spectacular night with my fiancé on a bed made of clouds. And chocolate.

I should have known it wouldn't last.

A spate of unseasonably warm weather for the beginning of May in Maine had generated a thick mist over the entire town of Mooselick River. The damp morning air turned my red curls into a frizzy mess as I stood on the porch of one of the rental properties I managed. The creaky old farmhouse needed some work before the next tenant could move in, but like most places in our quaint little town, it was charming in its own way. I glanced at my watch impatiently, wondering if I'd have time to run out for a coffee before I had to pay the plumber. He was an hour into unclogging the main septic drain, and from the sounds of things, it wasn't going well.

When I heard tires crunching toward me on the short

gravel road, I couldn't think who would have come out here. This was the most remote of my boss, Leo Hansen's, rental properties, and with the thick mist lending a creepy atmosphere, the one I least wanted to spend a spooky morning at.

I thought the plumber had called for reinforcements, but the vehicle that appeared out of the fog didn't belong to the plumber's helper.

"Everly Dupree!" a familiar voice called out the window of a dark green pickup truck with the Evergreen Christmas Tree Farms logo on the door.

"What are you doing way out here?"

Patrea Evergreen, my best friend and attorney, climbed out of the driver's seat and went around to the other side to retrieve a takeout tray with two large coffees. She handed one to me as she came up the steps.

"Bless you." The first sip burned my tongue, but I didn't care.

She'd let her hair grow long since her wedding and now had it pulled back to frame a lean and determined face. "You're welcome. I'm tracking you down. What else? You'll never guess what I've done now."

"You're pregnant?"

Her eyes lit with humor. "Not yet. That's only just gone past the discussion phase. Give me a minute."

"Then I guess I'm out. Just tell me," I raised an eyebrow. "I hate guessing games but can't resist a good mystery. Spill the details."

"Okay, okay," she grinned. "You know how much I love fixing up old houses, right?"

"Of course," I replied, smiling at her enthusiasm. "I think everyone in town knows that about you by now, so it's not exactly the shock to my system you were expecting."

"Then you won't be surprised to hear I've bought another one."

"Which?" I ran over the list of vacant homes. There were far fewer of them than when I moved back to town, and in some small part, I liked to think that was my doing. Mine and Martha Tipton's, anyway. We'd worked hard to begin bringing tourism back to our tiny town and, as a result, had slowed the exodus of people moving away to find better jobs.

"Wentworth mansion."

My chin hit my chest. Wentworth mansion had been empty for years. Decades, even. The place was shrouded in mystery. "How? I didn't think it was up for sale. Did you sacrifice a goat or something?"

"Ew. No." Patrea mounted the porch steps on long legs. Even in a simple pair of jeans and a sweatshirt, she gave off an air of elegance that I envied. After an hour's worth of toilet plunging before I gave up and called in a professional, I was a sweaty mess. No comparison. "But I was as surprised as you are when I got the letter accepting a cash offer that, between us, was just my opening bid. I expected to wear the owners down and pay at least thirty percent more. I just picked up the keys." She dangled them in front of my face.

The sound of booted feet on hardwood floors interrupted the conversation. Once we'd moved out of the way so the plumber could get to his vehicle and haul back some weird-looking machine, Patrea started up where she'd left off.

"Here's the thing—it's supposedly haunted." She paused for dramatic effect, watching my reaction closely. "I thought you might want to check it out with me, given your...unique skillset."

My curiosity piqued, I couldn't help but wonder about the lingering spirits that might dwell within the mansion's walls. Was someone trapped there, unable to move on? Or were they simply content to remain in a place that held memories of happier times?

"I'm on a ghost-free streak," I mused, tapping my chin thoughtfully. "Do I really want to yank the lid off that can of worms again? Besides, half the houses in town are said to be haunted—including mine. It isn't, so this one might not be haunted, either."

"You know you want to. Be honest, how tight is your worm can lid on, anyway?" Patrea wasn't above pushing for what she wanted. "I haven't even been inside yet. I bought it based on the limited view when I peeked in the windows. We could explore it for the first time together."

"I've always wanted to get a look inside that place." I was going with her. She knew it, and so did I. "The owners moved away before I was born. I'm surprised you haven't heard the stories before. The mansion figures highly in town legends."

"Right?" Patrea exclaimed, clapping her hands together. "Think of the history, the stories... and if there really are ghosts, who better to help them than you?"

"True," I agreed, feeling a mix of excitement and trepidation. Ghosts could be unpredictable, but my empathetic nature made it difficult to turn away from those in need - living or otherwise.

"You win," I sighed with mock exasperation, unable to resist her infectious enthusiasm. "I'll come take a look at this allegedly haunted mansion of yours. But first, I need to deal with the very real, very mundane issue of a stopped-up toilet drain."

"Deal," she said, grinning widely. "I'll wait with you. And then, adventure awaits!"

"Adventure indeed," I murmured, wondering what secrets and challenges the old mansion held in store for us.

Banging and grinding noises combined with the clatter of an electric motor drew us both to the upstairs bathroom, where the plumber had removed the toilet and stuck some sort of cable down the drain.

"You've got some scale in the pipes leading out to the septic," he said and showed me the footage from the camera at the end of the line. "Most people use plastic nowadays, but this is cast iron. I'm using the rooter to grind the scale away. Everything goes well, it should be good for another few years."

"Grind or hammer?" Patrea raised her voice to be heard.

"A little of both, I guess." The plumber responded to her smile, then turned back to me as I watched the little blade on the end of his line destroy the alien landscape of jagged stalagmites inside the metal pipe.

The noise was hideous, and the banging shook the entire house, but it only took fifteen minutes to break through the blockage. He spent ten more flushing out the debris with water, then another five gathering his tools. That step would have taken longer, but Patrea volunteered to help. She paced the porch while I paid the bill.

With the plumbing crisis finally resolved, I put her out of her misery. Exploring an old mansion with Patrea would be far more fun than spending the rest of the day cleaning up after sloppy tenants, and I had two weeks to get that done before the next family moved in. I made a show of locking up and checking my phone for messages in case any new crisis had arisen. None had.

"All right," I said to Patrea as I pocketed my phone, "it looks like I'm free for the rest of the day. Let's go look at your newest project."

"Fantastic!" she exclaimed, her eyes twinkling with anticipation. "I promise you, Everly, it'll be a day to remember. Ride with me. I'll bring you back to pick up your car after."

As I climbed into the passenger seat of Patrea's trusty pickup truck, anticipation shivered through me. After months of wanting to be rid of it entirely, I'd embraced and welcomed the full extent of my psychic ability only to have it, or maybe just the ghosts of Mooselick River, abandon me. Perhaps today would turn that tide.

The advancing day had burned off most of the fog as we wound along the narrow country roads that seemed to stretch forever. The sun cast dappled shadows through the canopy of newly burgeoning leaves above us, creating a serene atmosphere that belied the possibly supernatural undertones of our journey.

"Isn't it beautiful out here?" Patrea sighed, her hands gripping the wheel firmly as she navigated the twists and turns of the road. "I love how peaceful it is, away from all the hustle and bustle of town."

"Like you don't live in the country yourself," I teased. Still, I couldn't help but agree. There was something undeniably calming about being surrounded by nature, if only for a short while. I revised that opinion a minute later when the seat belt bit my shoulder as Patrea braked hard to keep from hitting the doe that darted across the road in front of us. Through the open windows, we heard a squirrel chattering in disapproving tones from its perch in the branches overhead.

"I know, right? Who ever thought I'd become a farmer's wife? I'm still getting used to all of this nature stuff, and you don't see deer every day," she grinned, her eyes twinkling with mischief. "Just like you don't see haunted mansions every day."

"True," I conceded, my thoughts returning to the task at hand. As the road began to climb, I felt an odd sensation in the pit of my stomach – a tingling that seemed to grow stronger as we drew closer to our destination. Probably just anticipation.

"Almost there," Patrea announced, her voice filled with excitement.

"There used to be a turnaround right there. Just the spot for parking after a date," I replied, pointing to the side of the road. "I haven't been out this way in years. I'm curious to see if it looks like I remember."

Since the Wade family lived nearby, Jacy and I had often ridden our bikes out to the old mansion when we were kids. On lazy summer days, with warm breezes stirring our hair, we'd sit on the front steps, blow dandelion clocks or weave daisy chains, and invent outlandish stories about the people we assumed once lived there.

"You've been here before. What do you know about the house?"

"Not much more than I've already said. The house has been empty for as long as I can remember, and there's no real mystery to that, as far as I know. Mrs. Wentworth got sick and couldn't handle the cold weather anymore, so they moved away and left the house to their kids. The kids had other plans, so it's been empty ever since."

"Mildly disappointing as far as stories go. How's the wedding planning going?" She changed the subject.

Her question elicited a heavy sigh. "Not good. I was going to call you today and talk about it. I think this wedding is cursed. First, the invitations had to be redone because they spelled my name wrong, and it looked like

Drew wanted to marry Every Dupree instead of Everly Dupree. My father took exception, and my mother used language she never uses."

"Tough break. What printer?"

"That's the thing. It was the one I usually use, so Mom gave me a hard time about not taking her advice. But that's not all." Letting out another sigh, I brushed my hair back off my face. "The woman we hired to do the alterations had a minor fire at her shop. They saved the building, and no one was hurt, but all the dresses suffered smoke and water damage. Ours were all ruined."

Patrea winced. "That's some spectacularly bad luck."

"You haven't heard the worst of it."

"Good grief. There's more? The woman didn't have insurance?"

"No. She did. She's getting reimbursed, and so are we. The worst is that I called the shop and asked if we could just reorder the same dresses in our sizes, but the bridesmaid line is sold out, and you know the deal with my dress."

"One of a kind."

Not that I'd commissioned it. Nope. Someone else ordered it to their exact specifications and then decided they didn't like it. If the look on the dress shop owner's face had been anything to go by, that someone had been a picky pain in the butt. She'd found fault with what I considered perfection. But none of that mattered now. The dress was gone, and not only did we need to go shopping soon, but we needed to find things that fit well enough not to need much sewing. So much for feeling fortunate we'd hit it out of the park at the second shop. I should have known luck like that wouldn't last.

"On the plus side, Mrs. Damson offered to do the alterations for us. She was at the library when the call came in and witnessed a rare Kitty Dupree meltdown."

"Including more swear words?"

"Apparently."

"So that means we have to go dress shopping again. Tragic. Don't worry. We'll find something just as good. Maybe even better. I heard of this place in Port Harbor called Bridal Heaven. It's supposed to be magical."

"It's just that I feel bad asking everyone to take another day off for something we've already done. And then there will be more fittings, too." A heavy sigh gusted out of me.

When Patrea slammed on the brakes again without warning, I pitched forward. The queen of cool was not feeling the chill, but I did when she turned to glare at me.

"I just showed up and hijacked you from work, did I not?"

"Yes." I was almost afraid to answer.

"And do you resent me for asking?"

"No. I'm excited to see the house."

"Then what makes you think your nearest and dearest will quibble over another chance to go dress shopping for your big day? I'm speaking for all of us when I say that if you start dropping apologies all over the place, we will make you pay." The threat came with a narrow look that got her point across quite well.

I held up my hands in surrender. "Okay. I won't apologize. We will shop, and we will buy new dresses, and we will have fun."

"Damn straight, we will." Relenting, she hit the gas and left a cloud of dust in her wake.

CHAPTER TWO

_A_s we rounded the final bend, the old mansion loomed above us like a grand but weary sentinel. Peeling paint and ivy snaking up the trim marred the once-elegant facade. Sunlight glittered off the shards of two broken windows, but otherwise, it looked as solid as ever.

"Wow," I breathed, suddenly aware of the tingling sensation intensifying in my fingertips.

"Isn't it amazing?" Patrea enthused, pulling the car to a stop. "According to my research, it was built in 1910 in a blend of Beaux-Arts and Mediterranean Revival styles. What's more, it was designed by the same architect who did David's Inn. I'm still annoyed with him for snapping that one up before I could."

"David didn't so much snap that one up as Martha forced it on him. I could probably hook you up with her if you wanted to lend a hand during the next event. Martha's always looking for fresh meat...I mean helpers." I might have only been half teasing. "You tell her you're looking for project houses. I'm sure she'll fix you right up."

"I think I'm good." Patrea shrugged and grinned. "Getting tangled up with Martha's more your thing than mine. I don't have your patience with people like her. Buying this place goes a long way toward mitigating my annoyance. It's a Gilded Age beauty. Those Doric columns on the sunroom get me all hot and bothered."

"Does Chris know you're cheating on him with architecture?"

Patrea grinned. "After the profit I made on the last restoration, he says he's willing to share me. Just imagine what she'll look like once we restore her to her former glory."

"Her? She's a girl house? I asked, stepping out of the vehicle.

"All houses are girl houses. They're like cars."

"But why?"

"I don't know." Patrea gave me a look. "It's a thing. Can we get on with it? I'm dying to see the inside."

We took a moment to survey the grounds. Despite the disrepair, the tender greens of spring lent an undeniable charm to the property. It was too bad the hyacinths had already lost their blooms, but an ocean of cheerful daffodils spread around the house's feet. I also recognized early azalea and lilac bushes that needed some pruning. Still, the pops of color reminded me of the embroidered hem of Grammie Dupree's favorite house dress.

I couldn't shake the feeling that we weren't alone as we approached the front door. Not unexpected since everyone said the place was haunted, and I could see ghosts, but I didn't see any of the usual signs.

It could have been my imagination.

Wishful thinking? Probably.

"Ready?" Patrea asked, her eyes sparkling with excitement as she fumbled with the key. A resounding creak echoed as the heavy wooden door swung open, revealing a dusty, dimly lit foyer. A strong sense of hope swept over me as we stepped inside. It made me giddy and dizzy for a few seconds, then dissipated.

Glancing left and right, Patrea searched and found a bank of light switches on the wall to her left. "The power was supposed to be turned on this morning."

Dim light flared when she used the side of her hand to flick them all on at once. I looked up at the chandelier hanging over my head, noted the strings of dust and cobwebs hanging from it, and shuddered. Of the ten bulbs, only three had lit.

"Better put new bulbs on that list I know you're already running in your head," I warned. "Lots of bulbs. This place is huge." My voice echoed off barren walls and windows so filthy you could barely see out. The undeniably grand style of the mansion seemed out of place in the humble environment of Mooselick River.

Gold and white tile marched in a diamond pattern through the foyer, past the base of a spectacularly curved staircase, through an arched doorway to create a path down the hallway beyond. What a showpiece this must have been back in its heyday. No wonder Patrea wanted to bring the house back to life.

"There's a sitting room over here," Patrea practically danced toward a nearby doorway. "One look in the windows, and I knew I had to buy this place. You'll see why."

Outlined by dusty drapes that might have once been red but were now faded to pink, three large windows with arched transoms soared from floor to ceiling along the far wall. Directly across from them, a scenic mural spread across three panels that mimicked the shapes and sizes of the windows.

"I'll have to get Neena out here to look at this painting. It needs cleaning and repair. Maybe a little touch-up here and there."

"You're keeping the mural? Most people would paint over it."

"Are you kidding? It's a piece of whimsy that's greatly needed in a house this size. I plan to build my color scheme around it and make this a nice, cozy space."

"Cozy? How do you plan to pull that off in a room big enough to park a tank?"

"It won't feel big once the ceiling is painted. I'm thinking of something on the gray side with strong blue overtones. A soothing color that should offset all this white trim quite nicely."

"You're leaving the molding white? I thought painted trim was an affront to your sensibilities," I joked.

"Not in this case." Patrea took me seriously. "Beaux-Arts style carries a strong sense of the eclectic, so while there might be a room or two that feature wood tones, most of the trim would have been painted to match the decorative plaster."

"Decorative plaster?"

"Sure." Patrea directed my attention to the smooth arch that curved from wall to ceiling. "There's a ton of it. In the days before we had flexible plywood, they built these deep cove moldings by adding cloth and wire as a base, slathering on a thick layer of plaster, and then running a template over it to get the final shape. Sort of like when you caulk around a bathtub and use a tool to get an even seam."

"Sounds like a lost art."

"An expensive one, but not entirely lost. Some of this will need a spruce. It's a good thing I know a guy. Or rather, I know a gal who knows a guy."

We wandered through the rooms, each one more lavish than the last. Despite decades of dust and grime, I could still sense the grandeur that once filled these halls. Every corner held a memory, and I tried to tune into the stories they told.

In what I assumed was the dining room, given its size and shape, some of the famous plaster had come loose from its moorings and lay in a crumbled heap on the floor. "Uh oh. That's not good," I said.

Shrugging, Patrea looked up to see more of the molding in danger of falling. "I'll make a call."

"How many bedrooms?" I asked, trying to focus on her renovation plans while also tuning into the lingering energy of the house. It was a delicate balance, but one I'd probably have to refine since ghosts were my life now.

"I'm not sure," she continued, leading me toward the

kitchen at the back of the house. "Just by eye, I'd say it's around six thousand square feet. That's on the small side for a home in this style. A mini-mansion, if you will."

My imagination supplied the delectable scents of holiday cooking and a faint whiff of lavender. I could almost picture the bustling activity that must have once taken place within these walls.

"This," Patrea waved her arm to encompass the room, "will be a chef's dream when I'm done. Six burner range, double wall ovens over there, walk-in freezer, pantry to die for, and a farmhouse sink with a yard of drainboard. It needs tons more cabinets and a butler's pantry in that little nook. I'll match the cabinet colors to the sitting room ceiling to pull both spaces together."

As she described it, the room came to life in my imagination. "What about one of those waterfall islands with space for seating?"

Nodding, Patrea took the suggestion on board. "It would be the perfect spot for the kids to eat breakfast or do their homework while mom or dad cooks a meal. I like it."

"Patrea, this place has so much potential," I said, my voice a mix of admiration and concern. "But we're talking a lot of money that needs spending, and the local housing market's still unstable. Are you sure now is the right time for a big project like this?"

Instead of brushing the question aside and offering reassurance, Patrea's face reddened slightly. "If I said this to anyone else, they'd give me one of those looks, but I know you'll understand. From the first minute I pulled into the drive, I knew something in this house needed me. Or someone?" She gave me a speculative look. "Is there someone?"

I hated to disappoint her. "Not that I've seen so far."

"But you've felt a presence?"

"Don't hate me, but no. Or not really. I don't think. Maybe." When she arched her brow, I sighed and admitted, "I'm getting tingles, but not the type that screams ghost. I'm not sure how this is supposed to work anymore. The process is different since the...half-life incident."

"Different, how?" Her eyes widened with interest, but she didn't seem scared or concerned. While everyone else considered Patrea a down-to-earth attorney type, I knew she had an open mind about the afterlife and a higher-than-average sensitivity to ghosts. She'd warned me once that my house was haunted. She'd been wrong because it wasn't the house ghosts sought out, but the person who owned it. Namely, me. But still, Amber Hale hadn't moved on right away, and Patrea had sensed her in my house.

I shrugged and tried to explain. "Maybe it's not. Before, I only saw ghosts of people if I'd been nearby when their bodies were found. During my unfortunate walk on the wild side, I met several ghosts in town and suspected there were more. Since I got my body back, I haven't seen a single one. I'm not sure why."

Eyes narrowed, Patrea leaned against the kitchen counter. "Do you want to?"

I shrugged again. "I don't know. And that's the truth."

Contemplating, she tilted her head. "I get that. I'm sure it's one of those things that looks a lot more fun from the outside."

See, she did get it.

"I felt something when I came in, but I haven't seen so much as a flicker of ghostly activity. There's probably someone here, but they're not reaching out. Does that bother you at all?"

"I guess not. It all adds to the charm, doesn't it?" She grinned, clearly comfortable with the idea of sharing her future project with spectral roommates. "And in some circles, a resident ghost is a selling point. So long as it's not one like that guy at the furniture store."

"Charm, yes—but also complications," I warned. "If I make contact, I'll feel obliged to help them move on if that's what they want to do. It might not be easy, but I'd have to try. What would that do to your selling point?"

"Ghost or no ghost, and even in the current market, this house will sell itself when I'm done," she assured me, clapping a hand on my shoulder. "I wouldn't force anyone to hang around if they're ready to move on. That would be selfish and unfair."

"Neither of which are words I would use to describe you," I conceded, smiling despite my reservations. "Cranky, yes. Selfish, not so much."

We continued to explore the mansion, discussing various renovation ideas and potential challenges. From repairing a few steps on the grand staircase to modernizing the plumbing, it was clear that Patrea had her work cut out for her. And as for me, well, I knew I'd have my hands full helping her with the work and lending aid to whatever spirits called this place home.

But as I stood there, surrounded by the echoes of lives long past, I couldn't tell if I was excited about the adventure ahead or filled with dread. Sometimes, those emotions feel the same. This old mansion held secrets, and I was determined to uncover them—one ghost at a time.

CHAPTER THREE

inished downstairs, we climbed the main staircase, and I suddenly felt the air shift around us. The temperature dropped a few degrees, and it was as if invisible fingers grazed my arm, sending shivers down my spine. My psychic senses went on high alert.

"Patrea," I whispered, not wanting to startle her. "I might have been premature when I said I hadn't sensed anything spooky here."

"Really?" Patrea's eyes sparkled with curiosity. "Who? What? Where?"

"I'm not sure yet." The sensation grew as she opened the first door on the left. Dark-stained panel molding accented walls painted a deep, masculine green. My imagination supplied the four-poster bed and heavy, antique furniture I assumed had once populated the room. "No painted trim in here."

"Total man cave," Patrea muttered. "Must have been the husband's suite. Any ghosts?"

"Let me try." I closed my eyes, focusing my energy on connecting with any spirits lingering in the house. While I still felt the chill, I sensed no immediate presence. I shook my head. "Not here." And yet, a niggling sense tugged me deeper into the upstairs rooms.

Patrea opened doors ahead of me, glancing into each room and commenting on what she saw. I didn't hear most of it as a tingling sensation drew me toward an oddly placed door on the right. Narrower than the rest, it opened to another staircase. Unable to stop myself, I followed the steps down with Patrea hard on my heels.

We descended, nearly tripping over one another in our haste. At the bottom of the steps was a door. Patrea reached out to open it, but I stopped her, feeling an even stronger flare of hope than before. The emotion seemed to radiate from within the room.

"I'm getting something," I said. "This is a new area for me, and it's hard to explain, but our being here feels like the answer to a prayer."

Patrea nodded and nearly knocked us both down, trying to get past me in the narrow confines. Finally, I pushed open the door and peeked inside. It was a smallish room filled with cast-off items that had either been forgotten or the previous owners hadn't wanted to take with them when they moved, but I had to look twice because my imagination insisted the room should have been bigger. Or different somehow.

A thick layer of dust coated everything. Really, can someone explain how dust gets into a closed house? No one had walked here for a very long time. My heart beat faster as I stepped inside, looking around as if expecting something or someone to appear out of the shadows.

There was no ghostly presence—just an eerie silence that seemed to hang in the air like it was waiting for the curtain to fall and for someone to cue action.

"Hello? Anyone here?" I gave it a shot but got no response.

Still, curiosity drove me to investigate further. Moving quietly around the room, I opened myself up, hoping to make contact.

"Nothing," I said. "But did you notice there's no door down here except for the one we came in? That's a fire hazard, isn't it?"

Shrugging, Patrea turned slowly in place, her gaze raked the room, missing nothing. "Probably." Leaving me alone, she clattered back up the stairs. "Stay there," her voice wafted back down from above. "I'll go back down the front stairs and see if I can figure out where this room is in relation to the rest of the house. Give me a minute and start knocking on the wall so I can orient myself."

"Okay." A strange feeling washed over me as I stood there, listening for Patrea's progress. It started as a tickle at the base of my skull but quickly grew into a full-blown sensation of being watched.

I spun around, but the room was just as empty as before. Even so, the feeling persisted, growing stronger with each passing second. It was as if someone—or something—stood directly behind me, breathing down my neck. Right before I was about to call out to Patrea for help, I heard a sound that made my blood run cold.

It was a whisper, so faint that I almost missed it, just on the edge of my hearing.

"Help me," it said.

I turned around, heart in my throat, to discover I was completely alone in the room.

"Who's there?" I asked, my voice a whisper to match the plea I'd heard.

Silence was my only answer, but the feeling of being watched lingered.

"Are you tapping?" Patrea yelled, her voice coming from closer than I expected. "I don't hear anything."

"I am now." My knuckles connected, but not with aged plaster. This wall sounded and felt newer than that. Well, duh, I thought. This space was closed off later, so they'd have used newer materials. I knocked again, the hollow spaces in the wall making the sound echo slightly.

"Okay, this is weird," her voice sounded faint. "There should be a door here, but there's not. Meet me in the foyer. I need to get something from the truck."

She wasn't gone long, and when Patrea returned, she wore a hard hat, carried a small sledgehammer in one hand, a regular hammer, and a pry bar in the other.

"What are you planning to do with those?"

"Knock a hole in the wall. What else?"

"Should you be doing that?"

Cocking the hat at a rakish angle, she gave me a look. "Why not? It's my place now. This isn't a load-bearing wall, and we agree there should have been a doorway here. I'm curious, aren't you?"

"Duh." I gestured for her to get on with it, and after pulling the hat back down and taking a two-handed grip on the hammer, she did just that. Fine dust filtered into the air with the force of the blow.

"Look at that," Patrea pointed.

"Okay." I did. "What am I supposed to be seeing?" It looked like a sledgehammer-sized hole in a wall to me. "I don't get it."

"That's not lath and plaster. It's drywall, see? This section of wall is made from newer materials."

"Same as the wall at the bottom of the stairs. It's hollow back there, too."

"Hand me the small hammer," Patrea held out a hand like a surgeon waiting for a scalpal. Glancing around, I found it, handed it over, and watched. Beginning at the hole she'd made, she gently tapped in a pattern that expanded a couple of feet in either direction.

"Did you hear where the sound changes to a duller thud here and also over there? That's what? Three and a half feet? Look at every other open doorway in this house. They're all around that size. This was open once. You know I'm right."

I didn't have long to wait before she enlarged the hole and proved her point.

"What did I tell you?" Patrea leaned the sledgehammer against the wall, wiggled her butt, and did a quick spin before pulling out her phone and shining the flashlight into the space. "There's another wall back there. Maybe it's a closet or something."

"Without a door? That's odd, don't you think? Why would anyone build a room without any access?" But it did satisfy my impression that the room behind the wall wasn't the size it should have been.

"People do the weird. Happens all the time." Shrugging, she grabbed the sledgehammer and headed back toward the stairs. "Grab that hammer and pry bar, would you?"

I did as she asked and followed her upstairs and back down to the storage room. "See, there's no door anywhere."

She didn't answer but set the hammer down and contemplated the wall for a long moment. "Oh, I think there is." Stepping forward, she crouched to look closer at the bottom of a shabby-looking wardrobe where a door would have made the most sense.

Regaining her feet, she offered me a delighted grin and took hold of the trim on the left-hand side. One yank and the hutch swung smoothly away from the wall on hidden hinges. "There you go."

What we stepped into wasn't exactly a closet. Patrea shined her light around the space to illuminate the pair of ladderback chairs that were the only things in the room. "What do you think they used it for?"

"Kids playroom, maybe?" The inside walls were finished and painted an off-white color.

"I suppose. It's what? Four feet by six feet. Give or take?"

"Around there." I'd have said the same no matter what

numbers she gave me. Calculating spatial distances isn't one of my strong suits. "I guess."

When she brushed past me, I followed her out and stood beside her while she contemplated the wall with narrowed eyes. "It's all wrong. Why would you make a four-by-six playroom when you could make a four-by-ten playroom?"

I had no answer and assumed it was a rhetorical question. "People do the weird," I parroted her statement back to her.

"Either way, none of this should be here, and it doesn't make sense for the house. I say we knock the whole thing down and open this back up to the main floor like it should be."

"You're hammer happy." I couldn't hold back a grin. "But it's my turn." I beat her to it, grabbed the handle, set my sights on the section of wall to the right of where the doorway should have been, and took a swing. The shock of the blow sang through my muscles. It made me feel powerful. "I guess I can see why you like demolishing things. It's a rush, isn't it?"

On the third blow, the hammer got stuck behind the wallboard. Laughing, Patrea grabbed the handle, braced her foot against the wall, and indicated I should do the same. I did, and on the count of three, we heaved.

It took two tries, and a whole section of the wall came down at once. So did we.

"Are you okay?" I looked over to see Patrea sitting on her butt, her head in her hands, shaking all over. "What?"

I scrambled to my knees and moved closer. "Where are you hurt?"

"I'm not." It was then that I realized she was laughing.

"You scared me," I tried for stern but giggled and ruined it. When I rose to look at the damage we had wrought. What I saw put an abrupt end to the hilarity and made me utter a word that my mother hated. More than once. "You've got to be kidding."

"What?" Patrea joined me, and when her gaze took the same track as mine, she sucked in a breath. "Well, hell."

Through a layer of dust too fine to hide the clear plastic tarp's grisly contents, we saw something unexpected. Nested in tattered remnants of pink silk and wisps of blond hair, the empty sockets of a skull stared back at us.

"You really are a murder magnet."

"Tell me about it." I rolled my eyes. "It has to be murder, though, doesn't it? Women who die of natural causes don't get rolled up in plastic and walled up in a house by accident." Based on the pink silk shrouding them, I assumed the bones belonged to a woman.

Whatever answer Patrea might have made was swallowed up by an inhuman howl that cut right to the bone. Arctic air crept under my clothes to chill my skin as a vaguely human shape rose from the bones and arrowed toward us. Grabbing Patrea, I dropped to the floor and barely avoided making contact with the vibrating energy that blew past us and headed up the stairs.

"What was that?" Patrea's voice finally penetrated the thrum of my heartbeat in my ears. She'd already regained her feet, so she reached down to help me up.

I jumped halfway out of my skin and whirled toward the sound when a voice spoke close to my ear.

"That's the Morgan girl, if I'm not mistaken, and I'm not."

"What?" Patrea said. "Is she here?"

"Someone is, but I don't think it's her."

The ghost wore a maid's uniform and was past middle age but not frumpy. Graying hair was carefully arranged in a bun, and her crisp white apron and cap were spotless. But the most striking thing about her was her eyes. They were so blue that they seemed to glow in the room's dim light. She floated around us, examining the hole in the wall with an air of curiosity and amusement as if she found it all highly entertaining. Every now and then, she would pause to peer at us intently as if trying to make sense of why we were there.

"Hello," I said softly, addressing the spirit. "My name is Everly, and this is my friend Patrea."

The ghost tilted her head in my direction, eyes unblinking. "I'm Charlotte Crane, keeper of this household for more than fifty years."

At first, all I could do was stare at her. Like other ghosts I had seen before, her body didn't glow with unearthly light, and she wasn't transparent. Instead, she looked nearly solid. As though she truly belonged in this room—and maybe even this world—in a way that the living couldn't match.

"We mean you no harm. We're here to help."

"Help?" The maid's voice echoed in the empty room, laced with skepticism. "You're not the help. Where's your uniform?"

"I never said I was the…never mind." Patrea was giving me one of those looks. "It's nice to meet you, Charlotte." To Patrea, I said, "Charlotte is with us. She was the housekeeper here and says the bones belong to a woman named Morgan." I could have added that her hearing wasn't great, but I figured it was too early in the day to piss off a ghost.

"I *am* the housekeeper, and that *is* Vanessa Morgan," the maid corrected me.

"Vanessa Morgan," I repeated for Patrea's benefit.

"Are you simple?" Charlotte said. "You keep repeating yourself."

"Not that I know of. Patrea can't hear you, so I'm just keeping her in the loop."

When Charlotte laid her hand on my wrist, I wanted to brush it off. The sensation wasn't pleasant, but I forgot all about the creepy crawly shudders when Patrea gasped. "I can see her."

"Of course, you can. You didn't think this was my first time around fleshies, did you?" Charlotte demanded.

"Fleshies?" Patrea's eyebrows shot up. "That's what you call the living?"

Charlotte shrugged.

"Is that like a thing?" I hadn't heard the term during my unfortunate dead period. "Among ghosts?"

Charlotte shrugged again.

Exchanging a look with me, Patrea cleared her throat softly. "Do you know what happened to the girl? Is that why you're here?"

"I'm the keeper of this house. Why are you here?" Charlotte's voice boomed. The force sent a cloud of dust into the air.

I stumbled back, nearly tripping over the debris on the floor. "Do you mind?" I gasped.

The ghostly maid didn't look so normal now as she floated in front of me, her pale face illuminated by some inner turmoil. "I've been waiting for someone to find her," she said. "To find out what happened to her. My job is to keep the house in order. Dead bodies do not mean order, and I'm not a detective."

Charlotte's words hung heavy in the air, and the gravity of the situation began to sink in. We weren't just dealing with a blocked-off door and a pile of bones. This was another murder mystery, and we had stumbled upon it completely by accident. But is it an accident if something happens over and over again?

"Neither am I. Not technically, anyway, but I have some experience with murder. Do you have any idea who might have wanted to hurt this Vanessa Morgan?" I asked Charlotte, my voice barely above a whisper.

Charlotte shook her head and began to fade. "Not my job. That's for you to figure out. Mind you wipe your feet."

"Everly?" Patrea's concerned voice pulled me back to the present. "Are you okay? You've gone quiet."

"Sorry," I said, opening my eyes to meet hers. "I was just thinking how much I dread calling Ernie Polk. It's been several lovely months since I've had to dial that number. Why don't you do it? I'd hate to break my streak."

But Patrea stepped back and held her hands up. "Why? So he can arrest me again? Nope."

I rolled my eyes but made the call.

"What's your emergency?" Carole Ann Wilmette sounded like she couldn't have cared less.

"I need to talk to Ernie." A minute too late, I realized I could have called his cell phone. "It's Everly Dupree."

"Who's dead?"

"I'm not sure. Just send him out to the Wentworth place. Tell him he doesn't need to hurry. These bones have been here for years. Another hour or two won't make a difference." Carole Ann was still sputtering when I hung up.

"Okay, that's done. We might as well keep exploring until Ernie shows up."

CHAPTER FOUR

An hour passed with no sign of Ernie's cruiser. Finding Vanessa's bones had put a damper on the fun, but we poked through the master's bedroom closets and cupboards while we waited and added several pages to Patrea's notes.

"If he doesn't show up soon, I'm ordering Berties. Do you think they deliver way out here?"

"Are you kidding?" I grinned. "I wouldn't be surprised if Bruno made the delivery himself just for the chance of seeing inside Wentworth mansion. You make the call. I'll spring for the pizza. Get an extra large so there's enough for Ernie when he arrives."

"House special?"

"That works. Don't forget drinks. I could go for a lemonade. Ernie will want unsweetened iced tea."

"I'm tempted to ask Sal to spit in his tea, but I won't."

"Arrest you once, pay for it forever?" I teased.

"Something like that," she said and made the call.

"Yoohoo!" A woman's voice called out from the doorway. It obviously wasn't Ernie, and we'd barely ordered the pizza.

"Who's that?" Patrea wondered.

"Anybody home?"

"We're upstairs," I called back when I recognized the voice. "I think it's Maryann Payne. She's a real estate agent I met at one of the rental houses. Nice woman. Kind of pushy, though."

"Be right down," Patrea yelled. "We have to get rid of her. Fast. Before Ernie shows up." Turning, she headed for the stairs, clattered down them, and practically railroaded Maryann into the room with the mural.

"Oh! Isn't this lovely?" Eyes twinkling in a good-natured face, Maryann clapped her hands and spun to take in everything she saw. "I've always wanted to get a good look at the inside of this house. You don't mind, do you?"

Determined to get that look, Maryann bustled toward the door at the room's far end. When Patrea caught up and gently took her arm, the older woman looked down at Patrea's hand. Looking back up, she tilted her head with its short wedge of hair dyed in lighter tones with a few darker highlights. I thought Maryann's new color looked better with her skin tone.

On the shorter side and stocky with it, Maryann cheerfully resisted Patrea's gentle effort at directing her back toward the front door. Like an eel, she slithered out of Patrea's grasp and kept on marching.

Looking like everyone's favorite auntie didn't do much to dispel my impression of her as a guard dog in a business suit over running shoes.

"Where's the kitchen?" Maryann wanted to know.

"Kitchens sell houses. You are planning to sell this one, aren't you? I can't see Chris Evergreen agreeing to move in here and leave his family home empty."

"Our family home now," Patrea said to Maryann's back.

"Right. Right," Maryann tossed over her shoulder and kept going.

"Might as well let her go," I told my annoyed friend. "She's a steamroller."

Having found the kitchen, Maryann let out a sound of approval. "Tell me you're not planning to tear up that tile. It's perfect. Very period."

Drawn to agree, Patrea discussed her plans for the room while Maryann prowled. "The tile stays. Cabinets will get updated with something that retains the period feel but has all the latest enhancements. Soft closing doors and drawers. Pull out storage, that kind of thing. For the rest, I'm going with a blend of what's here and what I can add to bring everything up to date while keeping the ambiance." That earned her a nod of approval.

"Glad to see you're not an idiot. When you're ready to sell, you'll list this place with me."

There was mild admiration in her voice when Patrea said, "Cocky."

"Cocky my butt. You took a bum deal on the last place. Just saying."

Patrea tilted her head. "How so?"

"Please," Maryann waved a hand. "Your listing price was low by a solid five percent, and I could have moved it in a week or less. That's a chunk of money left on the table. And speaking of tables, you could go with a waterfall island right here. Plenty of room for it."

"That's what I said," I pointed out.

"Well, you're right. Something sleek to match the era. White marble would be my first choice, and I know where you can get a bargain on a vintage light fixture that would set it off to perfection."

Despite herself, Patrea got interested. "Really? Where?"

Maryann named a shop in Augusta. "Bit of a drive, but the selection is great, and the prices are reasonable."

"Good to know."

Skillfully, Patrea led Maryann from the kitchen into the dining room, then circled through the mural room to return to the foyer. To keep her from going toward the rooms behind them or up the stairs, Patrea allowed the Realtor to pull her into a discussion of places to shop for architectural salvage that went on for some time. I got bored and wandered back toward the front door and onto the porch, hoping to see the driver from Bertino's. More than the pizza, I needed a drink.

Years of neglect had allowed nature to begin reclaiming the sprawling lawn. Bushes speared up from the tall grass of what might best be described as a meadow. Young trees dotted what had once been a swath of manicured green, a few early dandelions merrily dancing at their feet.

Patrea had her work cut out for her, I decided as the

sound of an approaching vehicle drew my attention. *Make that two vehicles*, I thought when Ernie's black and white turned in behind Bertie's delivery van. Food and an interrogation.

Whoop-de-doo.

"What's this about a skeleton?" Ernie's opening waited until I'd paid the driver.

"We found one behind a false wall. Maryann Payne's in there, so it might be best if you keep your voice down. We need to get rid of her before we show you. Plus, there's pizza. I figured you might want a slice with your iced tea." I handed him the tray of drinks and shifted the pizza box to a better position.

"Unsweetened?"

I nodded.

"And house special pizza. Are you sure you didn't kill someone?"

"I'm not trying to butter you up if that's what you're asking."

"Smells like lunch, and I've had a long morning, so I guess I wouldn't say no." He followed me inside, where Maryann was wrapping up her attempt to seal the listing deal. She looked at him speculatively but asked no questions and politely refused to eat with us, for which we were all thankful. When she left, she reduced the noise level in the place by more than half.

"Lot of loud with that one," Patrea observed. "Bones first, or lunch?" She gave Ernie the option while I looked for a place to put it and eventually carried the pizza box into the mural room and set it on one of the built-in cabinets.

"Add a couple of lawn chairs and a folding table to that list you've got running in your head," I told Patrea. She nodded.

"Bones ain't getting any deader, but the pizza won't stay warm forever." Ernie selected a slice, took his tea from the carrier, and strolled over to look at the mural. "I recognize this view."

Interested, Patrea joined him. "Really? Do tell."

"When my granddaddy was alive, he and my grandmother had a camp on Mayfield Pond."

The name didn't sound familiar to me at all. "Where's that?"

He held up a hand with his fingers together to indicate the rough shape of the state of Maine, then pointed to a spot at the base of his middle finger. "Somewhere around that area—Kingsbury Plantation. If you're coming in from Bingham, there's a moose wallow at the top of Cook Hill. We'd drive to Bingham, have supper at this little take-out place that served great fried chicken, then stop on the way back, hoping to see a moose cooling off in the mud. About a third of the way down the hill, the view of the lake opens up. I haven't been back there in years, but I remember it looking just like this. Real pretty."

It was probably the most I'd ever heard the man say that didn't have anything to do with murder, death, or the law. And—shocker—he sounded nostalgic, an emotion I hadn't credited Ernie with. Unfair of me, no doubt.

"It sounds lovely," I said. "Drew's always looking for new spots to put in the kayaks or go for a paddle in the canoe."

Ernie nodded. "You should still be able to launch a boat near the dam. Good fishing there, too. Or there was then. Pickerel and white perch, mostly. Hornpout and freshwater eel if you wanted to go out at night."

"Eel, I've heard of, but what on earth is a hornpout?" Patrea looked horrified at the sound of the word.

"Type of catfish. Bullhead. Quite tasty coated with salt and vinegar potato chip crumbs and pan-fried." With that, Ernie polished off his third slice. "I guess we'd better get down to business. Show me the bones."

"She's down there." Patrea pointed toward the evidence of our demolition efforts. "But the door's blocked off, so we'll have to go this way." Explaining how it happened, she led him to where we'd found the bones, then stood back to let Ernie get his first look through the hole in the wall.

"Stay back," he ordered. "You've done enough damage as it is."

Patrea and I exchanged a look but didn't bother to point out the irony while Ernie pulled out his phone and framed several shots of the skeleton coated in dusty plastic. He called in the unattended death to get the ball rolling with the coroner, who drove an ambulance as his primary job, and the medical examiner's office, then made us repeat everything we'd already told him. Twice.

When there wasn't a single detail left to explain, Ernie

sighed and grabbed the sledgehammer we'd left leaning against a wall. It took him mere minutes to break through the covered-up doorway. More dust filtered down to coat the plastic shroud. When he'd opened up enough of the wall for a person to fit through, he gave us a look meant to keep us in line, shot several more images with his phone, and then stepped through to wait for his team. The look had zero effect, nor did the stronger one he offered when we joined him without taking the long way around.

"This is police business."

"This is my house," Patrea countered.

"Don't touch anything." The order included me.

"I wasn't planning to." Not when my imagination had already supplied the sound of bones clacking together.

"Tell him her name." Charlotte had returned. Just what I needed at that particular moment. A ghost with a mission. I shook my head. She moved close enough to breathe an icy chill into the air near my face. "Now."

"Excuse me," I made my way toward the dining room with Charlotte hovering close enough to give me the creeps. When I'd closed the door behind me, I turned on her.

"Look, I realize you have your reasons for wanting this crime solved, but ordering me around in front of people who don't know about my abilities is not the way to get it done. I can't tell Ernie her name because he'd ask how I know. Do you really think he'll believe me if I tell him the housekeeper's ghost identified the remains?" This wasn't strictly true because Ernie had been exposed to ghostly shenanigans before but had chosen not to believe.

"I don't suppose he would." She dropped her gaze and gave me some space.

"You need to let me handle things my way."

Chagrined, she faded away. We'd have to talk about my ghost rules later.

CHAPTER FIVE

Charlotte stayed away while the hearse backed up to the front door. She stayed away while Ernie and the others zipped the plastic cocoon into a body bag and carried it out.

"What now?" Patrea faced Ernie as he watched the hearse's taillights disappear down the rutted driveway.

"Go home, that's what. Give me the keys to the place so I can get my guys in and finish documenting the scene, and I'll get them back to you when I'm done." When she opened her mouth to argue, he held up a hand. "For once, don't give me any guff. We both know there won't be much to find, but I have to do the job. Shouldn't take more than a day or two. I'll keep you posted."

A short but tense silence followed before Patrea gave in and handed over the keys.

"Fine, but I'm finishing my tour before I go. I haven't gone up to the third floor yet." She all but dared him to argue. He didn't, but he did glance in my direction. I kept my expression neutral but moved closer to Patrea to indicate solidarity.

Giving in, Ernie waved us off. "You've got one hour. No

more. That should give you enough time even for a house as big as this one. Who needs fifty bedrooms anyway?"

Getting her way made Patrea happy again. "It doesn't have that many," she assured. "We've only seen four so far."

"Still a white elephant."

"One man's elephant is another man's…okay, it's still an elephant, but not a white one," Patrea said, her dark eyes shining with excitement. "Come on, Everly. I'm not letting a decades-old murder put me off. It's too late to back out of the deal, so let's go see how to make the most of it."

That earned her a hard look from Ernie, but he clamped his jaw shut instead of offering an opinion. Probably wise of him.

The mansion's interior was a testament to its age, with intricate woodwork and dusty chandeliers draped in cobwebs—even way up in what had probably been used as a storage area. A layer of dust clung to crown molding, lending a ghostly air to the unused space.

The stairs opened out into a large, perfectly symmetrical room. Looking forward, we faced a bank of four deep-set windows that glowed with the afternoon light. Doorways on the left and right led to a pair of hallways that were identical in every way. Same wallpaper, same trim, two doors on the left, and two doors on the right. If you stood in the middle of the room, it almost felt like looking in a mirror. The urge to say "redrum" popped up, but I managed to resist. Barely.

Ignoring the architecture for once, Patrea headed for the left hallway, opened the first door on the right, dragged me inside, and closed it behind us.

She leaned on the door as if to pen me in. "Have you seen Vanessa yet?"

"Nope. Charlotte's gone for the moment as well. As far as I can tell, it's just us and Ernie. Why did you drag me in here?" The empty room wasn't anything special and had suffered some damage over the years. Strips of old wallpaper that had lost the will to cling to plaster littered dusty, wide-plank floors.

"Giving you a chance to do your thing without Ernie getting involved."

"My thing? What thing?"

Patrea shrugged, but her eyes glittered with excitement. "I don't know. Whatever you did earlier, only take it up a notch. Seance. Ghost hoodoo. Make contact with Vanessa since she's not reaching out to you."

"I think you're mistaking me for Momma Wade. I've never conducted a séance in my life, and I don't have any hoodoo.

"But you know how, right? Didn't your Grammie Dupree show you?"

"Not exactly. My mother had firm rules, and Grammie respected them to a point. She told me stories, but I never got to sit in on an actual event. Besides, I think there was more tippling than channeling going on at her séances."

"Still, you have to do something."

"I suppose."

Patrea stepped back to give me space.

"I don't know if it will work from up here, but I'll try."

For form's sake, I walked to the center of the room, held up both hands and closed my eyes.

"Is it working?" Patrea immediately asked.

I cracked one eye open. "I've hardly even started. Give it a minute."

"Sorry." Her expression said she was anything but.

Eyes closed again, I opened myself up to whatever forces might be willing to come through. Probably. I had no idea what I was doing or if it would work, but it felt right.

"What's going on?" It was Charlotte's voice that pulled my focus back to the present.

"Everly's embracing the haunted house aesthetic," Patrea joked, making me realize Charlotte had been talking to her and not me. For whatever reason, I felt miffed.

Patrea brushed a strand of dark hair away from her face and said, "So far, Vanessa's not responding. Any other ghosts we should know about?"

"Is this a joke to you?" Charlotte's annoyance sent out a frigid blast. Patrea shivered.

"No. I didn't mean to offend. I'll just be over here minding my own business." Contrite, Patrea crossed the room to take in the view through filthy windows. If she fooled Charlotte into thinking she wasn't listening, I knew better.

"If this is the best you can do, you need to leave."

Charlotte folded her arms and glared at me. "Before you get into trouble."

"What trouble? This is not my first time, you know. I've helped my share of ghosts find peace already," I tried to reassure. "I know what I'm doing." I wanted to say she couldn't make me leave, but we both knew that would be a lie. Ghosts can wreak plenty of havoc when they put their minds to it.

Charlotte looked at me like she thought I was either too stupid to live or just dumb enough to die. I didn't know what else to say to her. Not that I got the chance.

The room temperature dropped like a rock through water. Patrea gasped, her breath sending out a cloud of icy vapor, and stepped back. "What's happening? Charlotte, are you doing this?"

My vision went dark around the edges. My heart pounded in my chest. I couldn't catch my breath. Panic attack, the rational part of my brain insisted as it got swallowed up by the primitive need to find safety, except I couldn't take a single step.

Night-dark mist gathered in the far corner, building and rising slowly to form a vaguely human shape. After a tense moment, the dark spirit slithered over to Charlotte. A voice echoed as if coming from far away, "Have you been telling secrets?"

Charlotte went nearly translucent and moved closer to me, but fear paralysis kept my feet rooted. I am ashamed to say that I'd have abandoned the poor ghost to her fate without hesitation if I could have. Patrea, too. I could only stand and watch as it was, so I guess it amounted to the same thing in the end.

The inky cloud hovered an inch from the end of Charlotte's nose, then enveloped the poor ghost in darkness. When the mist lifted, both spirits were gone.

Patrea screamed and ran toward the door, realized I wasn't moving, and came back to grab my arm and drag me down the stairs with her. My imagination insisted the presence followed us, but I was too scared to look back. We raced out of the house into the safety of daylight with Ernie's shout trailing behind.

He appeared in the doorway, weapon in hand, and scanned the area for threats. "What happened?"

Patrea looked at me. I shook my head. "Nothing. Just a big hairy spider. Sorry. Didn't mean to scare you."

"You didn't."

We were both trembling, but Ernie couldn't tell from a distance, so he shrugged and went back inside. Neither of us spoke for what felt like a long time until I finally said, "I think it's best if we don't discuss what happened until we're well off the property."

Patrea nodded in agreement, still shaken from the encounter. "I'm not sure I could form a coherent sentence yet, anyway."

The dark spirit's words echoed in my mind. Was it warning Charlotte not to reveal something about the house? Or some other secrets? I had no idea. And why was the ghost so adamant about keeping things hidden? These were questions I couldn't answer, but they lingered.

"Should we go back inside? Or have you seen enough?"

"My purse is in there."

"Mine, too."

And still, some time passed before we felt up to walking back through the door. After retrieving our bags, we checked in with Ernie, who wasn't above getting in a subtle dig.

"There she is. The intrepid sleuth who finds dead bodies on the regular but screams and runs away from a little spider."

I could have pointed out that Patrea was the one who screamed, but that wouldn't earn me points with her, so I didn't. Instead, we watched Ernie tack crime scene tape over the opening to the room where we'd found the remains. Having worked together—reluctantly on his end—on several murder cases in the past, we'd developed a rapport. Maybe even some mutual respect. Still, he booted us out without a shred of remorse, locked the door behind us, and pocketed the keys.

"Don't come back here until I clear you. Understood?" he asked as he loaded his equipment into his car.

"You took the keys," I replied with a sigh. "But you can't stop me from doing some research online or dipping into the local gossip well. If I learn anything interesting, I'll share."

He nodded and gave me an enigmatic look before getting into his car and driving away.

"You're uncharacteristically serene, given you've just been locked out of your own property."

Her grin might have been a shadow of its usual self, but I offered a smile when Patrea pulled a lone key out of her pocket and dangled it by the chain. As we drove off, I glanced back at the house and saw Charlotte's face appear in one of the upstairs windows. At least she was okay. Now, it was time to check in with Patrea.

"How much of that did you see?"

"Charlotte. The weird black swirly thing of evil." She'd stopped shaking, but Patrea shook her head. "I thought Abner was as bad as it gets. I had no idea what you've been up against all this time." She took her hand off the steering wheel long enough to reach over and pat my arm.

I almost hated to admit that what happened hadn't been normal for me, but I did. I didn't admit that the whole way back to pick up my car, I couldn't shake the feeling of being watched. Or that it creeped me out. No sense in making her worry.

"Can we get rid of...whatever that was?" Patrea asked, breaking the short silence.

"I don't know," I admitted. "There are never any absolutes when it comes to dealing with ghosts. I'd like to think that finding out what happened to Vanessa would be enough to clear the house of bad energy, but I don't know enough about weird black swirly things of evil to say for sure."

Patrea got that look in her eye. "Research mode?"

"Looks like it," I said. "We need to learn more about

the Wentworth family, and I'll have to contact Kat to ask a few questions on the ghost side of things. There's something more than a typical haunting going on in that house, and we need to find out what it is."

"I'm glad you said we because there's no way you're leaving me out of this. It's my house, at least until I sell it later. I want to be involved in every step of clearing bad energy. Speaking of which, I'm sure Momma Wade would be happy to sage the place for us. What do you think?"

Patrea pulled in behind my car, left the truck running, and spun in her seat to see the effect of the question.

"When the danger is over, and as long as I don't have to get within fifteen feet of her sage ashes or whatever, I think it's a fine idea. Just don't blame me if you end up with a greased-up third eye and a new set of skills."

"Deal. And you'll let me tag along when you visit with Kat?"

"Consider it done. Are we on for Cappy's later? We missed you last Friday."

Her smile lit up her whole face. "I had a family dinner that included my brother. Can you believe it? My mother still cries every time. It was a moment."

I'd have hugged her if we weren't still sitting in the truck. As it was, I had to settle for squeezing her hand.

"You've been lighter in your soul since he came back."

That choked her up a bit, but she nodded.

When I finally got home, I took Molly out for a quick round of toss-the-tennis-ball. Two seconds later, my phone rang. Never a moment's peace.

CHAPTER SIX

"Where have you been?" I held the phone away from my ear, and my mother's voice still sounded inordinately loud. "You missed your hair appointment."

"What hair appointment? I don't remember making a hair appointment."

"It's on our shared wedding schedule if you ever bothered to check it."

Meet Kitty Dupree, MOB. Mother of the bride—or MOBzilla as I'd begun to think of her. She was taking this wedding planning thing quite seriously, but she had me there. I hadn't looked at our shared schedule before agreeing to go with Patrea.

"Sorry, mom. It slipped my mind. I'm sure we can—"

"I've already rescheduled for tomorrow at ten. Did you at least look at those links I sent you?"

"Links?" Because I had no idea what she was talking about, I must have sounded tentative because she let out a long-suffering sigh.

"Honestly, Everly. How are we supposed to decide between a tiara or a veil if you won't even look at the options? We're supposed to be testing hairstyles, remember? I'm bringing your homecoming tiara and your grandmother's veil, but I'd hoped you would have at least narrowed down your top picks by then."

"Since we have to get new dresses, don't you think it would be better to wait? The dress should inform the hairstyle, not the other way around. I don't think most people try on wedding hair beforehand."

Her tone took on the evenness that suggested she was keeping her temper in check. "I had to bump Mara up to next on the waiting list for that new Nora Roberts book and give Louisa your grandmother's sweet pickle recipe to get this appointment rescheduled so quickly. We are testing hairstyles tomorrow at ten. Do not be late."

My mother took her job as head librarian quite seriously. For her, finagling the waiting list for a new book was tantamount to high treason. If she weren't careful, she'd have to fine herself or something.

"But tomorrow's Saturday."

"And today is Friday. What's your point?"

"Nothing." So much for my plans to drive out to the lake with Drew. "I'll be there, but I do think I should pick out a new dress before choosing a hairstyle. It seems backward to me," I repeated.

If fury could somehow travel through the air on whatever magic makes cell phones work, I suspect my mother's would have melted my screen protector. Or frozen it since her voice now dripped with ice.

"Didn't you hear what I said? I bumped someone on

the waiting list for a book. We are doing the hair appointment tomorrow. It's a moral imperative."

"I'm sorry, mom. I really am. It feels like this wedding is cursed sometimes. First the invitations and now the dresses. What next?"

That softened her up a little.

"I think you've hit the end of the run of bad luck. Set a reminder on your phone. I mean it, Everly. We're at T minus forty-seven days, and I can't have another disruption to the schedule. Look at those links, and do not be late tomorrow."

She hung up without saying goodbye.

"Whoops, Molls. Looks like I'm on the naughty list." But my dog didn't care about wedding stuff. All she wanted was time with her person. When I sat on the back steps, she leaned in and rested her head on my shoulder— her method of asking for a hug, which I gave without reservation. That's how Drew found us a minute later.

Encased in a pair of jeans just tight enough to show it off to perfection, my fiancé's butt settled on the step beside me. As his lips met mine, Molly took the opportunity to give us both a swipe with her warm tongue. Drew laughed.

"There's my best girl." He was talking to the dog.

"And what am I?" I teased. "Second best?"

"My one and only." He meant it, too. "I heard you had an interesting day."

"How? I haven't been home for more than fifteen minutes."

"Carole Ann Wilmette joined Riley's guided meditation session this week."

"You mean the one where people aren't supposed to talk?"

His expression wry, Drew nodded. "That would be the one. Carole Ann struggled with that aspect of the class."

"You should apply for a job in the diplomatic service. That's the nicest way I've ever heard anyone describe Carole Ann's inability to shut her flap trap for more than thirty seconds at a time."

"That would be an accurate assessment." He smiled again, but only briefly before his face became serious. "Are you okay? It's not every day you stumble over a bag of bones."

"We both know I've stumbled over worse. Her name was Vanessa Morgan."

"Did she follow you home?" Drew glanced back at the house, his [color] eyes alight with fascination. After my first marriage imploded in such a spectacular manner, getting hooked up with another man hadn't been on my list of things to do. Ever. But Drew had come along and changed my mind. I collected ghosts like other women collected shoes. He didn't seem to mind.

"Not so far." Standing, I tugged his hand to get him to follow me inside while I told him the story of Charlotte, Vanessa, and the dark spirit. If I glossed over that last part, it had less to do with not wanting to scare him than not knowing exactly what I was up against. "Ernie booted us out for a couple of days. Patrea wasn't too happy to have her plans disrupted." And since I'd brought up the subject of disrupted plans, I told him about the hair appointment. "It shouldn't take more than an hour. Two at the most. We can go to the lake after."

"That works for me. Gives me time to catch up on paperwork for last quarter," Drew lied right to my face, but I didn't find that out until much later. "If you're doing the girl's night thing, I'll heat up some leftovers and get a couple of hours in tonight, too."

"I won't be late, and I'm nominating myself as designated driver. Somehow, I think showing up to this hair thing tomorrow with a hangover wouldn't go over very well."

"Give Kitty a break. She's trying to outdo the queen of planning, after all."

Drew followed me to the bedroom while I picked out an outfit that didn't have plaster dust and ghost cooties all over it. Wisely, he kicked off his sneakers before settling on the bed to talk while I changed. I could have used a shower, but the phone call from my mom had taken too long, and there wouldn't be time.

"What do you mean?"

"You're the planner of amazing events. With your experience, you could put a wedding together in your sleep, and while your mom has a highly organized mind, she wants your special day to be extra special. Perfect, even. It's a big deal for her."

I stopped in the middle of dragging on a pair of black slacks and stared at him.

"I know this isn't your first wedding, but she didn't get much say in how the last one went, did she?"

How had I missed this? "You're saying she's gone all MOBzilla on me because she's intimidated by my event-planning skills." It wasn't a question but a solidifying of his position.

"Makes sense, doesn't it?"

Because it did, I kissed him until his eyes glazed over. "I love you. I hope I tell you that often enough because it's true."

"You could blow off Cappy's and show me in great detail," he offered when he got his breath back.

"I could, but you'll have to wait until I get home instead. Besides, you have paperwork."

"Being a responsible adult takes all the fun out of life sometimes." He didn't mean it, and when he looked up at me, his innate good humor proved the point. "I'll wait up."

"I'll try to be worth waiting for."

"You always are."

No wonder I hadn't been able to resist the man.

CHAPTER SEVEN

"This place is dead tonight," Jacy Dean, my oldest and dearest friend, observed as we stepped through the door of Cappy's tavern. On a warm spring night, I was just as surprised as she was to see half the tables empty.

From her seat at our customary table, Patrea waved us over.

"Where is everyone?" Neena sat and craned her neck to look around. "It's Friday night, right? Did I miss the apocalypse or something?"

Patrea shrugged. "It was like this when Chris dropped me off. Maybe business will pick up before the band starts playing."

"Not likely," Miranda, our server, came up behind me. "Missy Tate and Cameron Jameson are getting married..." she checked her watch, "in about ten minutes. I figure we'll be slammed once the reception clears out, but until then, it's a quiet night."

"A little quiet might not be a bad thing," Patrea said, ordering a bottle of wine for the table, mozzarella sticks, and a garden salad. "Fried cheese for the sinner in me and salad for the saint."

"I'll go with the sinners and saints as well, but make mine onion rings and a chef salad. And since I'm driving tonight, I'll go with a strawberry lemonade." With some variations, the trend carried around the table.

"Okay," Jacy said, fixing her gaze on Patrea. "Everly gave us the gist of things in the car on the way here. Now, I want details. When and how did you talk the Wentworth heirs into selling that house? Many have tried, and many have failed in the pursuit."

Patrea shrugged. "Right place, right time, right offer, I guess." She brought Neena and Jacy up to speed on how she'd bought the house, and then we took turns describing the day's events until our food order came.

"Why are we always working when all the fun stuff happens?" Jacy asked her partner the rhetorical question.

"Because we're dedicated professionals." A touch of annoyance turned Neena's assessment scornful. "I'd have loved to see that mural."

"What's to stop us from going out there right now?" Patrea pulled the key from her pocket and dangled it over her plate. "What Ernie doesn't know won't hurt him."

"Let me finish my salad first," Neena said. "I'll need the extra energy if I have to run away from spooks and such."

Forty minutes later, we were on the road, and it seemed Neena was having second thoughts. "Tell me more about this painting." Framed by dark curls, her face looked as pale as the moon in my rear-view mirror. Patrea obliged her, which took up the rest of the drive.

"We're here." I pulled up in front of the mansion, thinking it looked even more imposing after dark. Again, Charlotte's face appeared briefly at one of the upper windows.

"I haven't been out this way in years. Not since Brian and I used to come here to do the wild thing in the back of his car," Jacy jumped out of the car almost before it swayed to a stop. "It's bigger than I remember." My headlights cast her in silhouette as she mounted the steps. Neena hung back with me while Patrea unlocked the door, then slipped inside to start flicking on light switches.

"See, there's power and everything," I reassured. "It's not so scary, and that painting is well worth seeing."

"In daylight, maybe. Natural light. It's a thing, you know." Neena wasn't convinced but had no intention of being left behind, either. She followed me inside.

"Look at the sweep on this staircase," Jacy's honey-blond hair swung as she bounced up the first few steps. "Doesn't it just make you want to slip into a fancy dress and make an entrance?" To illustrate, she ran halfway up, turned, lifted her chin, and let her hand hover gracefully along the banister as she came back down. Even in a pair of jeans and a pink and black checkered flannel shirt, she managed to look regal. "Before you put this thing back on the market, we need to have a party here. Everly can plan it."

"Better yet, she should get married here. Can you just picture it? Flowers everywhere, and candles. The glow from that chandelier—assuming it glows more when all the bulbs are working…and a gorgeous swirl of white as the bride appears at the top and walks majestically down the stairs." Getting into it, Neena sighed. As she did, I noted something different about the chandelier but didn't follow the thought far enough to realize what.

Because I could picture it, I echoed her sigh. "If this place could be ready in time, and if changing venues wouldn't send my mother into fits, I'd be on my knees begging to have the wedding here, but I'm wearing cream, not white. White washes me out."

"A house like this is too big for a single family these days, but it sure would make a great event space. Give that resort in Hackinaw a run for their money."

"Can I put you in charge of marketing?" Patrea wanted to know. "Because you're right, and that opens up a lot of options for the restoration. I'll need to think about it, but for now, let's take the tour."

We started in the sitting room, where Neena got her first look at the mural. "It's not in bad shape, actually. Needs cleaning, which is time-consuming on something this size that's done in oils, and a bit of retouching here and there, but that's nothing I can't handle."

While she and Patrea got into a lengthy discussion about what the work would entail, Jacy and I drifted back toward the main staircase.

"Neena's right, you know," Jacy stood at the foot of the stairs, her head tilted as she pictured the scene. "I bet they threw amazing parties here back in the day. With flappers and bathtub gin and handsome men wearing striped suits and those funny things on their shoes."

"They're called spats." Charlotte appeared nearby. Her presence sent a mild chill through the air, but other than a delicate shiver, Jacy didn't seem to notice.

"Spats," I supplied the word for Jacy. "Charlotte's here, but don't worry. She's friendly."

"Like Casper?" Jacy smiled in the general direction where Charlotte waited. "Nice to meet you."

"She's polite, at least." Charlotte approved and made the extra effort to show herself.

Jacy's eyes widened slightly, but her smile never faltered. Neena let out a muffled sound when she stepped out of the sitting room and saw us all standing, or in Charlotte's case, hovering there.

"Neena, I'd like you to meet Charlotte Crane. She's been keeping an eye on things here since the owners closed up the house. Even before, come to think of it."

Charlotte nodded, then tilted her head to give Neena an appraising look. "Boo," she said with almost no inflection whatsoever, then smiled when Neena's left eyebrow shot up. "Can't blame me for trying."

"I will never get used to this," Neena muttered.

"I'm glad to see you, Charlotte. I was worried after what happened earlier."

The ghost looked at me like I'd lost several sandwiches from my picnic basket.

"You do remember what happened, don't you?"

Charlotte waved a dismissive hand. "Of course I do. You and that one over there," she pointed at Patrea, "knocked holes in the walls. Made an awful mess, you did. Took hours to clean it up."

Patrea and I exchanged a look, but with her longer legs, she outpaced me on the trip to view the spot where we'd found Vanessa's remains. Charlotte had, indeed, cleaned up. Not a single mote of plaster dust had escaped her. Nor was there a cobweb in sight. That was what was different about the chandelier. Ernie would not be happy to find his bright yellow tape removed. And he would, without a doubt, blame us.

"You shouldn't have done that. This is a crime scene now, and you've tampered with evidence, but I was talking about what happened after we found Vanessa's bones."

Charlotte's face registered nothing but confusion.

"I don't think she remembers any of it," Patrea said, then turned to Charlotte. "Can you tell me what else you remember from when we were here yesterday? After the wall came down."

"I...you...oh." The effort to remember made Charlotte's edges blur as her body began to shiver and quake. The longer it continued, the more she looked like an old home movie on the wrong speed. And then, she went poof.

"What just happened?" Arms crossed against the chill, Jacy shivered. "I feel like a whole herd of geese just walked across my grave."

"I believe the correct term is a gaggle of geese, but I

feel the same way." Neena's face had gone white again. "What was that all about?"

They all looked to me for answers I didn't have, so I shrugged and shook my head. "I have no idea. It could be the dark spirit fogged her mind, or she had dementia when she passed, and it's still affecting her memory. I'm no expert in these things."

"You'll figure it out." It was nice to hear that Jacy had faith in me. And her hug was comforting as well. "But right now," she pulled away, "I think we'd better find Ernie's crime scene tape and put it back up. Then, I want to see the rest of the house."

We found the tape balled up in an empty container in the storage room, along with the bits of plaster and dust that Charlotte had cleaned up, and did our best to restore the crime scene to its former appearance. We failed, I'm sure, but it was the best we could do.

Patrea took the lead, naturally. I lagged behind as she began the tour. When they headed toward the kitchen, I felt a gentle pull in the opposite direction. I ignored the feeling, hoping it would go away, and listened to Patrea describe the fixtures and tile with great enthusiasm.

Drawn to the range, Jacy caressed the cast iron top as if it were a human in need of affection. "Aren't you the prettiest thing ever?" she crooned. "Probably weighs as much as a Buick. Do you know if it works?"

Patrea joined her. "Not yet, but I can't wait to find out. I thought I might pull this out to make room for one of those fancy numbers with a built-in grill and all the extras. Now, I'm not so sure."

"A shiny new range would ruin the ambiance," Jacy opened the oven door and peered inside before giving the rest of the room a critical look. "As much as I'd love to talk you into selling this through my shop, I'd leave it right where it is. If it works—bonus. But then, I'd add a second one on that wall over there. One of those fancy ones you had in mind, only in a vintage or retro style to match the decor. That way, you get the best of both worlds."

While they talked about the current value of antique ranges, the tug against my attention strengthened until I couldn't ignore it any longer. No one noticed when I drifted away. The niggling in my gut led me back to the entrance and then down a half-lit hallway toward what might have been a drawing room. Who drew what and why was still a mystery to me, but one I didn't put much thought into solving because I figured the tugging was Vanessa leading me to something that might help find her killer.

As if in a trance, head buzzing, I followed the pulling sensation toward a set of cupboards built into the corner. When I touched the handle, a spark of electricity jolted through me. Everything went quiet when I opened the door. Expectations flared, then died when I found the cupboard empty.

"Really?" Why bother leading me here?

"What?" I jumped at Jacy's question. They'd found me.

"Nothing. Nothing at all, and now I feel stupid. I had this weird urge to come in here and open this cupboard, and I thought it had to do with Vanessa's death, but the shelves are empty."

"Are you sure?" Patrea pulled out her phone, fired up the flashlight app, and gently nudged me aside to play the light over the space. "I guess so."

"Define urge," Jacy said.

"Define weird," Neena added.

After a moment, I admitted, "I don't know if I can, but I'll try. Have you ever had a moment of clarity that comes over you without warning? Let's say you've been looking for your scissors for hours, and they're nowhere to be found, but like a day later, when you've decided they're gone for good, the image of where you put them just pops into your head. It's kind of like that, only I wasn't looking for anything. I just knew I would find it if I came in here."

"But you didn't." Neena earned a pointy elbow to the ribs from Jacy.

"Exactly," I said. "I don't even know what I thought was in here." I walked across the room, and the sensation came over me again. "But I still do."

"Do what?"

"Think something is in here."

"But what?"

"That's the question of the day, isn't it?"

"I trust your gut," Patrea directed the light from her phone into the farthest reaches of the empty shelves, then leaned down to check their undersides. "Bingo!"

"What?" I knew she'd found whatever I was meant to see because my belly fluttered like a tattered flag in a hurricane. "What is it?"

"Envelope. Taped to the bottom of the shelf."

"What's in it?" We all crowded around her for a better look as she slid a fingernail under the flap and gave a tug. Brittle adhesive gave way under the pressure. We all sucked in a breath as she slowly slipped out the contents: a single sheet of blank paper folded around several photographs.

Patrea scanned the first and then handed it to Jacy, who did the same before passing it along to Neena. I was the last in line. They all featured the same beautiful young woman with a captivating smile.

"Do you think this is Vanessa Morgan?"

"Could be," I replied, feeling a strange connection to the woman in the image. "But since I haven't seen her yet, I can't confirm. It could be anyone. A daughter of the family who lived here, a guest, or even a relative. This is where Charlotte would have come in handy. She'd know exactly who this is."

"If it is Vanessa, she certainly deserves some closure." Patrea studied the woman's wide smile before slipping the photographs into the envelope. "She looks like a nice person who didn't deserve to be shut up inside a wall."

"I'm pretty sure no one deserves that," Jacy said, then amended. "Except maybe the jerk who killed her, and even then, I'd rather they'd be behind bars than behind a wall."

Since Jacy had summed up all our thoughts and there was nothing more to do about Vanessa, Neena suggested we finish the tour and head home. I couldn't shake the feeling that the walls were whispering, urging me to delve deeper into the mansion's secrets. And as the shadows lengthened and the air grew colder, I knew we were not alone in our quest for answers.

"You're late." My mother tapped her foot and pointed to the clock on the wall to show her annoyance with me. It didn't fly.

"Not even a minute. Does it even count if it's not even a minute?"

"You just come right in, honey." Soft-spoken, Mara Tibbets reminded me of someone from a movie, but I couldn't pinpoint who. Cruising toward her middle forties, she was bubbly and curvy and the second generation of Tibbets women to dedicate themselves to the art of cutting and styling.

"And let's get a look at that hair." Without asking, she pulled the frothing mass out of the band I'd secured it with and surveyed me with interest. "You've let it go wild. Needs shaping. Who did your color? Because I know you didn't get it done here. Peggy would have had a card on file for you."

"Mother Nature. It's my natural color." Which Peggy Sullivan had been told before but chose not to believe. "She's also behind the wild curls, what with all the humidity we've had. I know it needs a trim. I just haven't had time to deal with it lately."

What I meant was I hadn't had time to drive back to the city to visit my favorite salon.

Mara quirked one eyebrow but didn't argue, even though it looked like she wanted to. Instead, she practically dragged me to a chair and then turned to my mother. "What are we thinking? She's got plenty to work with if you're looking for a romantic updo with some volume."

"I'd like—"

"I've been looking at options online," my mother cut me off. "But we haven't decided on a headpiece yet. What styles work best with a veil?"

"I don't want a veil." I got that much in before they ignored me again. "Or a tiara."

"I've got some idea books in the back if you want to see them."

"Fabulous." Leaving me to sit in sullen silence, my mother followed Mara through the salon.

"Don't mind her." A smiling ghost shivered into view right in front of me. She wore a smock with the name Dolly embroidered over the left breast. "Dolly Tibbets," she said when she caught me looking. "I used to own this place. You're Kitty Dupree's kid, right?"

"Nice to meet you," I nodded and kept my voice down so no one would hear me talking to thin air. "You'd be Mara's mother?" The resemblance was hard to miss. Except for the differences in hairstyles and ages, the women could have been twins.

"That I would. This was my place before I handed it

along to her. She's done a good job keeping it going. Even during the rough times."

I nodded again as Mara and my mother returned. Mom plopped a book in my lap. "Since you couldn't be bothered looking at the links I sent, I've marked a few pages. Take a look."

"I looked at the links," I muttered and dutifully opened the book at the first sticky note she'd used as a marker. "I just didn't like most of the styles you chose. Too fussy and elaborate. Can't we keep it simple?"

"It's a wedding, Everly. Your wedding. Not a night out at Cappy's with your girlfriends. Don't you want to look special?"

Hurting her feelings hadn't been my intent, but it seemed I had. "Of course I do. But simple can be special, too." Dutifully, I flipped through the marked pages while my mother sighed impatiently.

"Let's try this one," I said, pointing to a photo of a woman with hair similar to my color pulled back from her face with combs. The back was a cascade of curls. "It's very romantic. Just right for my big day."

"No," Dolly said and shook her head. " You've got a great neck. You should show it off."

"She does," my mother said absently, then flushed when Mara looked at her funny. "Sorry, I was just thinking out loud."

Dolly rolled her eyes. "Your mother likes to pretend she can't see me. A body could do with a bit more conversation sometimes, but does she care? No, she does not."

Mom shot Dolly a raised brow but said nothing as Mara spoke up.

"Not that I don't love a good head of mermaid curls, but since you come by them naturally, there's such a thing as too simple." Taking the book away from me, she flipped several pages, ignoring those my mother had marked, and pointed to her choice. "This one."

The model had her hair loosely pulled back from a side part into an artful roll at the nape of her neck. The style was both elegant and romantic. Vintage but still current.

"Your hair's thick enough that you'll have to lose an inch or two to keep the bun from being too bulky," Dolly weighed in with her opinion.

When Mara made the same observation a minute later, Dolly beamed with pride. "That's my girl. She does good hair."

Dolly was right. Mara was good at her job. Once I agreed to try the style, her scissors slithered and snicked with a speed that made me nervous, but when she was done, I couldn't help but admire the results. She'd taken me from Ronald McDonald's love child to bombshell in about ten minutes.

"Did I hear that your lawyer friend bought the Wentworth?" Mara rubbed something that smelled nice into my hair and grabbed a round brush to tame the curls a bit. She had to raise her voice to be heard over the hair dryer.

"Word travels fast in Mooselick River," I said, bracing myself for the inevitable. The inevitable took about ten seconds to occur as everyone in the salon tuned into the conversation, and the questions began to fly.

Dolly's face fell into lines of sadness. "Junior and Gillian Wentworth's place? I used to be friends with Gillie. That was a long time ago." I made a note to myself to seek Dolly out when there wasn't a crowd of women around. She might know something about Vanessa Morgan.

"Carole Ann said they took a body out of there yesterday, and Ernie's up there today looking for more. Wasn't the lawyer, though, I guess. Too bad. The world could use fewer lawyers."

"No, it wasn't." Poor Mara was left holding her comb when I launched out of the chair and rounded on the woman who had spoken. "Patrea's a good person. If you don't know someone, you shouldn't talk trash about them."

She had a face like a carp and probably smelled like one.

"Everly." My mother's voice was sharp. "Sit back down. You're making a scene."

"Don't pay too much attention to Sylvie Warner," Dolly's lip curled into a sneer. "She's just annoyed her daughter couldn't land the Evergreen boy no matter how hard she tried, and then your friend came waltzing into town and took him off the market just like that." She snapped her fingers, and a pair of scissors flew off the table behind her. "Whoops," she said without looking too sorry.

"Keep your sour grapes to yourself, Sylvie," my mother

warned, then turned to me. "You weren't involved in anything dangerous, were you? And why is this the first I'm hearing of it?"

"It only happened yesterday. I was going to tell you all about it today."

"Maybe your position on the grapevine isn't as strong as you thought." Sylvie had to get a final dig in.

"Or I've got better things to do than pass the time spreading rumors."

"Well, there's plenty of them to go around," Mara said. "Did she really pay two million for it? Where does anyone get that kind of money?"

From guilty former mothers-in-law in my case, but that was a deep and dark secret, so I merely shrugged. "I didn't ask what she paid, so I can't say for sure."

"Wouldn't if you could." Dolly's eyes twinkled. She must have been a firecracker in her youth. "You don't strike me as a braggart."

"Enough with the money talk. I want to hear about the body." This from a dark-haired woman who had to raise her voice to be heard over the bubbling water of the spa bath her feet were soaking in.

"There's not all that much to tell. We found a wall where one shouldn't be, and the bones were behind it. She'd been there a long time."

"She?" Naturally, Sylvie picked up on the slip. "How do you know it was a she?"

Whoops. Said too much. "Ernie must have mentioned it."

"That's enough, Sylvie." Mara firmly directed the conversation back to my hair as she spun the chair and gave me a hand-held mirror to look at the back. "What do you think?"

"I think I love it." By the magic of hairdressing, she'd retained some of my natural curl and still made the roll at the nape of my neck look effortless and elegant. "What do you think, Mom?"

As annoyed as she'd been with me, she couldn't hold back a misty smile. "I think it's perfect. You'll be a beautiful bride." She came to stand behind me, her hands on my shoulders. We'd been at odds during my first marriage but had become close enough recently that we found it difficult to stay mad at each other for long.

"Stop, or you'll get me going, too," I told her when the pride I saw in her eyes brought the sting of tears to my own.

"Both of you stop, or I'll end up a sniveling mess. I can't do good hair when I'm blubbering, and we agreed to try a couple more styles." Mara was halfway there already.

As one, my mother and I shook our heads. "No need. This is the one," Mom put what we were both thinking into words. "It's perfect. You have a gift."

More than misty-eyed now, Mara waved away the praise, but she beamed when I practically begged her to be the stylist for the entire wedding party and booked a facial for the end of the next week.

When we got outside, I hugged my mother. "I know you

and Daddy want to pay for everything, but I'm covering this part and don't want any arguments. I'm planning a few pampering sessions for the bridal party, including you, so it wouldn't be fair for you to foot the bill. This will be my treat."

"I'd be delighted to be included, but don't think this gets you out of telling me what happened at the Wentworth house yesterday. You're not planning to get involved in anything dangerous again." It was a statement, not a question.

"I never plan for these things. They just happen. There's nothing more to tell than you've already heard. And why don't you talk to Dolly? She seems like a nice... formerly living person."

"She is, but the woman could talk the paint off the wall when she was alive. Now, even when I pretend I can't hear her, she has no other outlet but me, so she's even worse. Cultivating her would be a mistake."

"Duly noted." And ignored.

With the matter settled, Mom held out her hand. "Give me your phone."

Surprised, I did as she asked. "Why?"

"I need to add a few things to your calendar, and I'm setting up alerts so you don't miss anything. You settled things with Jacy and the others for dress shopping, so I've added that date, and the second set of invitations will be in on Thursday. We'll need to check that they're right this time and then get them addressed quickly. You'd better set aside the entire day. It's a good thing we sent out save-the-date cards, as these invitations will be unconscionably late."

"We could have ordered the invitations online. Save time."

The look she gave me could wither the most tenacious of weeds. "It's important to shop locally, Everly. The Internet's fine for some things, but for this, we needed to feel the weight of the paper stock, and you can't do that online."

"Well, we could at least print off labels so we don't have to address them all by hand."

If anything, her expression darkened. All I could do was hold my hands up in surrender. "Fine. It's on my calendar. I'll be there."

Her hug was warm, her tone not so much. "See that you are." Keeping a smile on my face, I waved her off. When she was out of sight, I returned to the salon.

"Do you mind if I use the restroom?" I asked Mara, then caught Dolly's eye and gave her a subtle nod.

Mara glanced over her shoulder. "Go right ahead, honey."

My skin prickled from the chill, but when Dolly joined me in the small space, she kept as much distance between us as possible. It seemed she knew a bit about ghost etiquette. What a refreshing change.

"What's up, Buttercup? It's been a long time since I had a two-way conversation. Your mother is an expert at the brush-off."

"I was hoping to talk about your experiences at Wentworth house."

Dolly grinned. "Happy to, but it'll take some time. If you don't want people thinking you've got something wrong with your plumbing, we should go somewhere else."

"Good point. I've got things to do today, and my schedule is busy all week. How about if you come by my place on Tuesday morning? Are you able to leave here at all?"

Gleeful at being asked to take a field trip, Dolly clapped her hands and bounced in place. The temperature in the tiny room dropped a few more degrees. "It's not my first day. Of course, I can."

"Do you know where Catherine Willowby's house is? I bought it a while back."

Dolly rolled her eyes. "Do I look like a tourist? I know all about how Martha Tipton worked you over. Go," she made a shooing motion with her hands. "I'll be there with bells on. What fun. I never get invited places anymore."

I hoped she didn't mean actual bells. My mother was probably right. Cultivating Dolly might be a mistake, but anyone could see the ghost was lonely. Maybe I could talk her into crossing over once I sorted the Vanessa situation.

CHAPTER NINE

Since Patrea and I topped Ernie's naughty list—he didn't consider the wind blowing through broken windows as a valid explanation for our botched recreation after Charlotte's clean-up of the crime scene—we agreed to stay away from the Wentworth until he declared it cleared. And so, still sporting my wedding hair, I stopped at the new shop to show Jacy and Neena before meeting Drew for our planned outing.

"A little fancy for Mooselick River on a Saturday morning, but it's a look. I like it." Neena saw me first since she was in the storage room unpacking boxes of consignment items. "Doesn't go with your outfit, but still, very flapperesque."

"Right? Mara nailed it on the first try, and since I loved it and it made my mother cry, we decided this is the look."

Neena grinned. "It's the bee's knees, and here comes Jacy. Get ready for more waterworks."

Walking and talking, Jacy didn't notice me at first. "You owe me a dollar. Judy just sold the unsellable doodad. I told you she—" Jacy broke off when she caught sight of me. "Oh." Her eyes went misty. "It's perfect. So elegant but still flirty and fun. You're getting married in that hair."

Nodding, I teared up a little, too. "I am."

"Sorry. I'm just so happy for you. I can't help myself."

We sniffled and hugged, then sniffled some more until we got Neena going. "I need a tissue," she said and went to hunt down a box. Not finding any, she detoured into the shop and grabbed a package of men's handkerchiefs from a basket of odds and ends near the counter.

"I'll note that in the inventory." Judy's voice followed her back.

"She's a stickler, that one."

Nodding her agreement, Jacy said, "She is. I tell you, that woman could sell feathers to a chicken."

"Is that why Neena owes you a buck?"

Her face lighting, Jacy grinned widely. "Yeah. We bought the entire contents of an estate in Hackinaw last month, and there were some beautiful pieces, but then... let's just say the poor elderly lady who died had some eclectic tastes. Wait here."

Neena and I exchanged a look while Jacy went to the front of the store and returned a few moments later holding a long, oddly shaped ceramic piece that my brain nearly couldn't process. "It looks like a clown and a wiener dog had a baby," was the best I could do. "What's it for?"

I had to ask because a handle shaped like a tail arched up at the back and six mug-style shot glasses hung on three hooks down each side of the clown/dog's body, and I just couldn't understand what I was seeing.

"I think it's a bottle. See. The clown's hat is a cork. It comes off." Jacy tugged and bobbled the piece. I caught the mug that fell off and handed it to Neena. "I figure you use the handle to pour."

Gently, Neena replaced the mug handle on the hook. "You'd better give that back to Judy to wrap before you end up owing the customer a refund."

"I know. I just had to show it to Everly first because my photos don't do it justice."

Neena snorted. "If Judy sells one of the Elvis heads, we'll have to give her a raise."

"The Elvis heads?" I had to ask while Jacy carefully carried the clown back up front to be boxed for shipping. "You have more than one? Are they like busts?" I had to know.

"There are two, and no, they're not busts. Or not exactly. Maybe the ceramic one is a bust. That one is hand-painted, while the other is made from plastic or rubber. I don't know which. It looks like it came from a life-sized doll or something. Highly creepy." Nodding that I should follow, Neena abandoned her unpacking and led me into the shop. "You won't understand until you see for yourself."

Now housed in the former furniture store, Curated Content's new space was three times larger than the one they'd rented from my boss. The building featured offices and studio space upstairs for Neena's painting, a cavernous storage area behind the showroom, and a larger parking lot. Patrea had bought the building with Jacy and Neena in mind, giving them the rent-to-own deal of a lifetime. All we'd had to do was get rid of the former owner—one Abner Mayfield, a cantankerous ghost with a territorial bent and unfinished business.

With Abner gone from the building, some careful restoration and refitting turned the area where he'd sold appliances into the perfect showcase for Jacy's growing stable of antiques. At Patrea's suggestion, they'd added a separate entrance and modern lighting to Neena's art gallery, which took up the left side of the former show-room. On the right, Jacy sold second-hand and consign-ment items. A partial wall divided the two front spaces but left room for customers to browse both, allowing for a shared checkout counter.

"You're right, of course," Judy Jackson, newly hired, told a potential customer. "You can't just plop that mid-century console table against a bare wall. It would be best to have the right art to hang over it. We have just the thing. Follow me." With a wink in Neena's direction, she led the couple into the gallery. "I have the perfect painting for you. I know you'll love it."

"She is good."

Neena picked her way past a selection of baby strollers. One of them looked like it should have carried a NASA emblem. Together, Jacy and I followed her.

"Judy is a blessing. She already knows what painting to show that couple because she pays attention. I predict she'll give them a package deal on the table and the art. They'll talk her down a percent or two, and she'll still be at or above the wiggle room we allow for dickering. They'll be happy they got a bargain, and we'll keep the doors open another day."

"Is that a concern?" I frowned. "Keeping the doors open, I mean."

Opening a shop had been Jacy's fondest wish, and Neena had always wanted to own a gallery. This business was their shared dream. I had the means to ensure they stayed open, but people can get prickly when you offer them money, so I needed to tread lightly here.

Tucking her arm in mine, Jacy shook her head. "It's just an expression. We're doing fine. Better than fine. We're doing very well."

"We're living the dream." Neena's voice carried no sarcasm but plenty of conviction, then she grinned and pointed to the pair of Elvis' heads sitting on lace doilies. "Not that everything in here is the stuff of dreams. Behold the head of Elvis. Or since there's two of them, maybe that's the head of Elvii."

For some reason, the doilies struck me funny, or maybe it was the term Elvii. But once the giggling began, it spread to them, and none of us could stop. Perhaps it was the relief of knowing the shop was okay. Or it could have been that Jacy laugh-snorted, which was funny, too.

Neena gasped, holding her stomach, "If Judy moves either of those, we should give her a raise."

"Challenge accepted." Judy had finalized the sale of

the console table and a painting to go over it before being drawn to the sounds of hilarity.

"Then it's a deal." Jacy sobered up a bit.

Her face solemn except for the twinkle in her eyes, Judy held out a hand to shake on it. "Give me a month."

"Five bucks says she does it in a week." I usually leave the betting to Jacy and Neena, but Judy wasn't one to rest on her laurels. Neena took the bet, and so did Jacy.

"Can I get in on that?" Tucking a lock of slowly silvering chestnut hair behind her ear, Judy's warm hazel eyes sparkled with good humor.

"I don't see why not." You couldn't help but like the woman.

We chatted a few more minutes before I left the shop and headed to the parking lot. Jacy's hot pink mini-van stood out like a beacon, making my red SUV look sedate. Adjusting my scarf, I hurried to my car and climbed inside. It wasn't until my butt hit the seat that I noticed a figure with long, pale blond hair sitting on the other side.

"Ack!" I bit back a scream in favor of a strangled exclamation as I realized who the woman had to be. "Vanessa Morgan?" Stupid question. Who else could it be? I'd seen her pictures, hadn't I?

She nodded. "I'm sorry. I didn't mean to frighten you," Vanessa said softly. "But I followed you when you left the Wentworth's house, and I've been working up the nerve to thank you for letting me out. I was trapped in that dark space for so long."

I took a deep breath and tried to compose myself but

failed as a shiver slid over me. I'm not claustrophobic, but that doesn't mean I'd want to be trapped behind a wall in the dark for thirty-odd years, either.

A second shiver wracked my chest when she reached out to touch my arm. Ghost touches still creep me out even though, for a short time, I walked among the not-quite dearly departed. But I didn't pull back because that would have been rude, and she seemed to need the comfort.

"It was my pleasure," I replied. Maybe pleasure wasn't the right word, but she smiled.

"You'll tell the other one, too? Patty, I think she's called."

"It's Patrea, but that's probably close enough. I'm not sure I'd call her Patty to her face, though."

Vanessa smiled. "I understand. My family always called me Nessie, and I hated it. I guess I wouldn't hate it so much now." Her tone turned sad. "I miss my folks."

This was my cue to press for details and fill her in on my rules for dealing with the dead, but I didn't. I felt compelled to pass on a message to loved ones for the first time. Vanessa had waited far too long to be found as it was, and her family deserved closure as much as she did.

"Is there someone I could call for you? Ernie will contact your family to let them know you've been found, but if there's anything else I can do, just say so."

"There are some distant cousins, but no one will care much, I don't think. I lost my parents to a house fire during my first year in college, but that's not why I wanted to talk to you. Since you got me out, I was hoping you would help me," Pleading, Vanessa reached a hand toward me, then yanked it back when I cringed. "I know it's a lot to ask when you've already done so much, but I think I need to know who murdered me, or I'll be stuck in this half-world forever."

Been there, done that. Not forever, but I got it. She wanted to move on, and while she wasn't threatening me with a long-term haunting—and wasn't that a nice change of pace—I already intended to help her.

"You're right, and I'm happy to do what I can," I sighed, feeling a surge of empathy kick in. "If you give me a list of the people in the house that night, I'll start doing some research."

I put my phone in its holder, turned on the voice recording app, dropped the car in gear, and drove out of the lot. I told Vanessa to give me her list, which I would repeat for the recording.

"A lot of people came to the party, and I didn't meet everyone. Is that okay?"

Absently, I tapped my fingers on the steering wheel. "Because of where you were found, I don't think it could have been a random guest. It had to be someone who lived there or was staying at the house. Who else would have the opportunity to hide you behind a wall?"

"That's true." Vanessa brightened for a moment, then sighed. "But it's not that simple. There were people in and out of the house all week. Workers. Well, not on the night of the party, but Mrs. Wentworth was always having something done to the place."

"Like remodeling? In the room where we found you?"

Vanessa nodded so hard I felt waves of cool air coming off her. "Have you ever heard of a panic room?"

Sure, I had. I just hadn't thought they'd been big in the...I looked at Vanessa to see if I could figure out during which decade she'd been killed. She styled her hair in long layers teased up for a bit of volume. Lots of makeup—mostly in pink and brown tones. Over a pair of what looked like high-waisted pants with a pleated front, she wore a slouchy jacket in a silky pink material with shoulder pads and the sleeves pushed up.

"You died in the 1980s?

"Yes. 1986. How did you know?"

"Lucky guess. I didn't know panic rooms were popular at the time. The movie didn't come out until the early two-thousands."

Vanessa tilted her head and squinted at me like I was speaking a language she didn't understand.

"Never mind. It's not important. You were telling me about the panic room."

Shaking off her confusion, she said, "According to Gloria, her family commissioned a prohibition room when the house was built. You had to go upstairs to get to it, and it had one of those hidden doors that looked just like the wall."

That explained the size and placement of the door we'd found.

"Once you followed the stairs down, it just looked like a small storage room, but there was a second hidden door, and that's where they kept the booze. Deke had the whole thing dismantled when he took over the house. They reopened all the hidden doors and turned the storage room into a reading nook until Mrs. W. Decided she needed a panic room."

That explained the room's odd dimensions and placement. "Did something happen to make Mrs. Wentworth feel unsafe?" This whole discussion got my crime-solving senses tingling.

Vanessa's expression turned grave. "Two weeks before the night of the party. Mrs. Wentworth was in the kitchen when she heard a loud crash coming from upstairs. When she went to investigate, she saw a man standing outside her bedroom door with a gun in his hand."

"There was a break-in?" Charlotte hadn't mentioned anything about a break-in.

"No one else saw or heard anything, and Mr. Wentworth flat-out accused his wife of imagining the whole incident, but she wouldn't let it go. I guess she kept at him until he gave in and told her he'd restore the prohibition room so she would have somewhere to hide if there was ever an intruder again."

"But that's not what happened, is it? I mean, they didn't just put in a pair of hidden doors and call it good, did they?"

"No," Vanessa confirmed with a shake of her head. "They couldn't find anyone with the skill to build the doors, and with the party coming up, Mr. Wentworth decided to have a room built at the foot of the stairs, and that would have to do. Mrs. Wentworth wasn't happy about it but got really annoyed when the workers couldn't finish in time for the party."

By then, we'd pulled up in front of my house, so I didn't press for details until she'd followed me inside.

"Is that your dog?" Charmed by Molly's welcoming dance, Vanessa's smile lit her narrow face. "Boy or girl?"

"Her name is Molly," I said as I let the dog out the back door and watched while she raced to her favorite pee spot. "You like dogs." Anyone could tell.

Having followed me, Vanessa stood a bit too close, but I didn't have the heart to say anything as she watched Molly streak back toward the house. "More than anything. I was studying to be a veterinarian." She sighed. What a waste of a life.

"You mentioned a party. Can you tell me about it?"

I pulled sandwich fixings out of the fridge while Vanessa talked.

"Sure. With the Wentworths, there was always a party. That's why Gloria invited me to stay with her over the winter break. But things didn't go smoothly."

Settling at the table, I prodded for more details. Vanessa paced while she talked.

"First, the workers didn't have time to finish Mrs. Wentworth's panic room. Then, Gillie was annoyed that they'd left a mess behind, and she tried to draft Arthur to help clean it up."

"And Arthur was who?"

"Wentworth. Arthur Wentworth, Gloria's older brother. He argued that it wasn't his job to clean up after incompetent tradespeople, but Mrs. Wentworth threatened to tell his father about something Arthur had done, and he gave in."

"Did you hear what it was?"

"Not exactly, but I figured it had to do with the man who came to see him the day before. Gloria wasn't up yet, so I'd gone to the library to pick out something to read and got engrossed in a detective novel. I was sitting in one of those chairs with the tall back facing away from the door when they came in."

We hadn't had much time to explore the house before finding poor Vanessa's bones, but I remembered glancing at the library so I could picture her sitting in a wing chair in front of the fireplace.

"Before I had a chance to speak up, they started talking about a business deal that sounded like it would generate a lot of money but at someone else's expense."

I'd have asked for more detail, but she kept going before I could.

"The whole thing felt off to me, and I couldn't look at Arthur quite the same way again. He noticed, too, and during the party, he asked me if he could speak to me in private, but we got interrupted. He said we'd talk later."

"Did you?"

Pausing to think, her forehead furrowed as she tried to

remember. "I don't know. I can't remember because something happened. Something bad."

Having edged too close to the topic of her death, Vannessa's body shook, then vanished from sight. I knew she wasn't gone for good; she would return when least expected. In the meantime, I would mull over what I'd learned. Besides, Drew would be home soon, and we had plans.

The rule is that the groom can't see the bride in her dress before the wedding, but I wasn't sure if that also went for the hairstyle.

"Better safe than sorry. One failed marriage is my limit," I said to Molly, who cocked her head but didn't weigh in with an opinion. My faithful shadow, she followed me to the bathroom and flopped down just inside the door while I took out the pins, let my hair down, and showered.

"There, that's better." I really was talking to the dog and not myself. That's my story, and I'm sticking to it. "Time to do some research." Grabbing my laptop, I headed for the kitchen, my thoughts already swirling with theories about Vanessa's murder.

When a basic search turned up little, I logged into the library website and scanned the local newspaper archives until I found an article on Wentworth House.

Built, as Patrea had said, in 1910, the Gilded Age beauty was the brainchild of Deacon "Deke" Wentworth the First. Riding high in the years before the First World War, Deke spent money left, right, and center. He built a home for his family that he felt befit a man of his station and stature. Sadly, Deke wouldn't survive the great depression. According to the article, he'd died by his own hand when his business went bankrupt. Deke left the house to his wife, Lizbeth, and his son, Deacon Jr. Lizbeth had no money of her own, but Junior held onto the house by the skin of his teeth until he met and quickly married heiress Gillian Dale. Lizbeth Wentworth passed just after the birth of Deacon Wentworth III, whom everyone called Arthur.

"Arthur Wentworth, huh?" I mused aloud, scrolling through search results until I located his online presence. There he was—a distinguished man in his late sixties with aristocratic features and piercing eyes that seemed to look right into my soul. "What are you hiding?"

After leaving home to strike out on his own, Arthur Wentworth began a new life in Port Harbor. He was now the head of a successful investment firm, and it seemed he had made quite a comfortable living for himself. Despite his success, however, there had been some bad press around him during the mid-nineties. Several of his clients got caught up in an investment scheme that cost them everything. From what the articles said, he hadn't been involved, but neither had he found out in time to protect his clients. Several hinted at a deeper involvement, but nothing was ever proved. Sounded about right after what Vanessa had said.

It would have been helpful to know the name of the man Arthur had made his deal with right before Vanessa's death, but I figured she'd have named him if she'd known. Since she didn't, I had as much chance of finding out as I did of seeing a pig fly over my house.

With wedding dress shopping in my future and a pile of money in the bank, I had a built-in excuse to drive to Port Harbor and talk to Arthur Wentworth about investments. If talk of family and home popped up, well, that's just what happens when you're from the same hometown, right? Sighing, I opened a blank document, typed Suspects at the top, and added his name to the number one slot.

A search for Vanessa's name turned up next to nothing. Only a single article in the Bangor Daily dated a few days after the murder, stated that police were still looking for the young woman who'd gone missing from the Wentworth house during a party.

It wasn't much, but it was a start. Finding Vanessa's killer after all this time wouldn't be easy, but since when had any of my cases been easy?

"You're in research mode. Dresses or ghosts?" Coming around to look at the screen, Drew figured it out for himself. "Ghosts, then." He leaned down to kiss me. "I'll just change, and we can head out."

We hadn't mentioned it to anyone, but we'd been talking about using some of my windfall money to buy a camp on the lake. The lake was where we'd met, after all, and would be a perfect wedding gift to ourselves and something we could leave for our kids when we had them.

Ideally, we hoped to find a place close enough to the Wade camp that our kids and Jacy's could hang out together.

"Some of the camp roads might still be muddy," I flipped my laptop closed. "But I know which ones to avoid. Another month, and it will be kayak weather. Speaking of which, I heard about a new spot." As we drove toward the lake, I told him the story Ernie had told me and promised to show him the mural as soon as we could get back into the house.

It was a nice day for the drive and for letting go of thoughts of death and murder for a while.

CHAPTER TEN

D rew and I drove to Bangor for date night after our trip along the east side of the lake. We hadn't found any camps for sale and had been home barely long enough to kick off our shoes when my mother called.

"Why didn't you tell me about the wedding expo in Brewer tomorrow? You know I don't work Sundays. We're going. I'll pick you up at eight."

I never even got a word in before she hung up.

"Don't tell me," Drew said and grinned. "You're going to Brewer tomorrow."

"I can get out of it." We'd tentatively planned to drive to the west side of the lake and check for camps there. "I'll call her back."

"Don't. It's okay. We'd probably do better looking on Marketplace or the Uncle Henrys." A statewide for-sale-by-owner booklet that went up for sale each Thursday. "Go with your mom. I've still got paperwork to catch up on." He lied to me again, but I wouldn't learn that until much later.

"Okay, but I'm going under protest. She's making way too big a deal over the tiniest details."

Still grinning, Drew turned me into his arms, lifted my chin, and kissed me gently. "She loves you and wants your day to be special. Let her pick out the perfect ring bearer pillow or flower girl basket. What does it hurt? If you won't do it for her, do it for me. I wouldn't want to get into her bad graces by being the excuse you use to get out of spending the day together."

"You're right." I kissed him back. "Do you know how much I love you?"

"If it's half as much as I love you, I'll consider myself a lucky man."

I kissed him again, then took him to bed to prove it.

Clutching a colorful brochure in one hand, Mom arrived on time the next morning and waved it in my face. "Over a hundred vendors are attending. I know we have the invitations and the florist, but there will be cake samples and photographers and a fashion show. I'm expecting great things." She talked excitedly through the entire drive.

"You know Mabel's making the cake, right? She insisted it would be her gift to us, and she's really good. And June Cobb at the new bakery is doing the groom's. We don't need to eat samples."

Mom waved that away with an impatient hand. "Maybe you don't, but I do. And why wouldn't we? It'll be fun."

"I hope this thing lives up to your expectations."

"It will." Stars wouldn't outshine her eyes. "Your day has to be special. I refuse to accept anything less."

"It's your day as much as it is mine." The comment earned me a sidelong look as we pulled into the parking lot, but she didn't respond.

As we wandered through the expo, admiring floral arrangements and marveling at the sheer volume of party favor ideas, I welcomed the distraction. Still, I couldn't keep my focus solely on what seemed like too many choices in wedding finery. Vanessa's face kept intruding, and it didn't help that I felt sorry for how she'd missed out on her chance at ever being a bride. I tried to stay present, asking vendors questions and taking notes on possible wedding ideas, but my mind kept wandering.

My mother, however, was in her element, dragging me from booth to booth as she excitedly chattered about color schemes and seating arrangements.

"Vanessa, I promise I'll get back to your case as soon as I can," I whispered while pretending to be engrossed in a display of headpieces.

"Everly!" Mom called out, snapping me out of my thoughts. "Come look at these beautiful place settings!"

"Coming, Mom," I replied, forcing a smile. As much as I wanted to solve Vanessa's murder, I had to strike a balance between my personal life and my paranormal pursuits. And today, that meant indulging my mother's enthusiasm for wedding planning—even when part of me insisted I should be chasing down leads to unravel the truth behind a decades-old murder. "Let's see if we can find a pretty basket for the flower girl to carry." I put Vanessa and her problems out of my mind.

In one of the corner booths, we came across a cake topper unlike any I'd ever seen: a tiny bride and groom perched atop a majestic unicorn, their plastic faces locked in expressions of pure joy as they clung to the creature's glittering mane. The bride wore a gown of intricate lace while the groom sported a suit of emerald green.

"Would you look at that?" I snorted, unable to contain my laughter, as I pointed it out to my mother. "Now, that's one way to make an entrance."

"It screams 'romantic adventure,' don't you think?" Mom's eyes sparkled with humor.

"More like 'adventures in questionable taste,'" I retorted, laughing as I placed it back on the table. "Unless you're marrying a Leprechaun or having one of those destination weddings in Fantasyland. Then it's probably perfect."

Kitty laughed along with me, her eyes crinkling at the corners as she studied the bright ornament. "You know, it's so ridiculous it's almost charming. What do you think? Should we consider it for your big day?"

It was.

"Only if you can find me a live unicorn to ride to the ceremony," I countered, still chuckling. "But I doubt you'll get Drew into a green tux."

"He would if you asked him to. The man is besotted. It's charming to see."

"He's not the only one, so I'll have to pass on the fantasy topper. His pride is worth a lot to me."

"Okay," Mom conceded, "maybe we should stick to

something more traditional." Still, she picked up another topper, this one featuring a bride dragging her groom by his ankles.

"Mom!" I exclaimed, trying to stifle my laughter. "You're not supposed to reveal our secret family tradition until after the ceremony!"

"Ah, yes, the sacred Dupree bridal kidnapping ritual," she whispered conspiratorially. "We mustn't let the unsuspecting groom catch wind of it."

Our shared laughter was a balm for my soul, and for a moment, the world outside the bridal expo ceased to exist. I threw myself into the experience.

The aroma of buttercream filled the air as we approached a table laden with cake samples. What could it hurt to taste a few? Mom and I took turns nibbling the decadent treats, our laughter ringing through the expo hall. The rich flavors of chocolate ganache and raspberry swirl mingled on my taste buds, making it difficult to decide on a favorite.

"Everly, you have to try this lemon lavender one!" Mom exclaimed, her eyes lighting up as she savored a bite. "It's divine!"

As I nibbled on the delicate floral confection, I heard someone call my name.

"Everly Dupree?" The voice didn't sound all that happy to see me, and when I turned to find Carlene Nicholson's beady eyes staring me down, the feeling was mutual.

"Carlene."

I'd have left it at that and walked away, but she had to get in a dig. Carlene and I had crossed paths in high school and more than once since. Not in a good way, either. Let's just say our chances of becoming friends were somewhere in the negative millions. But before I could protest, Mom engaged Carlene in face-saving conversation, her enthusiasm for all things wedding temporarily drowning out my apprehension.

"What are you doing here?" Since Carlene wore a badge proclaiming herself one of the vendors, it wasn't hard to figure out, but I wanted to hear her explain. I knew she'd moved back to the area recently, but I hadn't kept up with her job situation. Mostly, I pretended she didn't exist, and I was certain that sentiment went both ways.

"You're not the only one who knows how to plan a party. I've gone into the wedding planning business. I figured if you can do it...it can't be all that hard." She passed me her card.

"Indeed," I muttered, tucking the card into my purse without glancing at it. "I wouldn't expect a call from me if I were you."

Carlene's face gave nothing away as I dragged my mother toward the next booth.

"That was rude," she said, "but if there's a betting pool on how long Carlene's newest venture lasts, I'll take July 1st. She doesn't have the temperament or people skills to pull off a decent event."

Since I agreed, I leaned over and gave my mom a peck

on the cheek. "That's the nicest way I have ever heard anyone call Carlene an idiot."

She slung an arm around my neck. "If the shoe fits....and speaking of shoes," her attention zeroed in on a vendor offering a selection of pumps and strappy heels all aglitter with rhinestones, "look at those. What do you think?"

"I think I can feel the blisters already, and we should find a new dress first."

"You're probably right," she sighed. "But I'll grab a brochure if they have one, so we'll know where to shop later."

The mood between us had leveled out, and surprisingly, I was having more fun than I expected. Shared laughter and the simple joy of being together tamed my mother's overbearing nature, and as we continued our foray into all things bridal, I couldn't help but feel grateful. For now, the burden of responsibility could wait.

Sipping champagne, we sat through a wedding gown fashion show, sharing comments and taking notes on which styles I might want to consider. None of them hit me as the one, though.

"That one's lovely." I admired a dress with a more relaxed silhouette that featured a V-neck paired with a geometrically-inspired lace overlay and beading in a soft ivory color that would work better with my hair than stark white. The lack of corseting would make it far more comfortable on the day. Something about it seemed familiar. "What do you think?"

Head tilted, Mom assessed. "It's nice. The lace pattern reminds me of your Grammie Dupree's wedding dress. The shape is similar, too. Only hers had capped sleeves and a different neckline."

I snapped my fingers. "That's why it looked familiar. I've seen one like it in Daddy's photo albums. It's too bad she didn't save it. I might have been tempted, but this one is lovely, too."

"It's a modern take on a vintage design. Timeless and classic. I'll make a note of which store to visit so you can try one on."

Except I could see her eyes were constantly drawn to more elaborate confections similar to what she'd worn on her wedding day. A little damage control might be wise. "It takes a regal build to pull off a dress like that," I pointed to the number coming down the runway that featured yards of tulle ruffles that would have fit right in at Tara. "I don't have the frame to carry it off. I'd end up looking like a human shower pouf because I'm not statuesque like you. Grammie Dupree's genes skipped a generation and landed on me."

"I suppose you're right."

Amid the rustle of silk and satin as the next model passed, I heard her sigh, but she didn't seem annoyed. Score one for me. I didn't have time to gloat because the sensation of being watched washed over me and pulled my attention. Discreetly, I glanced around and finally spotted Carlene standing nearby. She looked away and pretended innocence, but she'd been staring at me. I just knew it. The question was, why?

CHAPTER ELEVEN

The welcome scent of coffee tickled my nose on Monday morning. So did the delicate swipe of Molly's tongue. I made a superhuman effort to drag one eyelid open and then pulled my head back into my pillow when the dog's face was so close to mine that she looked like a blur.

"Morning, Molls," I said, my voice husky with sleep.

"What about me?" Drew's voice rumbled from nearby. "I brought coffee. Shouldn't that earn me a greeting, too?"

Smiling, I opened both eyes and turned to see him standing in the doorway. "If you come closer, it will earn you more than that."

After one long kiss, he pulled back. "As much as I'd rather climb back in with you, Riley needed a day off, so I'm taking her morning classes." He set the coffee on my nightstand. "What's on your agenda for the day?"

"I'm back at the rental house in the woods today—just to meet Bennie's uncle, Sam, and give him a key. Part of the sill needs replacing, and it rotted the ends of two of the floor joists, so some jacking and repair needs doing. I didn't realize Bennie and Chris were distant cousins until we hired Sam and his crew to do the job. Sam likes to talk. After that, I was planning to go into research mode."

That was the plan anyway. Ten minutes after Drew left for work, the plan got derailed when my phone rang.

"Ernie's cleared the house," Patrea said without bothering to say hello. "I'm heading over to start outlining work orders for the various subcontractors. Want to come?"

"I do," I said, then told her I had a work thing I had to do first. We arranged for her to pick me up, and we'd detour out to the rental on the way. "But be warned. I'm drafting you to help clean this rental once Sam fixes the joists. It's only fair."

"Deal."

The damp morning air carried a chill as I paced back and forth on the porch half an hour later. Patrea would be late in another minute, which would put me late for meeting Sam. When she pulled in, I'd just about decided to get my car out of the garage.

"Sorry," she said when I slid into the passenger's seat. "The story about Vanessa broke, and I've been fielding calls from local news all morning."

"How did they find out?"

Patrea shrugged and pointed to a travel mug of coffee in the cup holder and a plastic container on the seat between us. I opened the lid to find homemade chocolate croissants, selected one, and sighed with contentment after the first bite. The woman should have been a baker by profession. I'd never tasted better. "My money's on someone in Ernie's office giving them the tip-off."

"Carole Ann Wilmette." If it came from there, she was the one who passed on the information. Had to be. Worse, it probably wasn't the first time she'd done it. I wondered if they paid her for the information. It wouldn't surprise me if she considered it part of the perks of the job. Either way, who told the press didn't matter since it was already done.

Dropping off the key with Sam took longer than planned. Like his nephew, Sam was a talker. He'd heard about the discovery at the Wentworth and wanted to know if we could scare up any work for him there. Patrea took his card, agreed to keep him in mind, and we made our escape.

The mansion looked as imposing as ever when we pulled up. More, maybe, since the pall of murder hung over it. And it was still chilly, which meant it would be even colder inside. I wasn't sure how that worked.

"A haunted house sells much better than a murder house," Patrea mused as she unlocked the door.

"Are you worried you won't be able to turn it around?"

She shrugged. "What will be, will be. But if you could solve Vanessa's murder, I'd be forever grateful." The door swung open.

"It's about time you showed up." Irate, Charlotte met us before we'd taken more than a few steps inside. "There have been people peeking in the windows all morning. It's put me in a right foul mood, I don't mind telling you."

"What people," I asked, then repeated what she'd said for Patrea's benefit.

"Nosy people, that's what." Popping her hands on her hips, Charlotte offered a wicked grin and put in the effort to show herself to Patrea. "Scaredy cats, the lot of them."

Uh oh.

"What did you do?" I figured I already had a good idea.

"Nothing much." Charlotte shrugged, her eyes twinkling now. "Just put the fear of Charlotte into them, that's all. It's not the first time I've protected the house. We haven't had a break-in since I returned to my post. Lost a couple of windows during a big blow a few years back, but that's it."

Catching my eye, Patrea allowed a wry grin. "Well, thanks, I guess."

"Don't get too excited," Charlotte warned as she faded. "I'm sure they'll be back once they figure out you're here."

Less than half an hour later, Charlotte's prediction proved correct when the Newscenter van pulled up behind Patrea's truck as we lifted out the stepladder she'd brought.

"Here we go," she said, gently setting her end. I followed suit but didn't go with her to meet the reporter who'd jumped out of the passenger side. The reporter's eyes were glued on Patrea as she stood in the driveway, blocking access to the house.

"What can you tell me about the bones discovered

here?" he asked, thrusting the microphone toward her face.

Patrea avoided giving direct answers as she danced around his question, "I have nothing to say at this time. Until the bones have been identified and the family of the deceased notified, I will make no further comment."

The camera operator panned the front of the house while the reporter continued to be aggressive, "You purchased this house only recently. Did you know it was the scene of a gruesome murder?"

"I have no comment to make at this time," Patrea repeated and moved close enough to the camera that the operator was forced to step back.

"Do you know what evidence the police have found?"

Patrea offered a withering stare and amended her statement to include that the police were still investigating. After a few more aborted attempts at asking questions, the reporter thanked her for her time and drove away.

Her shoulders heaved with a sigh of relief as Patrea turned back to me. "Well, that wasn't too bad," she said with a smile.

I smiled in return as we picked up the ladder again. It seemed like we might have dodged a bullet this time around—or at least delayed it until we had something concrete to report on Vanessa's case.

Inside, Charlotte grumbled about trespassers and promised to scare the pants off anyone else who came skulking around. I wondered why she hadn't done the same when Jacy and I were girls. Probably because she could see we hadn't meant any harm. I'd have asked, but she didn't stick around long enough to bother.

"I'd almost pay to see that," Patrea said, her eyes alight with humor, "except Charlotte has no need of money, so it's a weak bribe."

"You could set up security cameras. At least in a few strategic places."

Nodding, Patrea stood up the ladder and prepared to change some of the burned-out bulbs. "I'd have to get wi-fi hooked up first. Assuming the cable company runs out this far. Did they even have cable when this house went empty?"

"That's a good question. Let me call our friendly local librarian. I'm sure she'll have the answer."

"Say hi to your mom for me."

"Will do." I made the call.

My mom answered on the first ring, her voice cheery and bright.

"Hi, sweetheart! How are you?" she asked. "I know we already decided on wedding favors, but I can't stop thinking about those little wooden boxes we saw yesterday. What do you think?"

"Patrea says hello." I tried to deflect the conversation from wedding stuff. "There have been reporters sniffing around out here, so we're looking into setting up some sort of security system, but we weren't sure if there was Internet service out this far."

"Oh, that's easy," she said. "We all got cable in the late

seventies because the Wentworth family offered to cover a portion of the costs so long as the company agreed to run lines to the entire town, which included their own home."

"I knew you'd have the answer. We're considering webcams."

"That sounds quite practical," my mother chuckled. "Now, have you thought about personalized mementos for your guests instead of traditional favors? That would be much more meaningful than electronic surveillance!"

I laughed at her attempt at a joke and told her to send me a list of party favor ideas. It was the only way to get her off the phone.

"What's the consensus?" Patrea climbed back down the stepladder, flicked the switch, and grinned when the light in the foyer increased.

"There's cable."

Delighted, Patrea pulled out her phone to make the call. "Why do you have service and I don't?" Frowning, she held her phone up and wandered around to see if she could find a spot where she had more bars. "I know I can call from upstairs. Be right back."

As Patrea went up, Vanessa came down. She joined me at the bottom of the stairs. "Do you mind if we go out on the porch? I hate being inside, and it's nicer in the sun. Plus, the house being empty is unsettling."

"No problem," I followed her out and leaned against one of the columns, waiting for her to say what was on her mind.

"Being here brought home a few truths I hadn't

wanted to face," Vanessa finally said. "When you said it had to be someone who knew the house better than a casual guest, it didn't occur to me that meant it had to be someone in my close circle of friends. I was stupid."

"You're being too hard on yourself," I offered consolation. "I don't know anyone, living or dead, who wouldn't be unnerved by the thought of their nearest and dearest having homicidal tendencies."

"I suppose. What's the next step? It won't hurt any less if we put it off, so I'd like to get this done."

"Let's start by making a full list of suspects." I pulled out my phone, opened the notes app, and navigated to the entry I'd used since this mystery began. "I need to know who was in the house at the time of the incident."

When Vanessa paused for a long moment, it seemed she might not answer, but finally, she said, "Okay. There was Gloria Wentworth. But you're never going to convince me that my closest childhood friend would resort to murder. We went to the same boarding school and then to the same college where we talked the director into letting us room together."

"So, this wasn't the first time she'd invited you for a visit?"

Her hair never moved when Vanessa shook her head. A ghostly version of hair spray or the lack of wind on the other side of the veil, I wondered idly.

"I spent a lot of time with the Wentworths over the years. Enough that they stepped in as family when I lost mine. I think they funded the scholarships that let me attend the same schools as Gloria, but I never had proof. None of them would hurt me. I just know it."

"Well, someone did."

"True, but it wasn't Gloria or her parents. Gloria's not the type to resort to violence. She might talk a situation to death, but she wouldn't lash out physically. Junior and Gillie were kind people. Unfailingly kind. They took me in when I had no one left, and it didn't matter to them that I was technically an adult. I gave them no reason to hurt me. I loved them."

Except when pushed into a corner, nearly anyone would lash out. But we were going off her perceptions, so I had no choice but to take them as fact.

"I believe you. If it wasn't Gloria or her immediate family, then who else?" I noticed she didn't include Arthur in that list.

With no hesitation, Vanessa named names. "There was Evelyn Hartfield. She was a secretary in Deacon's office. I think Arthur got her the job, but Gloria was familiar with her, too. Enough to hold a conversation, in any case."

"Tell me about her," I ordered. "What do you remember?"

"Just that she was engaged to one of Arthur's college buddies. A man named Greg Thornton. But I doubt they ended up married. He didn't love her."

"How do you know?"

"If he loved her, he wouldn't have been making passes

at me, would he? Not my type at all, so I brushed him off. I don't think Evelyn was too happy with him."

I tapped the information into my notes app.

"Jealousy gives her a motive. Did she confront you about it?"

"Not that I remember," Vanessa mused, her pale hand absentmindedly brushing a strand of hair behind her ear. "But Evelyn always seemed more passive-aggressive than outright aggressive. She'd be more likely to spread nasty rumors about a person than make an effort to kill them. I know she had some poor woman fired from her job once."

"Describe them for me, would you? It helps if I can imagine what everyone looked like."

Vanessa smiled, the first real smile I'd seen from her since she had been called back from the darkness. "Gloria was always very stylish. Her upbringing gave her a taste for the finer things in life, which showed in her clothing choices. She was tall with long, dark hair that cascaded down her back like a waterfall. Her eyes were always so lively and full of mischief. Her laugh was contagious." The smile turned misty and sorrowful, but only for a moment.

"Evelyn was the complete opposite of Gloria," Vanessa said thoughtfully. "She wasn't as concerned about appearances but somehow managed to be a total Betty without trying too hard. She had blond hair, a few shades lighter than mine, and bright green eyes that missed nothing."

Vanessa hesitated as if she had more to say. "What else?" I encouraged her to speak.

"I hate to cast aspersions."

"Everything you tell me brings me closer to finding your killer. Every detail you can remember brings me closer. And I'm sorry, but I can't rule anyone out yet, or I might miss something. Someone got away with murder. Plain and simple. It's up to us to find justice, and we can't do that if we don't examine all of the possibilities."

That seemed to surprise her, so I elaborated. "Think about it. Who had access to the room where we found you? Only people who knew Mrs. Wentworth planned to build a panic room. Which means it's likely one of the family put you in there. Or maybe knew what happened. If not the family, it must have been someone close to them. Gloria moved away after Mrs. Wentworth fell ill, but she might have been suffering from a crisis of conscience."

"Not Gloria," Vanessa gasped. "She wouldn't put me in the dark. We were like sisters. She wouldn't do that, and neither would Junior or Miss Gillie. She treated me like I was one of her own. Gifts under the tree, birthday parties. I think she would have adopted me if she could have."

The temperature around me dropped a solid ten degrees as Vanessa's face darkened and her body began to vibrate. The last thing I needed was for her to go all angry ghost full of wrath on me again.

"Take a minute to calm yourself. I'm sure Gloria didn't intend for anything to happen to you, and there's no reason to get all keyed up until I've had a chance to talk to her. I'm here to help you. You're not alone and in the dark anymore. Can you hear me, Vanessa?"

For a moment, I thought she'd gone too far to pull it back, but somehow, she did. The feeling of ghost ants marching over my skin faded.

"Besides, you're wrong. Everyone knew about the panic room. Miss Gillie went on and on about her "harrowing event" and showed the unfinished room to all the guests. Not just the ones who stayed at the house." She settled back down.

Picking up on the key part of her sentence, I said, "Unfinished? In what way?"

"It didn't have a door yet. And she talked about waiting until after the party to have the room mudded. Which didn't make sense to me except for, I guess, it's mud, right? Mud is messy, and you wouldn't want someone slinging it around when there's a party happening. But I never understood what she meant. Unless it's something to do with that saying about throwing mud against the walls."

There'd been a time when I would have jumped to the same conclusion. Owning my own home and managing Leo's rental properties cured that bit of ignorance. "I always heard it was throwing spaghetti against the wall." Either way, she didn't mean mud from the backyard.

"Sheetrock mud is a white powder that, when mixed with water, forms a sort of paste that seals the spaces between sheets of drywall. The installers use a special tape on the joints, then spread more mud over the tape and let it dry. Once dry, the installer sands everything flat to create smooth walls and sharp corners. It can take a few coats to get it right."

"Well, now I feel stupid. That's not what I pictured in my head."

"Don't feel bad. I'd have thought the same thing before I bought my place."

"It's silly, though, isn't it? I mean, if you're going to all the trouble to create a safe place to hide in case of a break-in, why would you show everyone and their uncle where it is? Doesn't that defeat the purpose?" Vanessa picked up on a vital point.

"Seems like it. But it helps me understand a bit more about how you ended up where you did. If the room wasn't mudded and taped, anyone with a screwdriver could undo the wallboard, shove you back there, and put the wall back up. It wouldn't take more than fifteen or twenty minutes. Half an hour at the most."

None of that helped with cause of death, and just about anyone at the party had access to the room, so it didn't help with narrowing the suspect list much, either. It would have been one thing if the wall had been finished already. In that case, I'd have been looking for someone with knowledge of building and the ability to mud and tape a wall. Removing that qualification bumped the possibilities up to anyone who knew the screwdriver's handle from the business end.

"Tell me more about Evelyn, and don't worry about casting aspersions. I need all the information I can get, including your impressions, to help me narrow down the field of suspects."

"It's just that she was furious with Greg for talking to me, but she and Derek disappeared for half an hour the day before the party, and after that, neither of them could look the other in the eye."

"And Derek was?"

"Derek Montgomery, my ex-boyfriend."

I sat on the top step while the implications buzzed through my brain. "Love triangle? Or two of them. Intersecting lines. Intersecting people," I muttered while I updated my notes. "Bumps the jealousy motive higher on the list."

Standing quietly, Vanessa watched and listened but didn't speak until I'd worked through the possibilities.

"How did that make you feel? Seeing him with Evelyn?"

"Not bad enough to wrap myself in plastic and die in a dark room, if that's what you're asking. As if." Vanessa's smile took away the sting of sarcasm. "In truth, I felt sorry for Greg but glad for Derek. I figured that if he was knocking boots with someone else, he was over me. Evelyn and Greg could deal with their own relationship issues."

"Fair enough. Tell me more about Derek and Greg. What were they like?"

"Gloria used to compare Derek to Heathcliff as a joke. Tall, dark, handsome, and broody. He always wore jeans and a black shirt to set off his blue eyes and had a poet's mouth. Compared to him, Greg was much more low-key," Vanessa continued. "He favored slacks and polo shirts, but he could still look choice when he wanted to. He had short brown hair that was often unkempt and pale gray eyes that constantly searched for something new to explore."

"Something new? Or the next big thing?" There was a difference. Vanessa wasn't stupid, so she picked up on my meaning.

"You're wondering if Greg was an opportunist. Maybe so. I didn't know him well enough to be sure."

"Everly! Where did you go?" Patrea yelled from inside.

"I'm out here," I yelled back.

"I should bounce," Vanessa began to fade.

"No, don't. It's okay. Patrea can't see you unless you want her to, but she's ghost-friendly and has a good mind for crime-solving."

"There you are. The cable guy is on his way."

Turning to her, I let the surprise show on my face. "Who did you have to promise sexual favors to for that to happen so quickly? Last time I called them, it took a week to get anyone out, and I had to threaten to cut off the service to get them here that quickly."

"No sexual favors, but I did do a legal one. It helps when you get the local cable guy out of a nasty ticket."

Standing, I brushed off the back of my pants. "I didn't know you fixed tickets."

"Normally, I don't. In this case, it was warranted. He got busted in front of the lumber mill out on Lanyard

Road. They tried to hit him for twenty over the limit, which is a bigger fine and points off your license."

"Oh," I nodded. "I see. That's the one with the flashing lights that say you're going too fast, but there's no posted speed limit, and the flashing light runs twenty-four-seven."

"Ding, ding. Give the girl a prize. I didn't even have to go to court. I just told him to take a video of the lights flashing while he's standing still and another to show the last posted speed limit, which he was under. I didn't even charge him for the advice because that whole thing is shady. County mounties sit out there and pick people off, figuring most of them will be too intimidated to go to court and defend themselves."

"She's a warrior," Vanessa moved closer to Patrea and gave her a measuring look. "Just like you."

I snorted.

"What?" Patrea thought the snort was for her benefit. "You know I'm right."

"I do, indeed. It's only that Vanessa thinks you're a warrior. Just like me."

I heard Patrea's neck crack when she swiveled her head to look around. "She's here? Where? She's not going all ghost of vengeance again, is she?" The question came with an involuntary shiver.

Vanessa's shoulders slumped. "Tell her I'm sorry. I didn't mean to scare her when you let me out of the wall. All I could think about was getting out of the darkness. I wasn't myself, if you know what I mean."

At times like those, it bothered me that I couldn't hug a ghost. Vanessa really needed one. Maybe Charlotte could have offered comfort, but she hadn't come back. The best thing I could do was give Vanessa the chance to apologize in person.

"You can tell her yourself. You just have to want her to see you badly enough and put all your energy into the effort."

When Vanessa's face scrunched up with the strain, I had to bite my lip to keep from smiling.

"Hey," Patrea pointed. "I saw a flicker. Keep going. You're getting it." She took a short step back when Vanessa fully appeared. "There you are. It's nice to meet you, Vanessa." Waving away the ghost's apology, Patrea vowed, "I promise to do my part to help get you into the light."

CHAPTER TWELVE

Quickly, before Vanessa's ability to stay visible ran out, I filled Patrea in on the details the ghost had given me.

"A double love triangle and a possibly shady business deal. Slim motives, but it's a start. I'm leaning toward the ex-boyfriend. What else do we know about him? Maybe he wanted to rekindle your relationship and thought making you jealous would be a good way to get your attention. But when it didn't work, could he have snapped?"

"Anything's possible," Vanessa sighed. "Derek had a temper, and he didn't take rejection well. But I don't know if he'd go as far as murder. I wish I remembered more about my last moments alive. It would make things so much easier for all of us."

"Trust me, no ghost does. This is not my first time, so I know what I'm talking about." I squeezed her shoulder, forgetting for a moment that she was a ghost and my hand would pass right through her. But the gesture seemed to bring her some comfort, nonetheless. Worth getting a case of the creeps. "You can't tell me anything because that would be too easy. It's not your fault. It's just how this ghost thing works."

"Including the suspects you've already listed and the others who attended the party, there are just too many possibilities," Patrea added reassurance. "But I promise you, Vanessa, we'll find out who did this to you. And when we do, they'll pay for what they've done."

"Thank you. Both of you," Vanessa whispered, her eyes filled with gratitude. "I couldn't ask for better people to help me. It seems like no one else bothered."

I had theories on why there hadn't been a whole-scale investigation into the disappearance. One revolved around shoddy police work. The other, more sinister, involved a cover-up, which depended on whether the family knew exactly where Vanessa had gone. The latter was the one I put the most stock in.

"Arthur lives in Port Harbor these days. So far, he's the only one I've had time to research online."

"Online?" Confusion wrinkled Vanessa's forehead. "I don't understand."

Ever tried to explain the current version of the Internet to someone who died before it became available to the masses? Yeah, neither had I. By the time I managed to get through the clumsiest of descriptions, Vanessa's energy waned, and she faded away.

Once she was gone, I helped Patrea finish swapping burnt light bulbs, and as the rooms brightened, we made notes on the work that needed doing.

"Did you notice all the cobwebs are gone?" Patrea stood, clipboard in hand, and surveyed the smallest bedroom shrewdly. "I'm assuming that's Charlotte's doing since it's none of mine. Speaking of Charlotte, I'm surprised she's not following us around to make sure we don't make a mess or something. Don't you think that's weird?"

"Not necessarily. It takes considerable energy for a ghost to affect the living world. After all this cleaning, she's probably resting up or whatever it is that ghosts do to recharge. My stint on the other side didn't offer me that opportunity, so I still don't know how everything works over there."

"Looks like we're done down here. I'll send Chris over with a bigger ladder to do the chandeliers. This one isn't tall enough. Grab an end, and help me carry it upstairs." But she didn't move, which was unusual for Patrea, who rarely wasted time when there was a job to do. "We could start on the third floor—get the worst area out of the way first." Again, she didn't move.

I got it. We hadn't had a good experience the last time we went up there, and I wasn't looking forward to a repeat any more than she was. Still, outside of being scared half out of my skin and fully out of my wits, nothing bad had happened to us. It seemed like the dark spirit had been angrier with Charlotte than with the intrusion on the house.

The only way through a tough situation is to keep going forward. I picked up my end of the ladder. "Let's go."

And off we went.

I couldn't decide if it was a relief or a letdown to get through the changing of bulbs without incident, but the more time that passed, the more comfortable Patrea became. It took me a little longer, but eventually, I stopped worrying. Or got distracted by the view out the dormer windows.

"I bet you can see the lights in town from up here at night."

When Patrea didn't respond, I realized she'd gone into one of the other rooms and followed to find her trying to open one of the windows that faced the rear of the property.

"What are you doing?" She jumped at the sound of my voice.

"It's jammed. These old wooden windows swell up when it's damp. Especially when they haven't been maintained regularly." Demonstrating, she grabbed the sash handle, but the window wouldn't budge. Neither would the next or the third on that side. She crossed the room to test the front windows. The middle one rattled in the frame, then popped up two inches.

"Be careful. My father broke a storm window once. A shard of glass punctured the artery in his wrist. Scared me half to death. We're too far out to get you to a hospital in time if there was an accident." As it always did, the memory of blood pumping from the cut evoked a shudder.

"It's all about the finesse, not the force." With gentle

hands, she wiggled and jiggled the sash in its frame. Slowly, the window rose an inch and then another. "See. Easy."

I let out the breath I'd been holding, then sucked it in again when she got the window all the way open and stuck her leg through.

"What are you doing?"

"Going out to inspect the roof, of course. Come with me. Or are you scared of heights?"

"Not especially, but I am leery of a possibly sketchy roof."

She could have pooh-poohed my fears, but Patrea wasn't the type. "It's not sketchy," she said in earnest. "The house has been empty since 1987, and there's not a single sign of a current leak anywhere. This style of roof has a fifty-year lifespan, but most of them last a lot longer. Some even as long as a century."

Squinting, I ran over what I knew of the house. "Well, if the house was built in 1910, we're over the century mark, so how can you be so certain it's safe?"

"Because this isn't the original tile, and if I had to guess, I'd say this was installed in 1985, just a couple of years before they moved out. If my math is correct, it's got plenty of life left."

"How on earth could you possibly know when these tiles were replaced?" The path of her logic wasn't as clear as it could be.

"These are mission tiles, but this house had a French tile roof when it was built. I've seen pictures online."

"Okay. I don't know what that means, but I'll take your word for it."

She made a rippling motion with her hands. "It's not that complicated. French tiles and Mission tiles are all made from clay but in a different pattern."

Light dawned. "I'm sure I've heard them called something else."

Patrea nodded. "Probably Spanish tiles."

"That's it." I snapped my fingers.

"While Mission tiles are very similar to Spanish, both feature a larger, more graceful arch and less texture than the French."

I looked out the window again. "If you say so."

"I do. It wasn't a cheap repair, and most people don't put that kind of money into a house and then move out two years later."

"Again, I don't see how you could possibly know that."

Offering me a cheeky grin, Patrea shrugged. "I've done my homework. At least a little. The house was abandoned in 1987—"

"That's the year after Vanessa's death."

Patrea nodded. "Hurricane Gloria swept through the area in September of 1985—coincidence on the name, right?" When I nodded, she continued. "Based on the yellowing of the minor water damage I've noticed on the ceilings, I figure she ripped off enough tiles to force significant repair. French tiles are less common than the Mission style and harder to find—especially in the northern states. Given the time frame, they probably decided to replace the entire roof with what they could get rather than try to find matching tiles."

I couldn't fault her logic. I could, however, grab her arm when she slung a leg out the window.

"If nothing is leaking now, and you know all that, why would you need to inspect?"

"Because I want to see for myself. It's not steep, and you can see that the tiles are all intact. I'll be fine." Before I could argue against taking hasty action, she was out the window and stepping lightly across the undulating surface.

"If you fall and die, you're not allowed to haunt me."

"I'm not planning to fall."

"No one plans to fall," I leaned out the window and yelled to make sure she heard me. "That's why they're called accidents." Should I follow her? Or should I hit 9-1 and be ready to hit the final digit in case of trouble?

Listening to Patrea's careful progress, I kept pace below as she headed for the roof's peak and made her way down the other side. We arrived at the windows on the other side of the room at the same time. Whatever she saw when she looked closely at the window frames made Patrea happy because she gave me the thumbs-up sign.

"Just get back in here," I muttered in a tone too low to be heard through the glass. "Before you give me a heart attack." Heights don't bother me that much, and neither did being on a roof. Grammie Dupree used to throw stargazing parties on her roof for the two of us, but this one was higher, and I wasn't the fearless child I had once been.

Plus, there was a dark spirit in the house.

Instead of returning to the peak, Patrea's attention strayed toward the roof's lower edge. When she made her way toward the drop-off, I nearly peed my pants. As nimble as a tight-rope walker, Patrea tiptoed forward, then knelt to prod at something only she could see. I wanted to look away but couldn't because I somehow developed the irrational idea that if I watched closely enough, she wouldn't fall. Like my undivided attention was her saving grace. People's brains don't make sense half the time, and mine was no exception.

After two lifetimes and a dose of eternity, Patrea rose from her crouched position and picked her way back up the roof and over the peak. I met her at the window and waited until she had both feet on the floor before giving her a swat on the arm.

"You scared me half to death. What is wrong with you?"

"What? I like heights, and I have excellent balance. You should see me walk a tightrope. Don't you want to know what I found?"

"You're grinning like a goon, so it has to be something good, but...did you say tightrope? Never mind, it doesn't matter. I'm not done being mad at you until my heart rate goes back to normal."

Patrea has a great laugh. It's husky but somehow still

light, and it just rolls out of her, but I wasn't in the mood to hear it. "It's not funny."

"I'm sorry," she said. "Truly. I didn't mean to scare you, but you have to see what I found. I can't begin to think how it ended up where it was." She pulled a ring from her pocket and handed it over for my perusal.

"Holy cats," I turned toward the window and let daylight wash over the sapphire cabochon set into a circle of diamonds in a yellow-gold setting. "That's got to run close to ten carats on the sapphire and another couple in diamonds. Could be an engagement ring."

"It says VCA on the inside of the band. Do you think that stands for Vanessa? Maybe her last name wasn't Morgan."

For once, I knew something she didn't. "No, that's a maker's mark. Van Cleef and Arpel. VCA. My ex-mother-in-law favored them for watches, but everything they make is exquisite. And expensive."

Since Patrea's family ran in the same circles as my ex, she was familiar with the name once she heard it. "Too fussy for my taste, but the workmanship is flawless, which begs the question: How did it end up on the roof?"

"Only the one question?" I teased. "That seems a bit tame for the likes of Patrea Evergreen."

She tossed her head. "You want more? Here goes. Who did it belong to? Did that person lose it, or did they intentionally toss it away? Why didn't anyone come back for it? Is it a clue in Vanessa's murder? And finally, what should I do with it?"

"Starting with the last question first, I'd take it to a reputable appraiser and see what it's worth. Vintage VCA can go for hundreds of thousands. You might want to consider getting it insured."

"Hundreds of thousands? Really?" She held out a hand for the ring, then stared at it for a long moment. "That's a lot of money to spend on a bauble. Even more on one that someone tossed out a window."

"From the look of this place, the Wentworth family was rolling in it. I can't say the same for Vanessa because, from what she said, she came from people of more modest means. It's time to start researching the rest of the players, I suppose."

Long past time, if you wanted my honest opinion. But between work, dealing with ghosts, my mother, and wedding stuff, I'd dropped the ball. Still, Vanessa had been dead a good long time. A few more days shouldn't be that big of a deal.

"Where is Charlotte when you need her? I'm sure she knows all the dirty secrets." Patrea grinned at her attempt at humor. "Dirty secrets...housekeeper. That was a good one."

"I'm sure she's fine." I wasn't. Not entirely. Not that I knew what to do for her if she wasn't. "I'll get online tonight and start looking up the names I got from Vanessa. Until we know more about the major players, it's hard to know what questions to ask Charlotte. Plus, I have another line to tug as well."

I was thinking of Dolly, the ghost who'd been to

parties at the mansion. Maybe even the party where Vanessa died. Surely, she'd have insights to offer.

"Another line?"

"Well, maybe. It's a ghost. A very chatty one." I told her about Dolly during the trip back downstairs. Not that there was much to tell, but ghosts interested Patrea quite a bit, and she had some small ability to feel them, which she'd demonstrated when Amber Hale was a spectral visitor in my house. If I'd been a betting woman, I'd put money on Patrea making an appointment at the local salon just to see if she felt Dolly's presence.

"If you wouldn't mind spending another hour, I'd like to take a few more photos and add notes to get the ball rolling. I set up appointments with some of my subcontractors before Ernie locked everything down, so I'd like a working plan in place today."

"Take as long as you need. I'm not going anywhere."

We stood the stepladder back up in the sitting room with the painting and left it there while we cataloged the work needed on the exterior. "I can't believe how warm it has been for this time of year." I turned my face to welcome the sun's heat for a moment. The rising temperatures hadn't warmed the house up more than a degree or two inside.

"Don't get too excited for summer," she warned. "You know the older fellow who often hangs out at the hardware store? Well, when I was in there this morning to pick up a bunch of light bulbs, he told me his knees have been bothering him for nearly a week, which means a big storm is coming. He says snow, not rain."

"Eddie Mason? Yeah, his knees are more reliable than the weather report." With new grass coming up, daffodils showing their cheerful faces to the sky, and leaves just poking their noses out of tight buds, a snowstorm this late in the season could be bad. "Did he say when? A snowstorm this time of year can be catastrophic."

The alarm in my voice earned a concerned look. "Not really. Why? How bad could it be?"

"Fill the bathtub bad, as Grammie Dupree would say."

Patrea snorted. "Is that like a three on the Richter scale?"

The comparison wasn't as far off as she thought. "More like a five. Seven if you live far enough out of town."

Just inside the front door, Patrea stopped and turned to me. "Are you trying to scare me? Is it like one of those small-town things where you scare the city folk with dire weather predictions? We lose power in the city, too. Sometimes."

"But not for as long. And no, I'm not trying to scare you. I'm just saying things work differently here. You've seen that with a regular winter storm. This isn't winter anymore. It's May. We're in spring now, which brings other factors into play. The ground has thawed, so plowing tears up the ground. Most of the roads can't be plowed at all."

"So?" Patrea shrugged. "If the temps go back up, the

snow won't last. Who cares if people can't get to their camps for a few days?"

Since I wasn't done, I kept talking. Or lecturing, I suppose.

"There's more. The trees are starting to put on leaves, so they'll hold more snow. More snow means more weight. More weight means more broken trees. Broken trees fall on power lines, and it takes the power company longer to get back up and running in the rural areas because they send crews to the larger towns first."

Some of my concerns began to translate to her.

"It doesn't sound like you need to worry about the roof here, and the farm has weathered enough spring storms that Chris will know what to do. Just make sure you tell him old man Mason predicted a whopper."

She shrugged, and I could tell she only half believed there was such an elevated level of danger, but still, she had to ask, "Okay. But what does filling the tub have to do with anything? I'm not taking a cold bath no matter how long the power's out."

"That's not what it's for. You scrub and fill the bathtub if you're on a well and don't have a backup generator to run the pump. Gives you enough water to flush toilets, heat up for sponge baths, and wash dishes for a few days. Fill some gallon jugs for drinking water, and as long as you have a few kerosene lamps and a backup heat source, you can get by."

Patrea sorted through the sheets clipped to her clipboard while contemplating the scenario I'd just outlined. "And everyone does this when a storm is coming?"

"Some do. If they get enough warning. Grammie told me about this one time when she and Grandpa got blindsided. They spent five days hauling buckets of snow to heat over the wood stove because she didn't draw water in the tub. I don't know why that story stuck with me, but I still fill the tub if a storm's coming, and we have a generator."

"Did it get colder since we started talking about snow?" Patrea shivered.

"Feels like it." I agreed.

"Let's get this done. I'll record notes on my phone." She handed me the clipboard. "You mark locations on the charts."

I looked down at the first sheet to see a well-drawn diagram of the first floor with window and door locations already noted. "I can do that."

For the next hour, we focused on what the house needed, which, according to a delighted Patrea, was far less than she'd expected, even if it seemed like a huge amount of work to me. "My plaster guy's got his work cut out, but he's up to the task."

"If you mean the moldings, I'd like to come out and see the process. It sounds fascinating."

"You know what I find strange," she said as I noted down the location she wanted to turn into a second-floor laundry room. "Only two of the windows are broken.

Don't you think it's odd that kids haven't been out here with BB guns?"

"That would be my doing." Charlotte popped up out of nowhere, as ghosts are likely to do. "Kids can't shoot a BB gun with any accuracy when they're too busy peeing their pants."

Because I could picture the scene, I didn't hold back a chuckle. In the role of avenging fury, Charlotte would be a sight to behold.

To her credit, Patrea didn't miss a beat. "Well, thanks. You've saved me a lot of time, money, and headaches. Most houses wouldn't have fared as well after more than thirty years empty. I expected to find extensive water damage and the resulting loss of structural integrity, but there's none."

"I don't know from structural whatever you said, but I wasn't letting kids take potshots at the house. Not when I could put a stop to it."

"Again," Patrea's smile warmed the room, "I'm thankful. You won't run my floor guys or painting crew off the property when I get them in here, will you?"

"Can't promise nothing if they come skulking around after dark."

"Nor would I expect you to." Having gone into that mode, Patrea began explaining her plans for the mansion's updates. "I want to keep all the historical charm while adding plenty of modern functionality. That means updated wiring, plumbing, and a new heating system. I have people coming throughout the day tomorrow to work up estimates for everything. It doesn't look like it needs a roof, so that's a savings I can funnel toward other things." She named a budget for the project that would have made quite a dent in anyone's pocket.

With Charlotte trailing behind, we worked our way through the his-and-hers bedrooms with their adjoining bath. We found buckled hardwood flooring in the room where Chris had already boarded up the broken windows. I marked the spots on the chart while Patrea hunkered down for a closer look.

"This kind of thing happens sometimes. Wood needs room to expand and contract, so leaving the right amount of space between the flooring boards is crucial. Changes in temperature and humidity cause the wood to shift. It's sort of a Goldilocks thing. Not enough space between the planks means whole sections hump up if the wood swells with heat or humidity. Too much space allows the boards to come apart at the joints during the contracting phase. Then, when the wood expands, the tongues no longer mesh with the grooves, this happens." She pointed to where the two boards formed an inverted V shape.

"What a shame."

"I know. You don't see flooring made from wood of this quality anymore. Look at how tight the grain is. You only get that from old-growth lumber. I've seen worse, but there's also a bit of cupping here and there. These will have to be redone."

"Will you replace it all?" Despite herself, Charlotte showed interest in the plans.

Still crouching, Patrea looked up at the ghost. "Not if I can help it. *Restore if you can, replace if you must* is my motto." She rose and looked down at the bent and buckled wood, then walked over and opened one of the closet doors on either side of a wood-burning fireplace. "Oh yeah, baby. This is perfect."

"What?" Charlotte and I spoke at the same time.

"The hardwood runs into the closet. That isn't always the case, but it sure helps me here. I'll have my guy pull this up to replace the buckled areas and use new materials here. That'll keep the grain uniform throughout the rest of the room, and if it isn't as nice in the closet, no one will notice."

"That seems to be a theme around here, doesn't it?" Charlotte plopped her fists on ample hips and pointed a thumb in the general direction of the room where we'd discovered Vanessa's remains. "Things shoved in closets that no one talks about."

Eager to walk through the conversational door that Charlotte had opened, Patrea pulled the ring from her pocket. "Or tossed out on a roof."

Charlotte took one look at the ring and poofed.

"That didn't go how I'd hoped," Patrea's tone could have dried paint.

CHAPTER THIRTEEN

After Patrea dropped me off at home, I checked in with the crew at the rental house, took Molly out for a run, and put a chicken in the oven to roast for dinner.

Finally, with all the chores out of the way, I took my laptop upstairs to the room we'd recently cleared and outfitted as a home office. I didn't need an office, but the tiny desk in our bedroom wasn't the best place to work. Eventually, we planned to clear a second bedroom for Drew—good thing we had plenty—since he used the space far more often than I did. Molly followed me up and settled on the floor at my feet. Or mostly on them.

In under ten minutes, I'd run down the current whereabouts of our main suspects. Gloria had married a man named Henry Ashton and moved to Hackinaw less than a year after Vanessa's disappearance. Neither she nor her husband seemed inclined to post photos on social media, so the only one I found of her was from her engagement notice. She looked just as Vanessa had described her, though maybe, I fancied, a little sad around the eyes.

Ethan Middleton, Gloria's former flame, proved impossible to track down. How, in this day and age, did anyone manage to have zero online presence? Outside of a mention in the articles surrounding Vanessa's disappearance, where he was named as having attended the gathering, I couldn't find anything about him anywhere.

Evelyn Hartfield hadn't married Greg Thornton, which was no surprise, given what Vanessa had already told me. Her marrying Derek Montgomery, however, did raise my eyebrows. They were still together and living in Oxford, while Greg had settled in Bangor, where he ran a landscaping company. There wasn't a lot of information on his personal life, and he didn't appear to be active on social media.

As I'd already learned, Arthur Wentworth had moved to Port Harbor and married a wealthy socialite. He also kept a sparse online presence, but I found one thing notable when I scanned his public profile—Gloria wasn't on his friends list.

When an email pinged my inbox, I clicked over to find a rambling message from my mother. She'd used plenty of emojis and a bold warning in capital letters that I would be on time for our dress-shopping excursion on Wednesday. Or else. Two seconds later, I got a text from Jacy to say she'd received a similar email and assumed Neena and Patrea got them as well.

Better answer her. I texted back, *or she'll escalate.* And for that reason, I began to type up a response to reassure my mother that I hadn't forgotten our appointment. Besides, in a stroke of pure luck, that bridal shop Patrea recommended was on the same block as Arthur's office. If

I left early, I could pop in for a quick chat with him and kill two birds with one stone.

Halfway through, I thought the better of it and picked up my phone. "Want to come over for dinner tonight?" I said when Mom answered. "I've got a chicken in the oven, and I can make those sour cream biscuits Dad loves so much. It would be the four of us since Drew doesn't have classes tonight. We can talk about the wedding." That was the capper, and she agreed right away. Being a dutiful fiancée, I texted Drew to warn him we'd be having company for dinner. Not that he'd mind. He and my father had bonded deeply, and he got stars in his eyes whenever my mother patted him on the cheek.

Drew's response came quickly and as a series of emojis featuring food, hearts, and kissing lips, which I took as favorable to the change in dinner plans. Dad wasn't the only one partial to my biscuits.

The smell of roasting chicken filled the kitchen when I returned to put the rest of the meal together. The green beans sautéed with bacon, garlic, and almonds I'd planned wouldn't be enough to feed extra guests. This is what you get, Dupree, I told myself, when you issue those last-minute invitations.

With no time to shop, I surveyed the sorry state of my larder. Two small potatoes wouldn't be enough to mash but would work if combined with onions, a sad and lonely sweet potato, and a pair of parsnips rolling around the bottom of the veggie drawer. I could coat them with olive oil and herbs and roast them for a flavorful side dish. In the end, I tossed in a couple of carrots and found a head of fennel tucked in the meat drawer of all places.

Drew walked in as I was rolling out the biscuit dough.

"I wondered why it smelled like heaven in here, but it's easy to see why since there's an angel in the kitchen."

"Cheesy pickup line notwithstanding, welcome home." I turned my face up for a kiss and noted that he'd showered at work, probably to save time. "My folks will be here any minute. Be warned, there will be wedding talk."

I don't know why I said that. He was nearly as excited about the whole thing as my mother and had even agreed to wear the green tux if I wanted the unicorn cake topper. I'd have been happy if he never knew that thing existed, but my mom sent him a photo from the expo.

"It's never cheesy when it's true." He kissed me again, then offered to help.

"I'm good. I've got it under control." Holding the cutter, I pressed it into a small pile of flour to coat it, then jammed it into the raw dough. "Just finishing up now." The first biscuit landed in the pan while he watched me work, and I asked him about his day.

When the pan was full, I brushed the tops with heavy cream like Grammie Dupree taught me. Mom always insisted butter or egg wash worked better, but I preferred my grandmother's method and was glad I'd slid the pan onto the oven rack before Kitty could walk through the door and tell me I was doing it wrong. I beat her by mere seconds.

"We're in the kitchen," I yelled when I heard the front door open. "Come on back."

Dad walked in first, and while he nodded at Drew, he knew I wouldn't be satisfied with less than a hug. His were the best—sorry, Drew—they just were.

"Something sure smells good in here."

"It's chicken, dear." Mom came in and made him take off his coat. She'd already hung hers in the hall closet. "It does smell wonderful."

Small talk flew while Drew set the table without my having to ask, and when our plates were full, the topic of the wedding did, of course, come up.

"Did you know that the groom gives his new mother-in-law a live goose at the beginning of the festivities in Korea? Geese mate for life, so it symbolizes his intent."

"Is that a hint, Mom?"

"Heavens, no. Blue would lose his mind, and I am not interested in becoming a farmer of fowl."

Dad quacked and cracked himself up.

"Although," Mom drew the word out long, "it would be one way to get that water feature I've wanted in the backyard." The laughter stopped.

"Water features are nothing more than breeding grounds for mosquitoes. You know you hate mosquitoes."

Mom winked to let us know she was only poking at him for fun. "Yes, Dear."

He'd have put one in for her if she wanted a water feature badly enough, despite the mosquitoes.

My breath puffed into the sudden chill when I

laughed. Uh oh, I thought when Vanessa appeared in my kitchen. Without asking if it was okay, she put on the extra effort to show herself to everyone. My father's face froze, and Drew suddenly found the need to swallow half a dozen times. Mom merely cocked an eyebrow.

"Vanessa Morgan, I presume," she said.

"Yes, Ma'am. I didn't mean to intrude on your family time." Casting her eyes down, Vanessa began to fade. "I'm sorry. I've missed mine for so long, but I shouldn't have interrupted the fun."

How long had she been hanging out, and I hadn't noticed?

"Wait." Dad finally found his voice. And if his face was anything to go by, he also found his compassion. Not that it was ever that far below the surface. "Stay and be welcome."

Under the table, Drew's hand landed on my knee and squeezed. "It's nice to meet you, Vanessa," he said. "Was there something you needed?"

"I've just remembered someone else who attended the party but didn't realize Everly had company. I can come back another time."

She faded before anyone could stop her.

CHAPTER FOURTEEN

The ghost of Dolly Tibbets arrived right on time. I would have expected nothing less. Her bouffant bobbed into view as she wafted through the wall, bringing with her the sharp scents of perm solution and hairspray. "You rang, darling?"

On top, she wore a hairdressing smock in electric blue with pockets for tools and combs. Underneath, a pair of chartreuse leggings clung to stick-thin legs.

"Make yourself comfortable." I gestured for her to sit. "How are things at the salon?"

"Same as always." Declining the offer to sit, she roamed around the room. "You've cleared out some, haven't you? And I love that new sofa, but I recognize a lot of Catherine's stuff. I used to come by and do her hair once she couldn't get out as much."

Rising, I followed her from the living room into the kitchen. Apparently, we'd be doing the full tour before our chat got underway. "You've changed the colors in here, too. Nice and bright. She'd have approved, I think."

"I hope so." A widow with no children or other family of her own, the previous owner of my house hadn't left a will. The house and contents had gone back to the town once she passed and could no longer pay the taxes. When my first marriage imploded, I'd come home needing a place to live, and Martha Tipton at the town office had made me the deal of a lifetime. I ended up with the house and its contents for a paltry sum. Catherine Willowby hadn't intended to become my benefactress, but I thanked my lucky stars that she had. Someday, when I crossed into the light, I planned to find her and express my gratitude.

"You take my word for it, honey. Now, what can I do for you?" Dolly drifted back toward the living room, settling on the sofa while I took the chair opposite.

Taking my offer of making herself comfortable at face value, she stripped off the smock to reveal a bright yellow silk blouse. The colors should have clashed, but somehow, they only seemed as loud and eye-catching as her personality. She wore gold hoop earrings that sparkled in the light, and a bold leopard print scarf circled her neck. On her feet were a pair of rubber-soled sneakers that would have squeaked against the floor with each step she took if she'd been alive.

"I need your help. You mentioned attending parties at the Wentworth Mansion. By any chance, were you at the party where Vanessa Morgan went missing?"

"Oh, honey." Dolly's brown eyes twinkled with glee. "You came to the right ghost. Grab you a napkin, sweetie, 'cause I'm about to spill some tea that's been steeping for decades."

Molly watched Dolly with canine curiosity, her head tilting first one way, then the other. Dogs can see ghosts. I'd known that since Molly had come to live with me, but this one had her flummoxed. I suspect that living Dolly would have garnered the same reaction. Along with the scents of the salon that accompanied her into my living room, she brought a sense of life and movement that seemed to defeat death itself.

Settling in my chair, I curled my legs under and waited for her to speak, hoping Dolly could provide the lead I was looking for even if she possessed, as I suspected, a penchant for exaggeration. For now, though, I was desperate enough to chase any thread that could unravel the mystery of Vanessa's murder. All I needed was one loose end to pull.

"I was there that night, and it was both a wingding and a shindig. Child, there was every kind of drink you've ever heard of and enough food to sink a battleship. Gillie knew how to put on a spread. You know those little pickles on toothpicks?" She smacked her lips. "What I wouldn't give to taste one again."

"I'm sure they were very nice." I hadn't asked her over to discuss the food.

"But you don't care about the food, do you? You're looking to find out what happened to that poor girl who went missing."

I nodded along as Dolly dished the dirt.

"Let's start with Arthur Wentworth. Fine young man.

A bit too ambitious for his own good. Always wanting to prove himself, to live up to his family name, if you know what I mean."

"I suppose I do."

"Such a shame Deke went and did himself in. That kind of thing puts a lot of stress on a family." Dolly shook her head sadly, sending the phantom perm scent in my direction. "Not that Junior or Gillie were ashamed of what happened. It's just that people talked even after all those years."

"And you think Arthur was bothered by public opinion?"

"Enough to make more than one bad decision."

Did Dolly know about the funny business deal?

"But his heart was in the right place, and once he'd sowed those wild oats, Gillie thought he'd settle down. Just a shame things turned out the way they did."

"What things?"

Dolly's eyes filled. "He wasn't to blame."

For someone who could, as my mom had said, talk the paint off the walls, she wasn't being overly generous with the details.

"For what?" I prodded gently.

"Why, for Gillie's condition. What else? It must have been six months after the party. Maybe more. They'd had a bit of a dust-up, don't you see? Arthur and his folks. Something to do with money, but don't ask me what exactly because I don't know. Anyway, right in the middle of the argument, Gillie collapsed. That's when they discovered the cancer. Junior was beside himself, and Gloria blamed Arthur even though it wasn't any of his doing."

"Of course, it wasn't," I asked her to wait while I found a notebook to keep track of everything she said because it seemed like Dolly was just getting started. "Sounds like Gloria's worry took over, and she needed a handy scapegoat to let some of the fear out."

Dolly nodded so hard it sent a waft of icy air across the room. "If you ask me, that girl was never the same after what she considered the betrayal of Vanessa's disappearance. Those two were like sisters."

That wasn't news to me. Vanessa had said the same.

"I hate to ask, but is it possible Gloria had something to do with the murder? People sometimes deflect their guilt onto others, which might explain her extreme reaction."

All her good humor gone, Dolly leaned forward to make her point. "You've been friends with Leandra's girl for how long now?"

"Since Kindergarten. How do you know I'm friends with Jacy?" Was she spying on me? Creepy much?

"Please." Dolly rolled her eyes. "A good salon is the social hub of any town, and nothing goes on that your friendly, neighborhood stylist doesn't hear about. Your mother talks when she's getting her hair done. Leandra talks...well, just about any time you see her. How would I not know? Besides, you may not remember me, but I'm the one who fixed your hair after your mom gave you your one and only home perm."

Bam. A memory slammed into my head that I'd have been more than happy to have left firmly in my past. First, the tugging and tugging as my mother rolled my hair into what seemed like a million tiny curlers, then the horrible stench of chemicals that stung my scalp and made it tingle. And then the rinsing and yanking to get the curlers out, followed by a glimpse of myself in the mirror. The box of perm solution should have come with a red nose, floppy shoes, and a clown hat. I shuddered. "I remember."

With scissors in hand, Dolly had swooped in and saved my self-esteem with a cute pixie cut reminiscent of Audrey Hepburn's style in Breakfast at Tiffany's. Maybe I should consider going short again sometime.

"What about Henry Ashford, the man Gloria later married? Was he at the party?"

At first, Dolly squinted, then her eyes rounded. "Why, yes! I think he was. That's the thing about Henry. You tended to forget he was around sometimes." Dolly took a deep breath and let it out slowly. "Henry was harmless.

My instincts perked up. Wouldn't being invisible make for the perfect alibi? "Tell me more about him. What was he like?"

"Well," Dolly said, rubbing her chin. "He was quiet, kept to himself, and never seemed involved in any drama that went on around him."

She'd just given me the stock description of a serial killer. I needed to hear more.

"Can you remember if he had any connection to Vanessa or any motive to harm her?" I pressed.

Dolly shook her head. "I don't think so. Can I tell you a secret?"

"Sure."

"Gillie and I conspired to put Henry and Gloria together. You know how young girls can be—always so attracted to the bad boys they don't notice the nice one standing on the sidelines."

My mother had tried that trick a time or two. Now, she was getting her wish, but then again, Drew could be a bad boy if he needed to. Was that the same with Henry?

"Ethan was a bad boy?" That got my attention in a big way. "Do tell."

"Don't think I won't." And she did. "Have you ever gone to the store and found the perfect peach? One with rosy skin that gives slightly at the press of a thumb and smells like heaven, but when you take that first bite, you find it rotted from the inside out?"

I nodded. "I married that peach."

"And had the good sense to kick him to the curb when he showed his true nature, which means you know what Ethan Middleton was like. Your peach was born with a silver spoon in his mouth, but Gloria's was born with a wooden spoon in his hand. He used it to stir the pot, and I mean the chamber pot, not the one you use for soup."

It was a good thing I didn't have anything to drink in my mouth, or it would have sprayed everywhere.

"That boy took right after his shiftless father and never did an honest day's work in his life. Still, no one can get by on looks and false charm forever. Gillie and I took matters into our own hands the minute Gloria showed the first sign of seeing through him."

"What did you do?" I asked, fascinated.

Dolly smiled mischievously. "We figured if we could get Gloria to notice Henry, the rest would be history. So, we coached him a little before the party. Henry dabbled in the art of prestidigitation."

It took me a minute to remember the definition of the word. "You mean magic? Like pulling a rabbit out of a hat?"

Dolly nodded enthusiastically. "Exactly. Well, it wasn't a real rabbit. It was a stuffed toy. Very charming."

I couldn't help but consider all the ways a thing like that could go wrong. "And did it work?"

"Unfortunately, no," Dolly said with a giggle. "Poor Henry. He'd left his trick hat on one of the tables near the drinks cart, and someone accidentally spilled red wine in it. When he pulled out the cute and fuzzy bunny, it looked like it had been through a massacre. Gloria ran in the opposite direction, screaming like a banshee, and nearly knocked over the punch bowl in her haste to get away from him."

That was the type of story to tell grandkids when they came along. Cute and funny.

Still, I jotted down a note to find a way to speak to Gloria and her husband as soon as possible and circled it three times.

"Good. Take it from me. Gloria had nothing to do with Vanessa's death."

She leaned in. "But Evelyn Hartfield? Now, that one was a different type of girl. If you ask me, she wanted to get her hooks into Arthur, but he wasn't biting. I don't think he'd have noticed if she sprouted a second head." Dolly cackled out a laugh. "Which would have made sense since she had two faces to go with them."

It seemed expected, so I chuckled at her joke. "Did he have someone else in his sights?"

"Not Vanessa, if that's what you're thinking. She was nothing more to him than Gloria's little friend. And not Evelyn, either. Between us, Gillie worried that he'd turn out to be one of those confirmed bachelor types, if you get my meaning."

I did. I couldn't see how Arthur's mother's worries over his proclivities figured into Vanessa's death, but I added it to the list to consider later.

My hand raced to keep up as Dolly unspooled motives and grudges like yarn. Bit by bit, a tangled web emerged, with players becoming clearer in my head. Dolly may embellish, but she knew people—their pressure points, their jealousies. While I couldn't draw any conclusions from them, the secrets in her ghostly Rolodex filled page after page.

I scribbled down some notes about how all these

threads might connect. Still, I could feel it—the pieces were beginning to fit together, even if I wasn't sure exactly how yet. She confirmed what Vanessa had told me about Greg Thornton and Derek Montgomery, but her opinion of Ethan Middleton interested me the most.

She painted him in a different light than what little I'd gleaned from Vanessa. According to Dolly, Ethan hadn't been Gillie's pick for her daughter for good reason.

"Under the genial veneer, he was just the same as his father. That side of the family was crooked right to the bone. He'd have only wanted Gloria for her money. Did you know he didn't even ask Junior for permission to propose?"

"Did people still do that in the eighties?" I didn't realize I'd asked the question out loud until she laughed.

"Junior was old-fashioned in some ways. Ethan should have known better."

"From what I've learned, Gloria had had enough of him, so maybe she'd figured out he wasn't what he seemed." I made a note to talk to Vanessa about him in more detail.

When she finally ran down, I sat back. "This is incredible, Dolly. You've given me plenty to think about. I don't know how to thank you."

Dolly beamed, clearly relishing her role as an insider. "Anything for you, doll. Us gals have to stick together."

I sighed. "You said it. Promise you'll let me know if you uncover anything else?"

"Same goes, sweetie. I want to see how this plays out,

and if I think of anything else, I'll come by. Cross my heart." Dolly mimed the gesture across her translucent chest. "Now go get 'em, tiger."

With a wink, she vanished, leaving only the lingering scent of Aquanet hanging in the air. I breathed it in, feeling re-energized. The game was afoot.

I glanced down at the list of suspects Dolly and I had compiled and discovered it was roughly the same list I already had. Arthur Wentworth, Evelyn Hartfield, Derek Montgomery, and Ethan Middleton. She'd left Gloria off and done her best to convince me Arthur wasn't a suspect, but other than the inept magician, Henry Ashford, she hadn't added anyone new. Nor had she given me anything that changed the motives I'd already worked out for myself, which ranged from business deals gone bad to romantic jealousy.

Nothing new there, though. Murder motives always came down to love, money, revenge, or some variation on those themes. She'd bumped Ethan firmly into the top position on my list and had given me at least one reason why he might not want to be found online.

The next step was to talk to the rest of the players. Until I'd heard what they had to say, I'd get no closer to being certain who murdered Vanessa. I could get a start on that during the dress-shopping expedition with my friends. Speaking of which, I would be late for lunch with them if I didn't leave now.

I grabbed my purse, texted Jacy to tell her I was on my way and headed for the Blue Moon Diner. We'd eat good food and hash out everything Dolly told me. Surely, we could start piecing together the truth between us.

Raised voices didn't bode well when I walked through the door. Neena and Patrea were already there, nursing their first cups of coffee and listening to the argument coming from the kitchen.

"What's going on?" I asked as Patrea made way for me to slide into the vinyl booth at the back of the diner, our usual spot. The scent of fresh coffee and sizzling bacon enveloped me like a warm hug. Mabel did breakfast all day, and now that I'd smelled bacon, I wanted pancakes instead of the turkey club I'd planned to have.

"Thea and Mabel are going at it. I think Thea's getting fired." Neena's gaze flicked past me to land on Jacy, who'd just walked in. Sizing things up quickly, Jacy detoured behind the counter to fill a coffee mug for each of us, then headed toward the booth.

"Sounds bad. What happened? Thea make another little kid cry?"

"Something like that," Patrea leaned forward conspiratorially. "She told Billie Prescott's mother he was a heathen and a spoiled brat and would grow up to be a wife-beating baboon if Stacy didn't figure out how to employ a little discipline."

"Billie Prescott *is* a heathen," Jacy matched Patrea's subdued tone since Stacy Prescott, her face red with fury, sat three tables away. "And a spoiled brat. She lets him run wild in the shop, too. Last week, he tore the heads off three vintage Barbies before we could get him under control. I wanted to go all Willy Wonka on his butt, but you know, I don't have a golden goose chute to toss him down."

Unable to unsee that mental image, I snorted. We weren't the only ones who pretended we weren't watching when Thea and Mabel emerged from the kitchen with identically set expressions.

Apparently not fired, Thea went to Stacy's table and apologized for her comments, but anyone with half a brain could tell she wasn't sorry. Not when she refused to make eye contact and kept her nose pointed up. Arms folded against her ample chest, Mabel watched the half-hearted apology but made no further comment before returning to the kitchen.

"Dinner and a show," I muttered when Thea noticed us. "Or lunch, anyway."

"What can I get ya?" Thea snapped her gum but didn't mention how it would stick to my hips when I ordered a pancake platter with a side of bacon. We all knew what kept her from being snide was that Mabel was listening from the kitchen.

"I was planning to have a salad." Jacy flipped the menu shut and handed it to Thea. "But pancakes sound too good to pass up. I'll have the same and a glass of milk." Thea struggled to keep her mouth shut, and Jacy winked at me when Neena and Patrea also jumped on board.

"Four heart attack specials coming right up." Some

vitriol slipped out, but not enough to evoke the wrath of Mabel.

"So, what's the plan for the big shopping trip tomorrow?" Patrea asked, leaning forward eagerly. Her bright red nails matched her lipstick perfectly. "We're starting in Port Harbor and working our way back, right?"

"I'm," I opened my mouth to apologize for the inconvenience, then amended my statement when she raised an eyebrow at me. "Hoping this is the last of the wedding disasters. I don't think my mother's nerves can take another one."

Neena dumped more cream in her coffee. "The new invitations came in?"

"They did, and they're perfect, so that's one crisis resolved. Once we get the dresses sorted, we should be fine. The rest is all set. Dad booked the Lodge about five minutes after we showed him the ring. He and Mom had their reception there, and she put her foot down about having it at Cappy's. David offered the inn, which would have been lovely, but he was too late."

Thea returned to drop a couple of syrup containers at the table and top off our coffee cups. When she'd gone, Jacy nudged Neena. "Judy sold an Elvis head. That's why I'm late."

"You're kidding. Which one?"

"The ceramic."

I chortled. That was the worst one.

Left out, Patrea frowned. "I don't get it. What am I missing?"

Neena whipped out her phone and showed Patrea pictures. Patrea recoiled. "Those are really freaking weird."

"I believe someone owes me some money," I grinned. When Patrea frowned again, I explained. "We had a bet on how fast Judy would move one. She's a born salesman."

I dumped a bit more syrup on my pancakes than I normally would just because Thea was watching and asked Patrea how her morning appointments had gone.

She slathered hers with butter first, then added syrup while she answered. "Some bad news, but more good than bad. Electrical work starts on Friday. I lucked out on the timing, but the quote started at five percent over my initial estimate."

"Ouch." Jacy reached over to pat Patrea's hand. "That's a lot. Call Brian. He might be able to help." Jacy's husband worked for the power company.

"Already done. It's all good," She reassured. "Besides, the furnace company had better news. I don't have to replace any of the ductwork. New units won't match up perfectly, but they've got a fabricator who can make up the connecting pieces. That'll almost cover the overage on the electrical. Better, my roofer confirmed my findings. They'll pressure wash the tiles to make them look new and replace one or two cracked ones, but everything there seems solid. I'm heading back after this to meet my plaster guy about the moldings."

We all raised a coffee mug...well, except Jacy, who raised her milk glass to toast Patrea's good fortune.

"Charlotte behaving?" I asked around a mouthful of sticky, maple-coated fluffiness. Mabel is the pancake queen.

"So far. I never saw a sign of her. Vanessa, either. It was a ghost-free day."

"Not for me." I launched into the tale of Dolly's visit. "Bumped Ethan right up to the top of the list, and even better, she gave me a picture of Gloria's future husband. I think we need to talk to her soon."

"Is she a suspect, or is it the husband?"

"I'm not sure either of them are. Dolly is an excellent judge of character but has just enough imagination to conjure up some unlikely scenarios. She might have a blind spot for Gloria, but not Henry. She painted him as harmless and Gloria as heartbroken over the disappearance. I think she's probably right, but we still need to know for sure."

I'd transferred the suspect list to my phone, so I pulled up the app and laid my phone in the middle of the table for everyone to see.

"Short list. Manageable." Patrea said. "Not much of a party if those were the only people there."

"According to Dolly, it was a blowout, which is why they didn't notice Vanessa was missing until it was over. But I figured it had to be someone who knew about the panic room. We know Mrs. Wentworth showed it off some, but Dolly was positive she hadn't taken anyone through during the actual party."

"But we don't know for sure?" Jacy hit on the one snag in my theory.

"No. If she did, that opens the suspect list up to more than just the guests who spent time at the mansion before the party. We could be looking at fifty people or more. Dolly wasn't sure about the actual number."

I shut up when Thea came back around to check if we needed anything more. Or to subtly indicate we'd taken up a booth long enough. With her, it could go either way. Jacy ordered pie, which sounded good to the rest of us, and we all followed suit.

Before we could get back to the list, Ernie Polk walked in, noticed us, and stopped at our table.

"Dupree," he said.

"Polk," I responded. "Any news?"

"I don't know why I'm telling you this, but Vanessa Morgan's hyoid bone was broken. The ME has listed her cause of death as—"

"Strangulation." I cut him off.

"Been watching CSI?"

I wrinkled my nose at him for that one but didn't mention I'd been watching reruns of Bones. I like David Boreanaz. Sue me.

"Thanks for letting us know."

Ernie settling at a nearby table effectively ended our murder discussion. We switched over to finalizing plans for wedding shopping the next day.

"We've got to get back to work," Jacy said as she

motioned for Thea to drop off the lunch bill. "What are you doing the rest of the day?"

"I was planning to check in with the crew at the rental unit, but Sam already sent me an email with a bunch of photos. They found a bit more rot than expected, but he says it's under control, so I'm at loose ends."

"Come back to the Wentworth with me," Patrea requested. "I could use a little help laying out the dimensions for that waterfall island."

Since I had nothing better to do, I agreed and followed her to the mansion.

CHAPTER FIFTEEN

"Do you really think we'll get snow?" Patrea leaned toward the steering wheel and looked up at the sky. "Looks like spring to me."

"Looks can be deceiving. If Eddie says to expect snow, I'd make sure my boots weren't packed up for the season. He's rarely wrong. By tomorrow, I bet it'll be on the news."

Patrea's plaster guy was waiting for us when we pulled up the drive. Younger than I expected, tall, and his rawboned face cheerful, he stood next to the van with his business name splashed across the side and waved.

"Sorry, I'm late," she said as she shook the hand he offered. "Jerrold Kaminski, Everly Dupree." She made the introductions. From a distance, I'd judged him to be younger, but up close, some weathering had me revising his age to somewhere in the middle to late forties. A good-looking late forties, I was forced to admit, with unruly, raven-dark hair and ice-blue eyes.

"Call me Jerry. Pleased to meet you," he shook the hand I offered and held it maybe a second longer than necessary, but his attention kept straying toward the house. He seemed glad when we headed toward the front steps. "I have to tell you, I'm itching to get a look at this place, see if it's as grand as I remember. My grandfather did the plasterwork when this house was built. Then, my father got his hand in when Junior Wentworth had some rooms remodeled, but the house has been empty for so long, I never thought my chance would come."

Fascinated, Patrea turned to him before she unlocked the door. "Really? I had no idea your family had a connection to the place."

Grinning wider, if that was at all possible, Jerry nodded enthusiastically. "Third-generation plaster man —that's me. And that makes this your lucky day because I have the original molding forms, and they're all in great condition."

Patrea's grin matched his. "Fabulous." She unlocked the door. "I'll expect a discount."

"Don't tell her I said this," Jerry touched my arm, leaned in a bit too close, and lowered his voice conspiratorially, "but I'd have offered to do the work for free just for the sake of sentiment."

"I heard that."

"You mentioned you'd been here before. When was that?"

"Shoot," Jerry glanced up at the plaster medallion circling the chandelier over the grand staircase. "I was just a kid. Maybe eight or ten. That makes it somewhere in the mid-eighties."

A tingle shot through me. "Your father didn't work on Mrs. Wentworth's panic room, did he?"

Because he was standing so close, I caught the faint

shudder that ran through him. He'd heard the tragic news, but then again, this was Mooselick River. If he lived locally or even semi-locally, he'd have heard. The grapevine ran deep and wide in these parts.

In a sudden, surprising motion, Jerry slapped his right fist into his left palm. "My father had no reason to murder anyone. *He* didn't even know Vanessa Morgan. Thinking she might have been behind the wall when he plastered it has kept him up the last few nights. I can only imagine how he feels."

"It's okay," Patrea stepped forward to pat his hand gently. "No one's accusing your father of anything. "

"Appreciate that," Jerry sounded sincere. "But you know how this town loves to gossip, and they will if people find out he had anything to do with building that wall."

"They won't hear it from us," I said, catching Patrea's eye and getting her nod of agreement. "Not a word." Her cocked eyebrow said we'd talk about the implications when Jerry was gone.

Reassured, he followed us as we gave him a tour of the house, focusing on the rooms that most needed his expertise. By tacit agreement, we avoided the former panic room and kept the conversation centered on what the house required.

Being thorough, Jerry discovered more damage than Patrea had noticed, particularly in the room where the moldings had already fallen. "The molding didn't hold because this wall has issues. These keys are shot," the bearer of bad news poked at a section of wall that flexed slightly under the pressure. "It could be worse, though."

Patrea winced. "Define worse."

Shrugging, Jerry continued poking and tapping. "It's not the whole wall, so it's a patch job instead of a full replacement. Less time, not as expensive."

"Okay. Before you get started, I'll have my flooring crew lay protective pads or cardboard in here. These floors need refinishing, but there's no need to make things worse. When can you start?"

"How soon can you get the floor protected?"

"If I sweeten the deal with pastries and promise Chris will be here to help, probably tomorrow morning. At the very least, I can get them to drop off the pads or whatnot, and he'll take care of putting them down."

Jerry grinned. "Bribe me with pastries, and I'll be here in time to help. My crew can handle the current projects without me. This is one I want to do myself. Keep it in the family, you know."

"Done. I'll be baking all night since the electrician's also starting tomorrow."

Brows shooting up, Jerry said, "You bribe him, too?"

"Her," Patrea grinned. "And yes, but not with pastries."

"Well, if I'd known there were other options." He winked at me. "Now, let's talk money. I can give you a basic estimate, but it'll probably change depending on what's needed after the electrical is finished."

After coming to terms, they shook on the deal and

signed a contract because Patrea wouldn't have it any other way—and Jerry left whistling.

"That went very well, I think," Patrea said as he pulled down the drive. "We'll want to talk to his father at some point."

"The sooner, the better," I agreed and followed her into the kitchen, where we discussed the size and placement of the waterfall island and then marked the dimensions out on the floor. With that chore out of the way, we wandered into the storage/former panic room.

"Charlotte missed a spot," Patrea coughed, waving a hand in front of her face. "So much dust. My sinuses are screaming right now. Was it this dusty before?"

Glancing around at the haphazard piles surrounding us, I was surprised that we hadn't noticed how Charlotte had left only part of this particular room unaffected by her cleaning spree. Dust and cobwebs lay heavy on a chair with a broken leg, a couple of lamps with frayed cords, an old bicycle with deflated tires—a few bits of clutter tucked away and forgotten when the Wentworths cleared out of the house.

In fact, she hadn't come back to clean up after Ernie or the mess we'd done our best to remake around the area where Vanessa's body had lain for so long. Also odd.

"I think I need to check on Charlotte. We haven't seen her in a while and now, I'm worried the dark spirit might have done something to her. Do you mind?"

"I'm going with."

"Fine by me. I'm a firm believer that there's safety in numbers."

We found her gazing out a third-floor window where Patrea had discovered the engagement ring. "She's here," I said to Patrea. "We've been looking for you. Are you all right?"

No answer, and she didn't even turn around. Now what? Tapping her on the shoulder wasn't an option for obvious reasons, so I called her name, increasing my volume until she turned. At that point, I'd resorted to shouting.

"What?" she demanded, her tone testy and annoyed. "What do you want? Can't a body have a moment's peace in this house?"

"You don't have a body," I blurted without thinking, then stepped back when she tried to burn me with a look. "We were worried about you."

That softened her up a bit. "Why? I'm dead. What is there to worry about?"

"There's the weird swirly thing of darkness," Patrea said, making me realize Charlotte had made the effort to be seen.

"You've been watching too many horror movies, child. Haven't I done my duty all these years? Haven't I protected this house and kept it from harm? You're safe enough within these walls unless you let your imagination run wild. That's the one thing I can't save you from. Run along now, and leave me to my watching."

Since she seemed fine other than her temper, we left Charlotte alone to brood.

"She doesn't remember it, does she?" Patrea said when we were back in the storage room.

"That would be my take as well, and I don't know what to do about it other than talk to Kat. She has more experience in this type of thing than I do. "

"Call her and make the appointment. I'll go with you. In the meantime, we might as well get this mess cleaned up."

While I attacked the worst of the cobwebs with the broom, Patrea fired off the vacuum and used the wand attachment to start sucking up dust—some of it years old, some of it new. The high-pitched motor of the vacuum filled the alcove-turned storage room with a monotonous hum, but it didn't take long to clear up the bulk of what lay on every surface.

I blessed the silence when it finally fell.

"This bike is in decent shape minus the tires. For its age, anyway." When I touched the purple and white streamers tucked into the ends of the ape-hanger handlebars, old plastic turned brittle with age shattered into glittering shards. "Drew could fix this up for you. These banana bikes from the sixties go for decent money, and the seat isn't even faded." The glitter-shot purple vinyl still felt pliable. "Or you could just keep it for your firstborn," I teased.

"Put it in the keep pile, and I'll decide later."

"Will do."

"And stop smirking."

"Will do."

At Patrea's insistence, we carried piece after piece out through the newly opened doorway and into the foyer, where we created three piles: keep, trash, and sell.

As we reached the farthest corner, we uncovered an antique dresser. It was a monstrous thing, all carved wood and fancy trim, buried under a layer of dust the vacuum hadn't reached.

Patrea pulled out a rag and wiped off the worst of the dirt.

"Hello, beautiful," Patrea murmured. She ran a reverent hand over wood that badly needed polishing. "Wonder what stories you could tell?"

I felt a tingle of anticipation. Vintage discoveries were Patrea's passion, and I could see the sparkle in her eyes. Who knew what treasures might be hidden in this old dresser?

When my skin prickled in the same way it does during a ghostly session, my pulse quickened.

"I'm getting the spooky vibe. Should we open it?" I asked.

Patrea grinned at me. "Do you even have to ask?"

I reached for the tarnished brass handles, hesitating. The antique seemed to hum with energy. This had to be it. The breakthrough we were waiting for.

I took a deep breath and pulled. The drawer squealed in protest. Years of dust and grime must have built up in the tracks. The sound echoed eerily through the storage room.

Patrea coughed again as a plume of musty air wafted out. I waved a hand in front of my face, wrinkling my nose at the smell.

"Phew...smells like grandma's attic in there," I said, but the drawer was empty. She slid it closed with another squeal of wood on wood and tried the next drawer down. This one contained neatly folded linens, the pillowcase on top slightly yellowed with age but still crisp and monogrammed with elaborate stitching.

"Boring," Patrea wrinkled her nose. "I was hoping for something more...I don't know. Just more."

"Maybe there is." I dug through layers of lace and linen, pulling out three sets of sheets to see what was underneath.

"Any luck?" Patrea asked.

"Not yet. I'll try the bottom one."

It stuck, but only long enough that I gave it a harder yank and ended up on my butt in a cloud of more musty air with the drawer in my lap. Patrea didn't bother to hold back a chuckle.

"I'm fine. Thanks for asking."

She reached down and lifted the drawer off me, set it aside, and helped me up. The tingling across my skin increased until my arms itched. Absently scratching, I watched Patrea paw through the contents.

"What we've got here is your old standby," Patrea said. "A junk drawer."

Not precisely junk, I decided as she pulled out various items and laid them on the top of the dresser. Other than a set of dice that I thought might be made from bone and a rather suggestive cigar cutter in the shape of a nude woman reclining on a bed of marble, there didn't seem to be anything that should have alerted my senses.

Until...

"Everly, look." Patrea lifted an old, spiral-bound notebook from beneath a moth-eaten shawl. "That's new, right? Compared to all the rest of the stuff, I mean."

The humming moved from my skin to my bones.

"It's important. I can feel it." I motioned for her to open the cover. She did while I leaned over her shoulder and scanned the contents.

"It looks like a diary or journal," she said. "And I think it belonged to Vanessa."

My heartbeat quickened again as the humming along my body abruptly ceased. This might be it. The key to unlocking Vanessa's secrets and maybe even her murder. I met Patrea's eyes, seeing my own thrill reflected there and a dose of apprehension.

"Does it feel weird to read someone's most private thoughts?" It did to me.

"A little, but I can't not."

Vanessa's thoughts scrolled across fading lines in a looping script. The edges of the pages were soft and feathered with age. As I gently flipped through a few sheets, I caught a whiff of faded perfume—vanilla and jasmine.

I sneezed. Twice. Then again. "I think this room is

infested with dust bunnies, and they just keep multiplying."

Patrea shrugged, shoved the drawer back into place, closed it, and splayed open the notebook on top of the dresser.

"This part's dated two weeks before her disappearance," Patrea whispered, a quiver of excitement in her voice. One name jumped right off the page. Derek Montgomery. As Patrea read on, Vanessa described meeting the handsome man at the Wentworth's Spring Fling party the year before. He'd danced attendance on her all night, and she admitted she'd been smitten.

"I saw Derek again today by the oak tree. He said he's made a mistake, that he wants me back. After what I've seen this week, I said no, even if a tiny part of me wants to try again. We shared our first kiss under that tree. In some ways, it feels wrong just to let that go, but trust has to be earned and, once earned, must be maintained. I've lost mine."

Over the next few entries, Vanessa solidified her stance on reconciling as she described Derek's pursuit of her in unflattering terms:

"Every time I turn around, he's there. No means no, Derek. Besides, if he's so interested in me, why does he disappear every time Evelyn does? Maybe I'm being paranoid. But my gut says something is up with those two... like maybe they're sneaking around behind Greg's back.

Not that he deserves any better treatment from her. That man is a filthy pig in every possible way. Does he think I'm so stupid I can't tell when he's standing too close or finding an excuse to brush up against me every chance he gets? Ugh. It makes my skin crawl.

Does Evelyn know Greg is involved in that bad business thing with Arthur? Does Gloria know?"

Patrea paused and commented, "Sounds like a soap opera to me. Or one of those reality dating shows. People hopping in and out of bed with one another. I'm assuming this stirs up a few new motives."

"I'd think so. If Evelyn thought both men wanted Vanessa, she might have gone postal."

"Right," Patrea agreed. "And then there's Derek and Greg. Either one of them could have been angry or jealous enough to take her out."

Patrea leaned over my shoulder, both of us engrossed in the tragic story unfolding on the diary's pages. A picture was forming of the last days of Vanessa's life, her hopes and heartaches. Not to mention the tension she was under.

The final entry was abrupt.

"Party time."

My mind raced with possibilities. Derek and Evelyn, carrying on right under her fiancé's nose. Greg's interest in Vanessa and Evelyn's jealousy toward her. Shady business deals, secrets, and lies.

I turned the page, but it was blank. The diary ended there, on the night of the party that Vanessa did not survive.

"That's it?" Patrea asked in disbelief.

I flipped through the remaining empty and untouched pages. "She went down for the party, and that was that."

We were both quiet for a moment, the weight of Vanessa's fate hanging over us. Why had it ended this way?

"We have to talk to all of them," I finally said. "Someone named in her journal had to be the one who killed her."

Patrea nodded slowly. "My money's on Derek."

"I'm not sure," I admitted. "But clearly, their relationship was troubled before Vanessa ended it for good."

We still didn't have all the pieces, but the diary provided our first solid lead. After tomorrow, we'd arrange to meet some of the players and see if they could fill in the gaps about the fateful events of that final night. We had to keep digging for Vanessa's sake, no matter where it led.

Patrea tucked the diary carefully into her bag. We'd pore over it again later, searching for any other clues Vanessa may have left behind.

Just then, the creak of a floorboard made us both freeze. Patrea and I exchanged looks—we were supposed to be alone here. I felt my pulse quicken as footsteps approached down the hall. Who else was in this house?

CHAPTER SIXTEEN

figure appeared in the doorway. I stifled a gasp as I recognized the elegant woman from the photos I'd seen in the paper. She was older now, and the dark hair Vanessa had described as a waterfall showed threads of silver around a face that wore a look of shock that likely mirrored my own.

"Gloria Wentworth?" Patrea asked in disbelief.

The woman's gaze flickered between us warily. "I'm sorry to barge in unannounced."

Patrea and I shared a troubled look. She said, "I'm Patrea Evergreen, and this is Everly Dupree."

"You found her right here, didn't you?" Gloria's eyes were clouded with genuine distress. "I'm sorry. I'm trespassing, and I shouldn't have come here. This was my family's home once. I saw the news about...about Vanessa." Her voice broke on the name. "I don't even remember driving down here. I don't think I'm okay. I'll go now."

"Don't go."

"I'm sorry for your loss." Patrea and I spoke at once.

Pain flashed across Gloria's face. "She was my best friend. I thought...she just...disappeared. I never knew what happened to her after that night."

Her voice went husky with tears, then trailed off. My heart ached for her, for the years of unanswered questions and feelings of abandonment she must have carried from then until now. With her pain on display, I could see Gloria needed closure just as much as Vanessa did. Maybe more.

"We'd like to find out the truth," I said softly. "Will you help us do that?"

Gloria met my gaze, her expression turning resolute. "Yes. For Vanessa, I'll do whatever it takes." But her hand trembled as she lifted it to cover her eyes, and I couldn't just stand there and watch her fall apart. Crossing the short distance, I meant to touch her arm as a gesture of support, but she threw herself into my arms and cried on my shoulder for several long moments.

"I'm sorry." Gloria apologized yet again. "I'm handling this so poorly. You'd think after all this time, it wouldn't feel so raw."

"There's no statute of limitations on grief," Patrea's brisk tone didn't match her sympathetic expression. If anyone understood what it felt like to lose a sibling to uncertainty—and we all knew that's what Gloria had considered Vanessa to be—Patrea did. Her story of loss had turned out better than Gloria's, but she'd spent a long time wondering what had happened to her brother. "Not knowing is the hardest part. As hard as it is to face what happened, the healing starts now. It's what Vanessa would want."

Against my shoulder, Gloria nodded. "It is." She

sniffed back more tears and stepped back from my embrace. "Thank you for understanding."

The three of us exchanged solemn nods. With Gloria by our side, maybe we could finally uncover what really happened to Vanessa Morgan all those years ago. The secrets of this house couldn't stay buried forever.

"Loss is never easy."

Gloria gave a sad smile. "I appreciate that. Losing my best friend left a hole in my heart. For years, I thought she just abandoned me without explanation." She shook her head, eyes glistening. "But now I see there was more to the story."

"There always is." These two friends had suffered long enough and deserved to know the truth. Maybe Gloria didn't need the entire truth. I mean, I wasn't planning on telling her Vanessa still lingered in the house. Not yet, at least. Maybe I'd tell her later. Maybe I'd let them have a moment together. It all depended on what part Gloria had played in Vanessa's death.

At the moment, I was ninety-five percent certain she'd had no part in the murder, but ninety-five isn't one hundred, and until I hit that mark, I'd keep certain facts under wraps unless Charlotte showed up and showed out. That would change things considerably.

"We've already made a start on finding her killer," Patrea admitted. "Vanessa left a diary that mentioned some other guests who were here when she...when it happened." Her voice dropped off delicately. "Derek

Montgomery, Greg Thornton, and Evelyn Hartfield, for starters."

Gloria's brow furrowed. "You can't think any of them killed her." She paused, gazing into the distance as she sifted through memories. "But who else would it be? You forgot Ethan Middleton. And my Henry."

Patrea hadn't forgotten. She'd only intentionally mentioned people from Vanessa's notebook to allow Gloria to fill in the blanks. I might be ninety-five percent certain of Gloria's innocence, but Patrea had her own scale.

"There were others. My mother's parties were the stuff of legend. At least fifty people attended. It could have been any one of them or someone else entirely. Someone who blended in with the crowd but wasn't invited."

I shared another look with Patrea. Gloria hadn't mentioned her brother, but her perceptions would prove invaluable. With her perspective, we could begin piecing together the full picture of what happened to Vanessa Morgan and bring all the secrets to light.

Gloria reeled off a partial list of the other guests who had been present at the mansion that fateful evening. One name she left out was Dolly Tibbets, but from the beginning, I had my sights set on those who were staying at the house or who'd spent more time there than just attending a party or two. My shortlist included those Vanessa had already mentioned: Evelyn Hartfield, the secretary, and her fiancé, Greg Thornton, the charming entrepreneur.

Derek Montgomery, Vanessa's ex-boyfriend. Ethan Middleton, Gloria's ex. And finally, Arthur Wentworth, her brother. As she described their personalities and interactions with Vanessa, a timeline began forming in my mind.

"Vanessa's journal mentioned Derek wanting to rekindle their relationship. Did she discuss any of that with you?"

I didn't mention what might have been happening between Derek and Evelyn. But Gloria waved a hand to dismiss the notion.

"Oh, Vanessa and Derek were one of those on-and-off-again couples. Mostly off," she said wryly. "He only seemed to want her when someone else did, and she got tired of it toward the end. There wouldn't have been another chance for him, I don't think. Vanessa was done, and she made that clear. I think that's why he turned to Evelyn."

"Evelyn and Derek had a thing?" Patrea prodded to see how much Gloria knew.

"Thing might be too strong a word. I'd call it more of a flirtation, maybe."

Patrea sneezed again. "Let's take this to the mural room where we can sit in somewhat comfortable folding chairs, and there's far less dust. Can I offer you anything, Gloria? I've got bottled water in the fridge, fruit, and some cheese if you're hungry.

"I'd take a water, but I don't think I could eat anything. Coming here brings back so many memories."

When Patrea went to move past her, Gloria grabbed her arm gently. "You should know we've had multiple offers over the years, but yours just felt like it was the right time and the right person. I've always trusted my intuition, and this time was no different. You'll do what's right for the house, won't you? And for Vanessa?"

"You have my word." Patrea rested her hand on Gloria's for a moment.

"And mine as well," I added.

Eyes misty once again, Gloria nodded. "I can't tell you how much that means. Before I leave, would you mind if I walk through?"

"Be my guest," Patrea smiled.

In the end, Gloria had little to add to the stories Vanessa and her journal had already told other than her own perceptions of the relationships between Evelyn, Derek, and Greg.

"In her journal, Vanessa mentioned that Greg had taken several opportunities to..." I struggled for the correct phrase.

"Rub up against her? I know," Gloria picked up what I was putting down. "He was the type who thought sex with him could cure a woman of anything and anyone that ailed her."

Eyes rolling up, Patrea shook her head. "I know that type well enough. I'm sure we've all met a guy like that. Poor, deluded souls."

That sparked the first genuine smile we'd seen from

Gloria. "He tried it out on me once, and I shut him down hard."

"How did Vanessa respond?"

Maybe he thought she'd somehow led him on and went mad when he realized nothing could happen between them.

"She didn't take him up on it if that's what you're asking, and she's not to blame." Fury replaced the easy smile on Gloria's face. For the first time, she didn't look pale and shaken. "Even if he killed her, which I doubt, she did nothing to earn it."

Exchanging a glance with Patrea, I hastened to put Gloria's mind at ease. "I wasn't suggesting she did, and why do you doubt Greg's involvement?"

That stopped the anger and made her think. "Because he was too arrogant and too stupid to get away with murder. A person must be crafty to do something like that and keep quiet about it for over thirty years. And cool. Collected, even. Murdering someone in a house full of people is way too cold-blooded for someone like Greg. Even if he was capable of murder, he wasn't capable of keeping his mouth shut about it."

Now that she mentioned it, she was right. Whoever killed Vanessa had to have gone back to the party and acted like nothing had happened. Cold-blooded indeed.

"Who was?" I watched her face closely, as did Patrea, but Gloria merely shook her head.

"I wouldn't have said anyone I knew at the time was the kind of person who would kill an innocent woman.

Maybe that makes me naive. It probably does. After all, I was naive enough to believe it wasn't personal when everyone insisted Van had simply moved on."

"No, you didn't." The words popped out of my mouth before I had time to think them through. "You never believed that. Something else happened, didn't it, that you thought gave her a good reason to leave."

When her gaze slid away to rivet itself to the floor, I knew I'd struck a nerve. "What is it, Gloria? What's been eating at you all this time?"

"I think it was my fault. I think Van's dead because of me."

If there'd been any justice in the world, Vanessa would have popped up at that precise moment to confirm or deny, but there wasn't, and she didn't.

"Why?" Patrea asked gently.

"Because I asked her to do something for me. A favor. I never thought it would mean the end of everything." Her breath came out as a sob.

I moved closer and reached for her hand. "Tell us what happened, Gloria. It's important."

Through tears, she nodded. "It was Ethan Middleton. He was my Derek." And my Paul, according to Dolly.

When we both looked confused, she clarified. "In the off-and-on relationship sense. We'd been engaged until I broke it off. I couldn't face another scene when he showed up at the party, so I asked Vanessa to talk to him. To explain that we weren't going to get back together. I was afraid I'd lose my resolve if I talked to him, so I begged her to do it for me."

"Begged?" Patrea needed clarification. "Did she say no?"

"At first, but then she gave in and said if she handled Ethan for me, I was on Derek duty for the rest of the night. She laughed and told me to keep him away from her, and we had a deal."

"And you agreed?"

Gloria nodded, her body deflating until she slumped in her chair. "He killed her. Of course, he did. That's the only explanation."

It wasn't, but it was a good one, and I could see how she might think so. "It's one possibility, but she could have run into someone else after they spoke. We'll need to talk to him."

"To Ethan? Impossible." Gloria's gaze locked onto mine. "Ethan's car went off the road the next summer after we lost Vanessa. He died instantly."

"I guess that explains why he had no social media presence, but why didn't his obituary pop up when I searched?"

"I have no idea," Gloria shrugged. "But I did attend the funeral. Maybe he killed her, and maybe he didn't. I don't see how we'll ever find out for sure."

"By talking to anyone who might have spent time with Vanessa at the party. That will help us establish a timeline for the crime. You can help by running through the series of events as you remember them."

"Okay. I can do that." She seemed relieved. "I've gone over that night so many times trying to figure out what I'd done or said to cause Vanessa to leave. It's stayed fresh in my mind even after all this time."

These women deserved a chance to reconnect. I'd make sure they got one if I could.

As Gloria began to recite the chain of events, I got a better picture of what went on during the evening. Her retelling mirrored Dolly's in some respects, including the bloody rabbit incident.

"Poor Henry," she said fondly. "That was the end of his dream of performing on stage. It took him half the evening to work up the nerve, and to have it go spectacularly wrong was a blow to his ego."

"Was that before or after Vanessa disappeared?"

"Before," Gloria stated solemnly. "We laughed about it once I'd calmed down, and then, she amended our deal. Derek hadn't bothered her all evening, and if I wanted her to get Ethan off my back, I had to agree to find Henry and soothe his bruised ego. I think she knew we were meant for each other and that I needed a little push. I agreed, and we went our separate ways. It was the last time I saw her."

"Did anyone else see her after that?" Patrea asked.

She nodded firmly. "My brother did. He said she'd come in while he was playing pool and asked if he'd seen Ethan. He told the police when we called them. They spoke with him for quite some time and with Ethan as well, but nothing ever came of it."

"But he didn't see them together after that?"

Gloria shook her head. "As for the others, we haven't kept in touch, but I could reach out if that would help." Her eyes were alight with purpose. "Vanessa was the sister of my heart."

Patrea and I exchanged yet another glance, which Gloria caught and commented on. "You understand because you're the same way. I can see it in you, the way you talk without words. It was the same for us. I should have trusted my instincts and known she wouldn't leave me that way. If I had, she might have been found long before now."

Sisters of the heart wasn't a phrase I'd have come up with on my own, but once Gloria applied it to us, I realized how lucky I'd been because she was right. And not just about Patrea. There were four of us who qualified.

There was nothing more Gloria could tell us, but we exchanged numbers after she'd taken her walk through the house and promised to keep in touch.

"She didn't do it," Patrea said as soon as we were alone again.

I agreed.

Gloria hadn't been gone more than a few minutes when Vanessa showed up. I'm ashamed to say I found the timing a relief. In my less-than-professional opinion, Gloria wasn't ready for a reunion. Neither was I.

After a moment, I noticed something different about her.

"Hi, Vanessa. Did you change your hair?"

"Hey," Patrea said. "I can't see her. I want to see."

Vanessa obliged. "Dolly did it." Automatically, she reached up to touch newly-shortened bangs. "She said the shorter length would flatter my features."

"It does. It looks good. I just didn't know ghosts could change their appearance like that."

"Dolly can. She says it's because she was born to do hair and died with scissors in her hand."

"Oh." That put a bit of a damper on things.

CHAPTER SEVENTEEN

Road construction on I-95 slowed us down. We made it to Port Harbor with only twenty minutes left to spare. We'd have to pry information out of Arthur Wentworth quickly if we wanted to meet my mother at the bridal shop on time.

"We're expected," Patrea bulled past the young man at the receptionist station. "Don't bother yourself. I know the way."

We weren't, and she didn't, but it wasn't difficult to locate Wentworth's office. He looked confused when Patrea knocked and opened the door.

"Mr. Wentworth," she said. "Patrea Evergreen. Sorry to just barge in." His confusion deepened further when Jacy, Neena, and I followed Patrea inside.

The scent of stale cigar smoke permeated the man's tweed jacket, lending a fusty air to his office as we filed in, my heels sinking into the plush oriental rug. He sat behind his desk—a great hulking chunk of mahogany that likely cost more than my car. After quickly sizing us up, Arthur leaned back in his leather chair, bushy silver brows raised quizzically.

"Ladies." He nodded, eyes flitting between us. "Please,

have a seat. It's a rare occasion to have so many lovely women in my office at once. What can I do for you today, Miss Evergreen? Have we met before? Your name sounds familiar."

"It should since I'm the new owner of your former home in Mooselick River. And it's Mrs. Evergreen, by the way."

Wentworth's face went carefully blank. "A deal is a deal, *Mrs.* Evergreen. Caveat emptor and all that. You should have had someone competent look the place over before you made your offer."

"I'm not here about the condition of the house, *Mr.* Wentworth. It's in much better shape than I expected. Your sister was right to push for a sale when she did, though. No home is improved by long periods of staying empty. There's another matter we should discuss. You're aware Vanessa Morgan's remains were discovered on the property."

"I saw the news report, and I've given my statement to the police. Such a tragedy, but my sister would be the one to talk to about Vanessa. I had very little to do with Gloria's little friend. I can't think what help I could offer you at this time."

We settled into the plush leather chairs across from him.

"I realize we've barged in and disrupted your day only to bring up an uncomfortable topic. I'm Everly Dupree," I said and saw recognition. Not surprising given my former connections and the fact my face had been splashed all over the news for various reasons. Following that recognition, I caught a hint of speculation in his eyes. Had I come there to invest money with him? Looked like he hoped so

"You've already met my friend Patrea Evergreen. This is Jacy Dean and Neena Montayne." I pointed to each woman in turn. "We're here today because we thought you might have information that would be helpful in finding Vanessa's killer. She was murdered in your former home, after all. Anything you could tell us might help."

If he did know anything, his face didn't show so much as a flicker, which didn't bode well for us. "It was all such a long time ago," he said. "I barely knew the girl. It's hard to remember events that seemed insignificant at the time."

"You'd call the disappearance of a beautiful young woman insignificant?" Patrea laced her fingers together.

"That was in poor taste, I suppose, but Vanessa was young and known for being..." he hesitated over choosing the right words. "Flighty and over-dramatic as girls of that age often are."

Vanessa hadn't been that much younger when she died than I was now. Did the man think all women were drama queens? He certainly didn't do himself any favors with that attitude.

"And your point would be?" Patrea gave him her best blank face—the one she used when questioning a witness on the stand.

"Just that we thought the silly girl had gone off with a boyfriend or something, didn't we?"

"Your sister didn't," Jacy pointed out.

"I suppose not. At Gloria's insistence, our father reported the disappearance to the police, but when no evidence of foul play turned up, we decided to let the matter drop."

Arthur Wentworth enjoyed an untarnished reputation in his field, which made our footing somewhat tenuous. Had Vanessa threatened to tell on him, and after he killed her, he was too scared to go through with the deal she'd overheard? We'd never know unless we could squeeze more information out of him.

"How very noble of you." Neena's voice lacked any sense of warmth.

To his credit, Arthur flushed at the criticism, but any points he earned for it were offset by continuing to refer to Vanessa as a silly girl.

"Mr. Wentworth," I interjected, "were you aware that on the day before the party, Vanessa Morgan overheard you discussing an unsavory business deal?"

Arthur stiffened, his ruddy complexion paling. "Now see here, that was a long time ago. How could you possibly know about that?"

"A *woman* was murdered, Mr. Wentworth." I fixed him with an unwavering stare, willing him to cooperate. "One who died within a day of learning you planned to do something sketchy. She kept a diary. You can see how it looks, can't you? We need answers."

Arthur sagged, passing a hand over his face. "You're right, of course, but I can assure you that girl's death had nothing to do with me or that foolish deal. Greg Thornton got a tip from a friend of a friend and said if we acted fast, we could undercut a larger firm. Beat them to the punch. It didn't occur to me at the time that it would also tarnish an innocent broker's reputation."

"I see," Patrea said. "But your father did."

Nodding, Arthur continued. "My father caught wind of my plans and explained that rising to the top by stepping on the reputation of others wasn't the Wentworth way. Maybe Vanessa was the one who tipped him off, or maybe she wasn't. He never said how he'd found out, and I had no idea the girl had overheard anything."

He rubbed me the wrong way, and if he called her a girl one more time, the top of my head might pop off, but I believed him. Why? I couldn't say. Something in the eyes, maybe, and we were running out of time.

I nodded. "Gloria said you told the police the last time you'd seen Vanessa was when she came into the billiards room looking for Ethan Middleton."

"Ah yes, Ethan." Arthur's eyes took on a distant look. "He was engaged to my sister until Gloria came to her senses and gave him the boot."

Patrea leaned forward to ask, "What part did Vanessa play in that decision?" She watched his face carefully, as did the rest of us.

"How the hell should I know?" Wentworth's brows lowered as he scowled at us. "Look, I love my sister, and I'm glad she decided it was time to sell the house, but we didn't spend time in each other's pockets in those days.

There are six years between us, so while she and her little friend were off in their sorority world, I was out trying to make my mark on the real one."

"Condescending jerk," Jacy muttered.

I checked my watch. "Listen, we have another appointment. It would help if you'd tell us what you remember from the night of the party."

He shrugged. "There's not much to tell. I spent half the evening trying to convince Sue Ellen Kaminski to go out with me and the other half chasing balls around the pool table."

"Kaminski?" Patrea picked up on the name. "Was she related to the Kaminski who worked on the plaster at the house?"

"A niece, I believe."

Vanessa asked me about Ethan. I told her I didn't know where he was. It's all in the police report."

"And you're certain you didn't see Vanessa after that?"

All the bluster gone, Wentworth rubbed a hand over his forehead. "I've already told you she came looking for Ethan, and that was the last time I saw her."

"What about Ethan? Did you see him again that night?"

A ghost of a smile crossed Arthur's face. "I took him for twenty bucks earlier in the evening. He stayed away from me after that."

"What about Derek Montgomery and Greg Thornton?"

The smile deepened slightly. "Derek was too busy

chasing skirts. Greg was the better player. We were tied three games to three with fifty on the line. After I got the better of him, he went off to drown his sorrows. I poured him into bed before the last guest went home."

Wentworth shuffled some papers from one side of his desk to the other.

My phone buzzed with a text from Mom. We had five minutes to get to the bridal shop. I stood abruptly, the others following suit. "Thank you for your time, Mr. Wentworth. You've been very helpful." We made our way out.

"That guy is a grade-A prime misogynist." Jacy made a face at his door when it closed behind us. "Everything's a game to him. Pool-obsessed idiot."

"No lies detected," Neena agreed with my estimation.

We left the building and headed to Bridal Heaven with only about a minute to spare. Questions swirled in my mind. What had Vanessa stumbled upon? And what had it cost her?

"Put it away now," Patrea warned as we spotted my mother pacing outside the door. "Vanessa isn't getting any deader, and the rest of the day is for you."

"There you are!" my mother said when we got close enough. "I was starting to worry you'd forgotten. I've been waiting for nearly ten minutes." Taking the opportunity to meet up with a fellow librarian for an early lunch, she'd driven down from Mooselick River alone.

"Road construction on the highway. Didn't you hit it, too?"

"Yes, but I checked the maps app this morning and was prepared." The implication came without her usual level of condemnation, so I let it go.

"Well, we're all here now. Shall we pretend we haven't done this once already and go dress shopping?"

As we walked into the boutique, the scent of roses enveloped us. Pink ones. Vases of them. Soft music played while attendants fluttered around.

"This is nice," Jacy said. "That place I went to when Brian and I got married wasn't like this. All the dresses were in plastic bags, which made the place so full of static, my hair stood on end the whole time."

The next hour passed in a blur of satin and tulle. Beautiful dresses, every one of them, but none felt right.

"What about this one?" My mother leafed through a rack and pulled out a tiered confection that frothed and bounced and would make some lovely bride into a fantasy creature. Maybe a princess in a distant castle could pull it off.

Just not me.

"It's beautiful," Jacy put one arm around my mother and used the other to hang the dress back on the rack. "But it doesn't scream Everly, does it?"

On a sigh, my mother said, "I suppose not."

Then, Jacy got inspired and grabbed the dress again. "Neena, go try this on, won't you?"

Shocked, Neena burst out, "Are you out of your tiny mind?"

"No." Jacy put on her best innocent face. "I just

thought it would look good on you, and you could model it so Everly would know what it looks like on."

I'd have preferred to see it on fire.

Neena couldn't say the dress was too far over the top without hurting my mother's feelings, but Jacy wouldn't get the same consideration.

"I'm not tall enough to pull off that many tiers. Maybe Patrea should model it for us. She's got all that lovely height and those amazing shoulders. It's perfect for her."

If Neena expected Patrea to make excuses, she was about to be disappointed.

"I'm game, but I'm not doing this alone. If I try one on, we all do. How's that?" When my mother edged away from the group, Patrea pointed a finger in her direction. "You, too, Kitty. It's all or nothing."

"Oh, but I don't think…"

"Uh uh. You started this." That might not have been technically true, but I wanted to see if she'd do it. "I'll pick you out something nice."

And that was how we all ended up wearing white when a tall blond consultant named Marguerite introduced herself.

"You're all looking lovely today, but which one of you is Everly?"

I raised my hand and hoped we hadn't broken any unspoken rules. When she smiled at me, I assumed we weren't in trouble and relaxed a bit.

"Well, Everly. Why don't you describe your wedding

vision for me, and then I'll see what I can find for you, hmm?"

If that was a hint to get down to the business at hand, her cheerful demeanor softened it. While the others went to change, I couldn't help smiling back as I described the dress we'd seen at the expo.

"I'm looking for something with a vintage feel but not the poofy type of vintage. The dress I saw evoked the 1920s, with intricate beadwork, slim lines, and a nice, creamy color to keep my hair from looking like the flame on the top of a candle."

Marguerite's eyes lit up. "I have the perfect dress for you. I'll be right back."

She disappeared through a set of curtains and emerged a moment later holding the most gorgeous gown I'd ever seen. It was a silk number, very Gatsbyesque, with a deep V dropping from capped sleeves in the same fluid material. Delicate beadwork flowed in graceful lines from the bodice to an inverted fan pattern just below the waist. Similar shapes echoed their way to the scalloped hem.

My breath caught and held for a moment as I pictured myself in the dress. The color wouldn't clash with my pale skin or make my freckles stand out more. It complimented my hair rather than contrasting it, and the beading glittered in the light.

In a dreamlike state, I followed Marguerite into the changing room but declined her help getting undressed. Instead, I wrestled my way out of the dress Patrea made me try on and left the tiered confection in a puddle on the floor, forgotten. Beaded silk slithered over my body as if made for it and hugged every curve. As the dress fell into place, so did the very essence of being a bride.

I was getting married.

Not news to me, obviously, but suddenly, it felt different. I felt different. Like I'd been let in on some cosmic secret that came with a dose of timeless wisdom. It hadn't been like this when I married Paul. He'd swept me so thoroughly off my feet that there hadn't been time to absorb the import or the enormity of it all. My entire marriage to him had been a dress rehearsal for the real thing. Drew was the real thing, and our wedding would be more than just a day. It would be a marriage. One that lasted a lifetime.

I was getting married in this dress.

It made me look like I'd stepped out of an old photograph. Unable to stop grinning, watching silk swirl around me, I spun. The beads caught the light, winking like tiny stars.

My purse hung on a hook in the changing room. From it, I pulled a hair tie and a few pins and did my best to hastily recreate the hairstyle I'd decided on for my big day.

When I stepped out, every eye in the room went misty.

"It's perfect!" Neena stepped close to twitch the beaded skirt into place. "Bombshell."

"Oh, Everly." Jacy dabbed her eyes. "You're glowing."

Patrea merely grinned and patted her hand over her heart.

My mother stood frozen, tears slipping down her face,

but saying nothing. When her eyes met mine, the jolt of love hit me. That's when I started to cry. And to move. We met in a hug that jarred my bones, and I wouldn't have had it any other way.

"You're beautiful," she said, her voice as shaky as her hands. "Inside and out. I'm a lucky woman."

"Me, too. To have you."

We held each other for another long moment while smiles broke through tears.

"Thank you," I turned to Marguerite.

"It was nothing," she waved my thanks away. "This is the best part of my job, and you were easy."

"Easy or not, it takes a good eye to find the right dress on the first try. You have a skill."

Waggling her left eyebrow, Marguerite grinned. "You haven't seen anything yet. Wait until I show you the bridesmaid dresses I have in mind." Tilting her head, she gazed at each woman in turn, including my mother, then left us alone to gush for a moment while she returned to the curtained area.

"Did you see the back?" Jacy patted my arm, then led me to the funny little pedestal with mirrors angled to show me the whole effect. Cut low and beaded to enhance a woman's natural curves. The back was as spectacular as the front.

The curtains parted to allow Marguerite and a rack of dresses through. I grinned as Jacy deserted me to see what the capable consultant might have in store for her.

"I went with cocktail-length sheaths in the same

weight of silk, but we can order them in full length if you prefer. These come in a variety of colors and necklines and have just enough glitter to go with, but not compete against the main event."

"Did you see the hemlines match?" Neena reached for a dress in a soft, watery blue, fingering the beaded hem. "And isn't this close to the color we had before?"

"The very same. Marguerite is a genius." I pulled the dress off the rack and held it up in front of her. "Try it on. It looks like your size, and that V-neck will be perfect for you. Show off that glorious cleavage."

Jacy went for a scooped neckline that framed her face.

"I'll take the sweetheart style," Patrea headed for one of the changing rooms.

"Now," Marguerite reached for the only bagged garment on the rack. "For the mother of the bride."

"Oh, I already have my outfit," she begged off. "It wasn't damaged with the rest."

"Yes, I'm sure it's lovely." Marguerite continued unzipping the bag as if she hadn't heard my mother's comment. When she pulled the dress out of the bag, I saw why.

A shade darker than the bridesmaid dresses, this sleeveless sheath would hug my mother's body gently and then swirl away at the ankle. The long-sleeved, beaded overlay in dark tulle made it perfect.

"Try it on," I ordered.

"Oh, I don't think I need another dress." But she fingered the material anyway.

"Try it on." Jacy stepped out of the fitting room.

"Try it on," came a chorus from the other two fitting rooms.

"Try it on," we all chanted together until she finally held up her hands in surrender.

"Okay. I will."

When she came out of the fitting room, we all stood together and looked at ourselves in the mirror.

"You're having that dress, Mom." I wasn't taking no for an answer. "Because we all look fantastic, even if I say so myself."

"This calls for a celebration," Marguerite declared. She hurried to a small fridge in the corner and pulled out a bottle of champagne and plastic flutes. Popping the cork, she poured us all a glass.

"To Everly!" Patrea cheered. "The most stunning bride Mooselick River will ever see!"

"I think stunning's a bit much, but I'll amend that to the happiest and say cheers."

"To Everly!" my friends echoed, raising their flutes.

We clinked glasses and drank, the bubbles tickling my nose. I gazed at each of their faces, feeling incredibly grateful. It was a perfect moment. When a pang of regret on Vanessa's behalf threatened to sneak in and put a damper on the day, I pushed it back.

We finished our champagne and hugged each other tightly. The dresses were perfect, but sharing this experience with my best friends made the moment truly special.

I paid for the dresses and arranged to have them

shipped to Mooselick River. We were halfway home, and I was still feeling the blissful bridal glow when Patrea's phone rang. She glanced at the screen.

"It's the insurance appraiser about the ring," she said. Answering, she listened for a minute, her face falling.

"Uh-huh. I see. Thanks for letting me know."

She hung up, shaking her head. "Well, the ring's a fake. Or at least the stones are. The setting is authentic, but the diamonds and sapphire are paste. They said the ring would have been worth over a quarter million if the stones were genuine."

"What does that mean?" Jacy wanted to know.

"It means someone pried them out and replaced them with fakes."

"I know that," Jacy grumbled. "I meant, what does that mean for Vanessa's case?"

"I'm not sure," I said. "It didn't occur to me to show it to her, and I didn't think to have Patrea show Arthur the photos. Until we know who it belonged to, I don't think we can estimate its effect on Vanessa's death."

"We should send the photos to Gloria," Patrea suggested. "Where's your phone? I'll do it."

"In my purse," I said without taking my hands off the wheel.

"How does this sound? *Gloria, we found this ring at the house. Any idea who it belongs to? Let me know if you recognize it!*"

"Perfect."

She hit send. "Now we wait.

"I'm hungry," Jacy complained. "Can we stop for snacks or something?"

"I could go for a drink," Patrea chimed in.

But it was Neena who clinched the deal with, "I have to pee."

"Fine," I took the next exit and followed the signs for the nearest gas station, hoping it had a mini-mart. It didn't, but the one across the street did. Neena beelined for the restrooms while Patrea headed for the drink coolers, and Jacy peeled off to see if they carried her favorite brand of whoopie pies.

I spotted the coffee station and found it well-stocked. Thank goodness this wasn't one of those places that quit filling the urns after noon. As we waited in line, I pulled out my phone. Still nothing from Gloria.

"Maybe she doesn't recognize the number," Neena said, coming up behind me.

"Or the ring," Patrea said.

"Or maybe she's avoiding the question," Jacy added. "Could be she knows something but doesn't want to get involved."

I nodded. "Could be. Or she's just busy right now. Hopefully, she'll respond soon." I tucked my phone away again and waited my turn to pay.

Back in the car, we continued our discussion.

"In the meantime, what did we learn from Arthur?"

Patrea rolled her eyes. "He's smug and superior, which is the worst combination. But I think he definitely knows more than he's letting on."

"I agree," Neena said. "When you brought up Vanessa, he got all twitchy and evasive."

Merging back onto the highway, I thought back to the encounter. "He said his dad threatened to cut him off financially. If he found out Vanessa passed along the information, it speaks to revenge as the motive."

Patrea leaned forward eagerly. "Ooh, maybe Arthur was secretly in love with Vanessa and thought running to his father was the ultimate betrayal. That makes it both love and revenge."

I smiled. It wasn't like Patrea to conjure up dramatic theories. Still, Gloria would surely know if her brother had a thing for her best friend, and it was a question worth asking. I added it to my mental list. For now, though, it was time to set mysteries aside and simply enjoy the rest of the trip home. I steered the conversation away from Vanessa.

"Who's your date for the wedding, Neena?" That should do it. "Has David asked you? Or since you're in the wedding party, maybe he's expecting you to ask him."

Her face pinked. "He's expecting no such thing. We're just friends. It's not like that."

Turning in her seat, Patrea shot Neena a look. "The hell it's not. There are more sparks between you than the Fourth of July fireworks. You can't tell me you're not attracted to the man."

If the lie jumped to Neena's lips, she bit it back, then sighed. "He's not hard to look at."

"Not hard to look at," Jacy scoffed. "If I hadn't seen the

two of you together, I might buy that line of crap." Then it was Jacy's turn to sigh. "Look, if you tell me Hudson was the love of your life and ruined you for any other man, I'll respect that. But you're young and vital, and if you're keeping yourself on the shelf because you think Viola Montayne will give you a hard time, you're also an idiot."

"Whomp," Patrea said, breaking the rising tension. "There goes Jacy dropping those truth bombs again. I say snap him up before someone else does."

"Fine. Why don't you all gang up on me?"

Because I understood some of what Neena might be feeling, I caught her eye in the rearview mirror and tried for a reassuring smile. "Lay off, okay? When Neena's ready to date, I'm sure David will be the first to know."

"It's just that wedding dates aren't like other dates," she said. "A movie and dinner, I'd go in a hot minute, but a wedding says something more. I'm not sure I'm ready for something more."

"David's been through some stuff." I knew because he'd told me his story, but since it was his and not mine to tell, I wouldn't betray his confidence. "He may need a little time, too. Why don't we change the subject?"

I probably should have specified to what because Neena and Jacy bickered light-heartedly about work stuff until Patrea broke in and recounted a hilarious mishap while baking pastries the night before. I mostly listened, interjecting an occasional thought while my mind drifted.

A ray of sunlight slanted through the window, catching the ring on Patrea's finger. The real diamond glittered, mockingly bright, reminding me of the fake ring and all of the questions I hoped Gloria could answer. Anticipation grew once more, like a steady humming beneath my skin. We would get to the bottom of this mystery one way or another. For now, we had friendship, a wedding to plan, and the promise of revelations still to come.

With that thought buoying me, I tuned back into the conversation and let myself enjoy the moment. The rest could wait a little while longer.

CHAPTER EIGHTEEN

*J*ust because she'd promised to help clean the rental house didn't mean Patrea wouldn't grumble about it, but despite her litany of complaints, we had the place sparkling by noon on Thursday—a full week ahead of the new renters because Sam's crew finished early.

"I'm starving," she said when we'd put the last cleaning supplies back in my car. "Gas-n-Go sub sound okay?"

"I could go for one. Ham and provolone. Extra pickles. Iced tea. Call ahead, and it's my treat."

We made it to the Wentworth just before one.

"Weird," Patrea frowned as we pulled up to the house to find the driveway deserted. "The electrician was supposed to be here today. She's usually more reliable than that."

"Maybe something unexpected came up."

"I guess." She didn't seem convinced. "I just want to check on the progress. The furnace should be done by the middle of next week. I've got a pair of windows being shipped on Monday."

"That was fast."

Grinning, she unlocked the door. "I found this amazing salvage place in Rhode Island. They had six that were a close enough match to the originals I bought the entire lot. He gave me a good deal on them, so it only cost ten percent over replacements, and these are historically accurate."

"Won't they be less energy efficient than new?"

We'd taken our lunch into the mural room to sit in folding chairs and eat off a camp table. Patrea waved her sub at me, dropping one of the pickles in her eagerness to make a point. "That's balderdash."

"Balderdash?" I curled my lips under to keep from smiling at the term.

"I could choose another word that starts with B if you'd rather, but it all amounts to the same thing. Replacement window companies have perpetuated the myth that historical windows can't be updated, which just isn't true."

I love it when Patrea gets fired up. The light of conviction transforms her face. I could see her in armor battling alongside Joan of Arc.

"These windows have lasted longer than any replacement window you'll find. They just need proper weatherstripping, paint, and some insulation tucked around the frames."

Holding my hands up in surrender, I said, "I'm convinced. What's on the agenda for today? Besides calling the electrician, I mean."

She balled up the paper her sub came in and tossed it

toward the trash can. "Nothing, except I'd like to go look at the progress on the furnace system."

"In the creepy basement?"

She cocked an eyebrow at me, grabbed my sub wrapper, balled it up, and with her gaze fixed on mine, sank another shot into the trashcan. "Chicken?"

I was, but not enough to admit the fact.

"Nope. Let's go."

"You know there's no basement here, right? The furnace is in the utility room, but I appreciate your willingness to follow me into creepy spaces. Maybe you'd like to help me clean the attic at our place sometime."

"I work for pastries."

"That's because you're an easy touch," she grinned and opened the utility room door, flicking on the lights so I could see to follow her inside. It wasn't as big or creepy as I expected, and there was plenty of evidence that workers had been busy there. "They had to cut up the old furnace to get it out of here without damaging anything. That's the new one over there," she pointed to several boxes stacked on a pallet. "Or new ones, to be precise. We decided to go with three. One for each wing and one for the central spaces. Plus, they've all got modulating variable speeds and multiple zones."

"Which means?" I understood all those words, just not in that order.

"They're energy-efficient. All three of them take up less space than the old system, and having so many zones allows the main rooms to have separate controls."

"Fancy," I said just as the slammed shut behind us.

And locked.

"Charlotte?" I called out. Aside from the ghosts, we were alone in the house, and Vanessa stayed outside as much as possible. "You unlock that door right now! This isn't funny."

Not even the tiniest breath of cool air stirred in response to my order.

"At least the lights are—" Patrea began just as the lights went out. "Great." And they didn't come back on when she tried the switch.

"It's Charlotte. It has to be."

"Tell her to cut it out." In the light reflected off her cell phone, Patrea's features took on shadows and angles that fit right into the eerie atmosphere. Then she flipped the phone so I could see its face. "No service. First thing I'm doing when we get out of here is changing my carrier. You probably have service."

"I probably do. What I don't have is my phone. I left it in the mural room because the pocket on these pants is too shallow, and it kept poking me in the ribs."

"Great," she repeated. "What did you do to piss Charlotte off?"

"Me? Who says I did anything?"

"I can only see her sometimes, and I know I haven't talked to her without you around, so it had to be something you said or did." She tapped the flashlight app and shined it into the far corners, hoping to see the telltale flicker of a ghostly presence. When none appeared, she turned it toward the door to see if it unlocked from the inside. It didn't. Frustrated, she rattled the knob, then kicked the door.

We bickered for a few moments more until Patrea declared she knew how to pick a lock. Did I have a hairpin?

Of course, I didn't. So we hunted around for something in the room that might work.

"Some kind of a poker or a piece of wire would be really useful. Or a damn screwdriver. The pins are on this side of the door, so I could get it off the hinges if I had something to pry them up with."

We didn't find a single tool left by a careless furnace worker and had no luck whatsoever using our fingers on the pins. Ruined a couple of nails, though.

Sighing in defeat, Patrea pushed her hair back from her face. "Looks like we'll have to wait for someone to realize we're missing."

"It will have to be Chris because this is Drew's late night. He might get concerned if I don't answer messages and come out sooner, but he's not super clingy, so he might just assume I got caught up in something."

Annoyed, Patrea kicked the door. "Ow."

"Feel better?"

"No. And Chris won't be riding to the rescue. Not until late, anyway. He took the big truck to Kittery to pick up an order of supplies. He won't be back until at least eight. Looks like we're stuck in here by ourselves for a while."

By ourselves but for the thin stream of black smoke rippling in from under the door.

I think one of us screamed, or maybe that was just in my head. I know we both moved away from the door as if it had gone red hot, and one of us said a four-letter word.

Once the dark figure began to rise, I didn't have enough breath to do more than squeak. The room flashed from empty-house cold to arctic cold as we huddled together and waited for whatever might come next.

"If I pee my pants, you won't hold it against me, will you? Patrea whispered.

"Same goes." The words had to squeeze past the lump in my throat. "Don't turn off that light, whatever you do."

"Long as my battery holds."

My ears popped under the building pressure as the dark spirit fed off our fear, growing larger until the first tendril of black snaked toward my face. That time, I was sure it was me who screamed. But then again, so did Patrea.

Where was Charlotte when you needed her?

"Charlotte," I shouted, hoping she'd come and save the day.

"Charlotte isn't here right now." The evil thing's voice hissed like the skittering of spider feet across floor tile. If touching a ghost gave me the heebie-jeebies, this was like that on steroids.

In lockstep, we retreated until our backs hit the wall, and still, the dark thing came until Patrea held up her phone and used the flash to take a photo. Why? I have no idea. Worse, the camera app turned off the flashlight, so once the glare died down, we were in the dark again while she fumbled, trying to get it back on. I swear I felt the icy fingers of doom sliding down my cheek.

I'm not ashamed to say I screamed again.

"What's wrong?" The door popped open. Jerry, the plaster guy, stuck his face inside as he flipped on the light switch. As we blinked back at him, he was the most welcome sight ever. "The front door was unlocked." Eyes wide, he scanned the room for threats. "So I just came in."

As if jet-propelled, our backsides left the wall, and we didn't stop moving until we were back in the hallway.

"What happened? I could hear you screaming from the driveway." Eyes wide with concern, Jerry approached us like he might have approached a frightened animal. Moving close, he grasped me gently by the upper arms and looked deeply into my eyes. "Are you all right?"

What was I supposed to say? *We got locked in by an evil spirit, and if you hadn't come, who knows what would have happened?* I'm sure that would go over well. Plus, he was standing a little too close for my liking. I could feel his breath on my face.

Patrea was the first to recover. Her face still pale, she tried to laugh the whole thing off. "These old houses." She shook her head slowly. "Things are unpredictable. The door locked behind us, and in our attempt to get it open, we managed to hit the light switch, and when we couldn't find it again, I guess we panicked."

Frankly, the explanation burned at the very heart of

being a strong woman, but what could I say? The man had heard us screaming from the driveway. Better he thought us a bit silly than the alternative. I had no intention of telling him the truth. I did, however, gently extricate myself from his grasp and move away.

"It wasn't locked," he piled insult on top of injury, but he did it with a smile, and it seemed like he bought the story. "Who's Charlotte?"

"A friend." Patrea didn't lie. Not exactly. "What are you doing out here today, Jerry? We didn't have an appointment, did we? I'm sure I mentioned the furnace wouldn't be working until the end of the week. You can't install plaster without heat this time of year, right?"

A hesitant pause echoed between question and answer.

"No. We didn't have an appointment. I was just passing by, saw Everly's car in the drive, and thought I'd stop in to see how things were going. Looks like it's all on track."

I didn't have any reason to be skeptical of his answer, yet I was. Still, whatever his intentions, he didn't push the issue, and he didn't try to touch me again. When he'd gone, Patrea grinned and pointed at me.

"Someone's got a crush."

"Did we not just shop for my wedding dress? Besides, I don't go for older men, and you know it."

"Not you. Him."

When I stared at her in disbelief, she laughed and

rolled her eyes. "You really have lived a sheltered life. Can't you tell when a man is into you?"

"You make me sound like Mary Sunshine or something. Of course, I know when a man is interested." Okay, so maybe I had and didn't want to admit it, even to myself. Sue me.

"He saw your car in the drive and knew it was yours. What does that tell you?"

When I stared at her blankly, she shook her head. "We were in my car the day you met him, weren't we? That means he took the time to find out what you drive. That's what someone does when they develop a crush."

"Only if they're a creeper and have nothing better to do. Are you telling me I have a stalker?"

Now, Patrea didn't seem quite so amused, either. "I hope not. Why didn't Charlotte show up?"

"That's a question I plan to ask next time she does. It's been a while since we've seen her, too. I think it's time to call in an expert. I'd better give Kat a call."

When I got to my phone, I found a text from Gloria.

I don't know where you found it, but that looks like the engagement ring I returned to Ethan.

Eyes wide, I spun the display to show Patrea what she'd said.

"What do we do now? Should we tell her where we found it?"

"I guess so." I sent the text. This time, the little scribbling pencil came up to show she was answering.

On the roof? I have no idea how it got there, but it must

have been the night of the party because that was the first time he'd returned to the house since I gave the ring back. I hope that helps.

It did not. Nor did it explain Charlotte's reaction to seeing it. Or that we hadn't seen a sign of her since we'd shown her the ring. A mystery within a mystery that only Charlotte could solve, and she wasn't talking. Or couldn't.

"Maybe Kat will know. She got back to me last night. I'm going to Oakville in the morning."

"Not without me, you're not, and you'd better call Jacy. You know she and Neena will want to go, and while we're out, we'll hit a few more stops along the way."

"You're right." It seemed another road trip was in order. By the time I got off the phone, it was all planned. We'd visit with Kat, and on the way back, we'd stop in Augusta to chat with Evelyn and Derek Montgomery.

CHAPTER NINETEEN

The trip to Oakville passed in a haze of conversation punctuated with pastry.

"It's a good thing calories consumed in a car don't count," Jacy waved the curved tail of a cream horn toward where Patea sat in the back seat. "Chris must thank his lucky stars daily to have found you."

"Trust me," Patrea grinned. "He does. Baking is my second best wifely skill."

The snorts and giggles that followed the comment cut off as we crested the hill overlooking our destination. Nestled against the sun-sparked water of the lake, Oakville made a pretty picture of a small town on a perfect spring day in Maine.

"I need to come back here with paints." Neena leaned forward in her seat to get a better view.

"We should ask about cabin rentals. Maybe do a long weekend in the summer as a group."

"Oh, sure," Neena said. "That'll be fun for me as the quintessential fifth wheel. No thanks."

"We'll invite David," Jacy said sweetly. "Problem solved." She ignored Neena's murderous glare.

"I'm not jumping into bed with David just to make up

the numbers," Neena crossed her arms and set her face in mutinous lines.

"I don't know," Jacy teased. "He's one of those still waters types. It could be fun. I bet he's got serious moves."

"Maybe he does, but I'll find out if and when I'm ready and not just because you think everyone needs to be coupled up. We're almost there. Can we please change the subject?"

Tenderhearted to a fault, Jacy backtracked. "I don't mean to push. I just want you to be happy."

"Then quit nagging."

"I will, but you can't tell me there's no chemistry. We've all seen it."

"There's more to life than hormones," Neena chided while avoiding the implied question.

Thankfully, pulling into Oakville ended that part of the conversation. With the start of tourist season just a month away, it was too early for the ice cream shop, or take-out stands to be open, but I noted the seafood restaurant at the water's edge had a sign out front listing crab cakes as the daily special. Sounded good to me.

Just past the restaurant, I turned left, then pulled up behind the car already parked in front of Kat Canton's sunny, yellow house. "We're here."

"What is that?" Patrea pointed to the car we'd parked behind. "It looks like something from a kid's toy box come to life."

"Best guess, it's Gustavia's car. I think it's a Pacer," Jacy responded before I could.

"A what?"

"An AMC Pacer. Weird little vintage hatchback and rare, too. They only made them for about five years at the end of the seventies."

"Weird is right," Neena came up beside Patrea to stand and stare. "It didn't come like this, did it?" She pointed toward a few modifications Gustavia had made to the interior, including tasseled trim hanging from the headliner, which had been painted to look like a cloudy sky. Quite appropriate, considering hunks of plastic grass rug decorated the floorboards and the seats had been covered in floral fabric. Splatters of automotive paint coated the exterior. Pollock would have been proud. Or mortified. It could go either way.

"One of the perks is I never have to scour the parking lot to figure out which one is mine," Gustavia came down the steps to pull me in for a hug. Today, her hair was pulled back from her face in a single braid that fell halfway down her back. Instead of her normal comple-ment of dangly bits and bobs, she'd opted for winding a scarf printed in eye-watering colors through the twists.

Everyone got the same treatment before she linked arms with me. "Come on in. Kat's inside with Julie. Amethyst will be along in a minute. It's so good to see you again."

It's rare to meet someone and feel like you've known them forever. It's downright spooky when it happens times four. Or would that be sixteen since there were four of us and four of them? Friend math. Very complicated.

Inside, we were met with another flurry of hugs and excited chatter.

"Come right in and sit down." Kat led the way to the living room, where she'd already set out plates of cookies and a tray of drinks on the coffee table. "I want to hear all about your recent encounter."

"Not yet. Don't you dare start without me!" Before we could sit, Amethyst dashed through the front door, several shades of purple chiffon fluttering around her slight form like an errant cloud at sunset. As soon as she spotted me, she stilled and stared. "Whoa."

"What?" I looked down to see what put that look on her face because it wasn't good.

"Your aura."

"What about it?"

Instead of answering, she approached and stuck her face close to mine. Really close, and it was no mean feat since I had at least six inches of height on her. Instinctively, I reared back so my eyes could focus again. "You're freaking me out."

Nodding absently, she took half a step back and, with tiny fingers, began to pluck at the air around my head. Like a milder version of touching an electric fence, a tingle ran through me with each motion. It wasn't pleasant, but it wasn't exactly unpleasant, either. When she was done, I felt lighter, cleaner somehow.

"That's better," Amethyst said, then turned to Patrea. "Yours is nearly as bad." Which was why Patrea got the same treatment. It was a point of pride that she didn't flinch at the first shock of sensation. "There. You're clean. Let me wash this ick off my hands, and then you can explain what type of dark energy you've been fooling with."

"It was me." Since she hadn't come with us, Vanessa's appearance shocked everyone. Me included. "I didn't realize you thought of me as something foul." Sorrow dripped down her ghostly face.

"Ghost," Gustavia pointed out quite literally since one hand went to her heart while the other pointed at Vanessa's feet that hovered just above the floor. "That's a ghost."

"I'd have thought you'd be used to seeing them by now," I said.

"Um. No." Gustavia's wasn't the only head shaking. None of the Oakville contingency seemed comfortable with the chain of events—including Kat. "Not since Julie's grandparents, and that was a special situation. Does this happen to you every day?"

"I shouldn't have come." No fool, Vanessa picked up on the tension. "I didn't know."

"Stop that right now. You're not foul, and you haven't done anything wrong. You just surprised everyone because we weren't expecting you," I tried to put her at ease while everyone stood frozen.

"Please," Kat regained her composure. "Let's all sit and be comfortable." Still, I caught the look that passed between her and her friends. They were still a bit freaked out. I needed to know why.

"What am I missing here?" I asked once we'd ranged ourselves over the sofas and chairs. All except for Gustavia, who settled on the floor near Julie's feet. "Aren't ghosts kind of your thing?"

"Not like this, and I tend not to refer to my calling as a thing." Casting an uncomfortable glance toward Vanessa, Kat tried to explain. "With one or two notable exceptions, I serve as a channel for those who have gone into the light. That means the departed go through me if they want to contact someone on this plane. They usually give me a series of symbols or impressions, and I have to figure out the message from there. Occasionally, I get one strong enough that they can speak to or even through me, and rarer still, I might see an apparition."

"Oh."

Dryly, Kat confirmed, "They don't just pop up in my living room in all their ghostly glory looking like regular people. You'll have to tell me how you get them to do that."

"I'd rather you tell me how I can get them to stop. I don't seem to have any say in the matter." My life is such fun sometimes.

"I'm sorry," Vanessa said, beginning to fade. "I didn't mean to cause trouble."

"Don't go!" Gustavia nearly shouted. "You're not causing any trouble. We were surprised, is all. Please, don't go." When her sentiments were echoed, Vanessa's form solidified.

After a round of introductions, Kat got right to the point. "What can you tell us about your death?"

"Be careful what you ask for," I warned. "If she gets too close to certain events, she'll poof."

"Poof?" Kat's left brow shot up.

"Poof," I affirmed but didn't explain. "It's not a technical term, but it's the best I've got."

"Go ahead then." Pinning on a welcoming smile, Kat motioned for Vanessa to speak. "From what Everly's said, you were staying with friends when you crossed over. Or didn't cross over. Why don't you tell us about them? It will help us," she waved a hand to indicate her friends, "get up to speed."

"Okay," Vanessa said, her face taking on a determined expression. "Let's start with the Wentworths. That would be the family I was staying with. Junior and Gillie Wentworth always made me feel like I belonged there. I'd been friends with their daughter since we were kids. Gloria Wentworth was like a sister to me. Sisters of the heart. You understand?"

Gloria had used the same term.

"Totally," Julie spoke for the first time. "Blood makes families, but so does love."

Vanessa nodded. "That's exactly it. Then there was Arthur Wentworth, Gloria's brother, who treated me the same as he did his sister," she smiled again. "We were the pesky younger siblings when he bothered to notice us at all."

"I have an older brother, so I can relate." Gustavia

tilted her head. "There was always friction between us, but we're over it now. Was it the same with you?"

"Not with Arthur, but Gloria didn't approve when I started dating Derek. That's Derek Montgomery. He wasn't a bad guy. He simply wasn't the one she'd have picked for me, and she wasn't shy about letting him know it. If anyone had friction, it was Glo and Derek, for sure."

Tilting her head, Amethyst observed Vanessa speculatively, making me wonder if ghosts have auras. I made a mental note to ask later and then promptly forgot. "Did that translate to problems between the two of you?"

"Who? Me and Gloria?" Brows shooting up, Vanessa shook her head. "Not the kind of problems that end in murder. Besides, what would be the point? Protecting me from hooking up with the wrong guy by killing me seems a bit extreme."

"True," I mused, twisting one of my curls around my finger as I tried to envision Gloria as a murderer and failed utterly. My ninety-five percent certainty had hit the top of the line at some point. "As motives go, that's probably the worst one ever. It would take a sick mind to think of it, and having met her, I can categorically state that I don't think she's a suspect."

Patrea backed me up on that one.

"Arthur's on the list still, but since we talked to him and he didn't give off the vibe, he's way at the bottom."

As if it were second nature, Jacy began to pour drinks from the pitcher on the coffee table, handing them out to the others. Gustavia guzzled hers and set the glass down on the table. "Why?"

"Why's he on the list? Because Vanessa heard him conducting a shady business deal on the night of the party. He's on the bottom because we've already interviewed him. He said he had no idea she'd overheard anything, and we believed him," Neena supplied the details.

Intrigued, Amethyst leaned forward to snag a cookie from the plate, then circled her hand to encourage the next revelation.

"Next, we figured we'd look at Vanessa's circle of friends. At least those who came to the party that night," I said.

"That's right. There was Evelyn Hartfield," Vanessa continued. "She had a motive, all right. She was furious when she caught her fiancé, Greg, flirting with me at the party. But is that enough to drive her to murder?"

"Jealousy can make people do crazy things," Patrea said.

"Still, I'd have thought if she wanted to kill anyone, it would be Greg since I had absolutely no interest in him, and I think I made my feelings fairly clear." Vanessa shrugged. "I told him to keep his grody hands off me if he didn't want me to turn them into bloody stumps. Evelyn was there."

"For some, those might be killing words," Julie mused as if she had experience with that type of man. "He stays on the list, and so does she. Do you know if they ended up getting married?"

I shook my head, then smiled when I noticed each of my friends doing the same.

"They did not, and here's the twist. Evelyn ended up married to Derek Montgomery."

"Really?" Vanessa seemed surprised, which surprised me. I thought she knew, but when I thought about it, I realized she wouldn't have since I hadn't told her.

"Speaking of Derek. He spent half the weekend trying to rekindle our relationship and the other half following Evelyn around. I turned him down. He didn't take it well and was known for being dramatic. Gloria called him Heathcliff light."

"Definitely worth looking into," Kat nodded. "Anyone else who might have wanted you dead?"

"Be careful what you ask her," I muttered.

"I'd like to think no one did," Vanessa sighed. "But it's painfully obvious that wasn't the case." When she paused to organize her thoughts, I could see she was beginning to fade around the edges. We'd need to hurry things up.

"The last two on the list would be Henry Ashford—he's the other guest I meant to tell you about—and Ethan Middleton, but since they were both gone over Gloria, and she didn't turn up dead, I'm not sure if either of them should be on the list."

"Speaking of Henry," I took the chance to give Vanessa the latest news. "He and Gloria ended up married."

She grinned. "Even after the bloody rabbit?"

"Even after," I confirmed amid curious looks from everyone except Patrea, who knew the story. Before Vanessa faded completely, I told her what we'd learned about Ethan. "There's bad news, too. We learned that Ethan was killed in an accident a few months after you passed."

"And we wanted to ask you about the ring." Patrea pulled out her phone and quickly scrolled to the photo. "We found it on the roof of all places, and it turned out to be a fake." She studied Vanessa's reaction, which wasn't what we expected.

"No surprise there. I don't know how it came to be on the roof, but it being fake doesn't surprise me."

"Well, it certainly shocked Charlotte when we showed it to her." I turned toward Vanessa just in time to hear her squeak as her body began to vibrate. Half a second later, she was gone.

"Poof?" Kat looked at me with great humor.

"Poof." I nodded. The tone of the room changed.

"That was seriously cool," Gustavia flipped her braid over one shoulder. "I'm a little hazy on the details of the murder, but that was an experience."

Taking turns, the four of us filled in the rest of the details for the four of them. The rabbit story went over with a laugh.

"Once we leave here today," I said, explaining where we were in the investigation. "We've got a meeting lined up with Evelyn and Derek. Greg's on the list for later."

"What about Charlotte?" Waving a cookie in my direction, Amethyst squinted to bring back the memory. "Who's she? Did you notice Vanessa poofed right when you started talking about her?"

I hadn't, but now that she mentioned it, I realized Gustavia was right. Still, Vanessa had already begun to fade, so it could have just been unfortunate timing.

"One of the things we wanted to ask Kat about is the Ethan problem," Patrea admitted. "Even though both Gloria and Charlotte said he was the last person known to speak to Vanessa, he passed on some years ago."

"Did you want me to try and make contact?" Kat smiled.

My face pinked. "No. That would be presumptive. Mostly, I wanted your take on the dark spirit, but now that we're talking about Ethan, I wonder if it's him. If he's the murderer, I mean. Would that turn his soul black? Or is that even what's happening here?"

A moment's silence fell while Kat considered the question. "It's possible. I've only dealt with one dark spirit before, and the circumstances were nothing like this. That was a full-on possession by the ghost of a deranged killer."

I'd only heard parts of the story, but an evil spirit had possessed Julie's ex-fiancé, causing these fine women all manner of trouble. Kat downplayed the experience, but the waves of tension coming from her said all I needed to know. We were in potentially dangerous territory.

"Still," she continued, "the circumstances are somewhat similar. Certain deeds darken the soul. A person whose heart was blackened by vengeance at the time of their death won't be allowed to cross into the light. Their thirst for it binds them to the earthly plane until they see the error of their ways. They're what I'd call gray ghosts."

"I've heard of shades, but only in fiction. I had no idea they were real."

Kat nodded, then continued. "Shades are fairly harmless since the thirst for vengeance only hurts the one focused on it. Then there are specters—ghosts who can't cross over because of willfully committed misdeeds who haven't repented at the time of their deaths. They're a bit darker on the scale."

"Is that what you were up against?"

"No." Nudging Gustavia out of the way, Amethyst rose from her chair and leaned over to look at my aura again. "That wasn't the same type of thing at all. We were dealing with someone who'd already crossed into the dark place but found his way back. For all intents and purposes, he was a demon."

Neena went pale. "You're scaring me."

"Don't worry," Amethyst shook her head. "You're not dealing with anything like a demon. I could tell when I cleared Everly's aura. The stains weren't nearly dark enough to be on that level."

Even so, I felt like a bug on a stick.

"Are you sure?" Jacy asked, drawing the aura reader's focus.

After a moment of head-tilting consideration,

Amethyst grinned. "You've got a whiff of ability there. Want me to show you?"

"What," Jacy went preternaturally still, "did you just say?"

"I said you have a spark. It's tiny but there if you'd like to try to see."

Whatever Amethyst expected as a response, I didn't think Jacy dissolving into giggles was it, and yet, that is what happened.

"My mother would have a field day with this. All right, go on then. Show me. But if anyone tells Momma Wade I saw an aura, I swear I'll send her to your house, and you'll pay."

"Well, I don't know her, so I guess I'm safe. Come on then," Amethyst took Jacy's hand and pulled her off the sofa with more power than a woman her size should have had. Then, she pointed at me. "You, too. Come and stand in the hall."

"Can we watch?" Patrea was already on her feet, determined not to be left out.

"Why not?" Amethyst grinned. "The more, the merrier."

The next thing I knew, my back was against the hallway wall, and Amethyst was telling Jacy to focus on the area just outside my body. "Let your eyes relax. If you try too hard, it doesn't work at all. Have you ever seen one of those 3D stereoscopic things with hidden images?"

"You mean the ones that look like a kaleidoscope threw up on paper?"

Amethyst nodded. "It's the same basic idea here. You relax your focus while not looking directly at the subject, and you'll see the aura begin to appear. Anyone can do it with some practice, but it's easier if you have a little something extra to start with."

"I see it," Patrea's eyes went wide. "Whoops. Lost it."

"Good for you," Jacy stared until her eyes crossed. "I got nothing. So much for the spark. Momma Wade will disown me."

"I don't think so," Amethyst laid her hand on Jacy's wrist, allowing a hint of her power to flow. "Try again. Just relax. It's better to let it happen and not try too hard."

"Oh," Jacy said. "Oh, I see it. It's like that haze over hot pavement. Kind of a wavering light outlining your body."

"Is that all?" Neena huffed. "Everyone has one of those. I thought you were talking about something interesting. Aura reading sounds so woo-woo." She caught the look on Amethyst's face. "Sorry. I didn't mean that in a bad way."

"Is there a good way to mean it?" Amethyst's chuckle took some of the sting from the question.

Neena's face flamed anyway. "I suppose not." Then, it all sank in, and she turned to Jacy. "Not a word of this to your mother. Do you understand me?"

"I won't tell on you if you don't tattle on me." A smile lurked behind Jacy's eyes, but her face stayed solemn otherwise. "Scout's honor."

"Deal."

With the demonstration over, we headed back to the

living room. Taking turns, Patrea and I described both encounters with what she still called the weird black swirly thing of evil. It was then that I remembered she'd taken a picture of it with her phone.

"Doesn't matter," Patrea grumbled. "Nothing showed up."

"Can I see?" Kat held out her hand. "If you still have it, that is."

"Sure." The phone made the rounds. I didn't see anything, but Kat and Amethyst stared at it for a long time before handing it back.

"Send me a copy," Kat ordered. "I've got a theory, but I'd like to run it by someone with more experience before I say anything more. I'll get back to you by tomorrow."

After asking for the number, Patrea did as she'd been told, and with our business concluded, we said our good-byes. Kat followed us out, giving me time to ask one final question.

"If Ethan was the murderer, wouldn't his death have canceled out Vanessa's unfinished business and allowed her to go into the light?"

"Good question." Kat didn't seem to have an answer, but she hugged me warmly and ordered me to call if I needed her.

"That went well, I think," Jacy said when we pulled back onto the main street.

"Did it?" Patrea mused. "I'm not sure we got any of the answers Everly needed."

"At least our auras are clean."

CHAPTER TWENTY

"I can't think what we could tell you that we haven't already said to the police," Derek Montgomery said once we'd passed the introductions phase of our interview. "Then or now."

He is Heathcliff, I thought—minus the hunger strike. All grown up with silvered hair and those piercing blue eyes Vanessa had mentioned peering out at me through dark-framed glasses. Since, according to him, his wife was running late, it was just him and us for the moment.

"You can see, can't you, Mr. Montgomery, how I might have concerns now that I've purchased the house where Vanessa died?" As we'd planned, Patrea took the lead. "I'd dearly like to get to the bottom of this mystery, and anything you can tell us might help open up another line of pursuit."

"Well, sure." He said, solemn eyes meeting Patrea's gaze head-on. "I get that, and I don't mind saying the news gave Evvie and me quite a shock. It's all we've been able to talk about since we heard."

"We'd appreciate it if you could give us your version of what happened that night. It might help put some of the ghosts to rest." He had no idea I meant that literally.

"It's all such a long time ago, but I'll do my best and ask that you not judge my actions too harshly. I like to think I've grown into a better man than I was then."

With that, he laid out a timeline that matched everything we'd heard so far.

"I treated Vanessa badly at the time, and my one regret is never having the chance to apologize." He looked up when his wife entered the room, his expression softening. "And to thank her for dumping me so mercilessly. If she hadn't, I might not have turned to Evelyn for comfort."

Evelyn snorted. "Comfort was the last thing on your mind, dear. You were looking for revenge sex, and so was I. It was just our good fortune we found something more. My one regret is not being able to thank Vanessa for putting us together." She crossed over to sit next to him. "I'm Evelyn, by the way, and you are?"

After a second round of introductions, she offered her rendition of the night of the party, which matched his. It didn't sound rehearsed, but they'd had plenty of time to figure out the details and present a united front. At this point, I couldn't take anything at face value.

Despite our hastily concocted plan for dealing with the couple, Neena went for broke. "Who do you think killed her? Since you were there and all, you must have a theory."

Removing his glasses, Derek passed the palm of his hand over his eyes. "I haven't slept much the past few nights going over everything in my head. I always thought it was my fault she left, and finding out she never did put a whole new spin on things. I know I didn't kill her, but I might have been the last one to see her alive. Well, besides whoever hurt her."

"Derek, you don't have to—" Evelyn tried to stop him, but he put his hand on hers and shook his head.

"Yes. I do. It helps to talk about it. I went looking for Vanessa not too long after Henry Ashton pulled that bloody rabbit out of the hat. I planned to tell her I'd been with Evelyn, and in great detail. I was angry, and I wanted to hurt her."

Jacy sucked in an audible breath.

"Not that way." Derek held up a hand to stop our minds from following the natural track. "I thought I loved her at the time, and she'd dumped me. I wanted her to think I'd moved on, and she meant nothing—was nothing to me. It didn't work out that way."

"You never found her?"

"No, I did. I ran into the housekeeper, and she told me she'd seen Vanessa go upstairs with Ethan Middleton. I just about lost my mind." He swallowed hard. "It's a universal truth that people judge others by their own behavior. I thought she'd gone into one of the bedrooms with him for the same reason I went into one with Evelyn."

"More than one," Evelyn added, not helpfully.

He offered her a brief smile, then continued. "Seeing I was in a foul mood, the maid tried to stop me but followed me up when I kept going. They weren't in any of the bedrooms, but when I passed the open doorway to Gillie's folly, I heard her arguing with Ethan Middleton about Gloria."

Every cell in my body went on full alert. "Gillie's folly?"

"That ridiculous panic room."

My breath caught in my throat. This was it. "Tell us everything you heard. It's important."

"I only caught the tail end of her telling him Gloria didn't want the engagement ring and him refusing to take it back. Then, he muttered something I didn't catch, and she said, 'That's the thing, Ethan. Second chances aren't given. They're earned, and if you want one, you'll have to become a better man.' And that was when I realized I'd made a horrible mistake."

"What happened next," Jacy leaned forward to catch every detail."

"I heard footsteps on the stairs. Middleton. I didn't want Vanessa to know I'd been listening, so I ducked behind the door. He didn't even glance in my direction as he stormed off."

"But you said you were the last person to see her," Neena pointed out.

"Besides her killer." He nodded and sighed. "I waited a minute, thinking she'd follow him, but she didn't, so I decided to go down and talk to her, but when I saw her standing there, at the foot of the stairs, holding that ring in her hand, I lost my nerve. I went back downstairs and found Evelyn."

"Don't you see?" Evelyn chimed in before anyone else could speak. "Ethan must have come back after Derek went back downstairs and killed her."

"If I'd waited a few more minutes," misery etched itself into Derek's tone. "I might have seen something or someone. I might have been able to stop it."

"If you live your life looking at the might have beens, you'll miss out on the could bes." I'd never heard Neena sound so brusque. I wondered if she was talking about Hudson or David. Probably both. Either way, now wasn't the time to talk about it.

"She's right," Evelyn said, her expression going serious. "And I like to think Vanessa would be pleased with what you've made of your life. Everything seems so immediate in your early twenties, doesn't it?"

Goosebumps prickled across my arms. "Tell them I'm happy for them," Vanessa didn't show herself, but she did whisper in my ear. That was a first for me.

"If she was the kind of person Gloria described, I think it's safe to say she'd be happy for you both. If you think of anything else that might help, would you give Patrea a call? You have her number, right?"

Back in the car, Jacy was the first to speak. "He didn't do it."

Even the skeptical Patrea agreed. "Unless they're Oscar-caliber actors, neither did she. Worse, unless Greg turns out to have some crazy motive we couldn't possibly fathom, we're back to Ethan, who is dead, and we'll never find proof. What happens if we can't solve this thing?"

"You'll find out if murder house beats ghost house when it comes to high-value real estate, or I'll have to find another way to help Vanessa cross over. Maybe Ethan's stuck on the wrong side of the veil. I suppose I can look deeper into his death, visit the crash site, see if he's hanging around."

But my gut insisted there was more to Vanessa's case than chasing a ghost, and a few miles ahead of the Newport exit, I discovered Patrea felt the same.

"I need a landscaper," she said. "Anyone know a good one? Maybe one named Greg?"

"You want to go to Bangor and talk to him now?" Jacy didn't seem annoyed at the thought of adding an extra hour and a half to our trip.

"I suppose we could if everyone agrees," I glanced at Neena in the mirror to gauge her response.

"Judy's closing up for us anyway." Neena was in. "I've got no other plans and nothing but time."

"I'll call ahead just to make sure he'll be there," Patrea fired up her phone and searched for the number.

"I'll call Brian. The baby's with his parents for the weekend anyway. They've got Shanna and Caleb over there, too. They're calling it Grandbabypalooza. I think they want us to have lots of sex and make them another one, but I could be wrong."

"Have him let Drew know. What do you say we skip our usual Friday thing and go co-ed at Cappy's tomorrow night?" I said. "We haven't done one of those in a while."

"Sure. I'll have him call the guys and let them know.

David, too?" Jacy glanced at Neena, who kept her face carefully blank but nodded.

She made the call while Patrea wrangled us an appointment with the head of Fresh Start Landscaping.

Twenty-five minutes later, we trooped into Greg Thornton's office.

"Well," he said when he looked up from his computer, "I wasn't expecting a bevy of lovely ladies."

He might have come off badly if his smile hadn't been genuine and welcoming and his gaze hadn't remained at eye level instead of several inches lower. Vanessa's description of him had been accurate enough, even if years of outdoor work had etched weathered lines into his skin.

"I'm Patrea Evergreen," she introduced herself and then the rest of us. "I was hoping you could help me with a property I recently purchased in Mooselick River. It's a house that was owned by the Wentworth family."

That got his attention.

"Junior and Gillie's place?" His eyes went wide. You could almost see the wheels turning as he absorbed the shock.

"You knew the family." It was a statement, not a question.

He shrugged. "Through their son, Arthur."

"Yes," I said. "We know. I'm afraid we're here under false pretenses."

"Not entirely," Patrea corrected. "I need a landscaping service, but we were hoping you might speak to us about the party you attended on the night Vanessa Morgan was killed."

His expression shuttered. "I've already talked to the cops. A guy named Ernie Polk came by yesterday. I'm happy to tell you exactly what I told him. Vanessa was a beautiful young woman, and it's a damned shame what someone did to her, but I don't know anything about her death."

"Greg, we've talked to Gloria. We know you found Vanessa attractive enough to make passes, and we know you and Evelyn were on the outs. Vanessa wasn't interested in you the way you hoped. That had to make you angry."

He was already shaking his head. "It wasn't like that, but I can see how it might have looked that way to Gloria. I knew Vanessa wasn't into me, just like I knew Evelyn was using Derek Montgomery to make me jealous. I figured maybe Vanessa wanted to play the same game, so I gave it a shot. But she didn't and that's all there was to it."

I didn't know whether I believed him, but we needed to hear his version of events. "What can you tell us about that night?"

When he hesitated, Jacy was the one who pushed. "Please. For Vanessa. She deserves a chance to rest in peace."

Spearing a hand through silvered hair in need of a trim, he sighed. "You're right. It's difficult to think of such a bright spirit being locked away, and if I knew anything remotely helpful, I'd tell you."

"Just take us through the evening. That will help a lot."

To his credit, he didn't gloss over the parts where he made advances on Vanessa, but his face went dull red. "I don't blame her for not wanting to play the game. Too much alcohol had me pushing harder than I should have, but I wasn't angry with her over it. Truthfully, if I'd have wanted to do away with any woman that night, it would have been Evelyn."

When he got to the bloody rabbit part, he grinned.

"Gloria sure had a set of pipes on her. She just about screamed the house down, but who could blame her? It was a hell of a thing to see. I heard she married Ashton, so I guess it worked after all, hey?"

"So it seems," I said. "What did you do after that?" We were getting to the part of the evening when Vanessa had disappeared.

"Got my butt handed to me in a game of pool. Arthur took me for fifty bucks, which was more money back in the eighties than it is now. My own fault for drowning my sorrows over Evelyn, but let's be clear here. She did me a favor. It would never have worked out with us. Anyway, after I lost all my cash, I wandered back to the bar."

He shook his head ruefully. "I ended the night in one of the downstairs toilets, worshiping at the porcelain altar. Gillie found me there and got Junior and Arthur to take me up and put me to bed."

After a few more questions, it seemed he had nothing to add to his story, so we moved on to his impressions of the rest of our suspects. Maybe he'd give something away there. We didn't. Not really.

According to Greg, Junior and Gillie were the salt of the earth. Arthur had a few rough edges and a willingness to step on toes. His opinion of Derek Montgomery was exactly as expected, but as far as he was concerned, he didn't see Derek going so far as murder.

"We've spoken to Derek and Evelyn, and I'm inclined to believe you." Leaning forward, Patrea pinned him with a look. "They pointed the finger at Ethan Middleton, which is handy since he's no longer around to defend himself." That was a point I hadn't considered. Maybe they'd been lying after all.

"Ethan Middleton was shady. I know it's not polite to speak ill of the dead, but you could see it in his eyes. Still, I don't see why he'd want to kill Vanessa. If what you've said is true, she hadn't done anything but give him a really good piece of advice."

"People kill for their own reasons," Patrea pointed out. "They don't all have to make sense."

But Greg shook his head. "The news report said she'd been hidden behind a false wall. I realize landscaping isn't the same as hanging sheetrock, but my dad offered him some work one summer when we needed a little extra help, and let's just say Ethan was about as handy as a broken finger. Didn't last two days on the job, and every time he picked up a tool, which wasn't often enough, he whined like a girl."

At Patrea's arch look, Greg allowed a sheepish grin. "Pardon the expression. But if you ask me, Ethan wouldn't have had the skill to take down a wall or put one back up. Happens that way sometimes when a man's raised by a single mother and doesn't have a father figure to show him how things are done. No. If you ask me, Ethan Middleton couldn't tell a hammer from a nail, which is why it had to be someone else."

"Who?"

"That's the thing, isn't it? I have no idea." Lips pursed in sorrow, he shook his head. "If you're sure it wasn't Thornton, it must have been one of the guests."

"But you didn't notice anyone taking more than a casual interest in Vanessa?"

"Not that I remember, but if you leave your number, I'll let you know if anything comes to mind. I just can't get my mind around it now."

We exchanged numbers, and then, he looked at his watch.

"If you don't mind, it's getting near closing time, and my wife will be expecting me for dinner. If you're still interested in my services, we could set up a time, and I'd be happy to come out and look at the grounds."

Patrea made the appointment, and we left.

CHAPTER TWENTY-ONE

ack in the car, we waited until we were on the road to begin picking apart the interview.

"It all comes down to motive," I said. "And no one seems to have one."

"Which could also mean everyone does," Jacy pointed out. "Not that I can think what it might be. Every single person we talked to has said Vanessa was a nice person, except for Arthur, who thought she was a twit, but I got the impression he thinks all women of a certain age are twits."

"Bah," Neena spit, "if the certain age is birth to death, maybe."

When my phone rang, I pulled over, fumbled it out of my pocket, and looked at the screen. Martha Tipton. Who else would call me at the worst possible time?

"Hey, Martha. What's cooking?"

"If I need bail money, can you swing it?"

And then some. "I'm sure I could manage. Catherine stashed a few pantyhose eggs filled with change around the place. What's the crime?"

"Assault and battery at the very least, but possibly murder."

"What has Bess done this time?" I figured if Martha was that fired up, Bess Tate had to be behind it. The two women traversed the space between bosom buddy to frenemy territory and back on any given day. But together with Patricia Croft, the third of the unholy trinity, they got things done. Things that made the town a better place to live.

"She's hired a band to play at the Spring into Easter event."

"Okay." I didn't see the problem since we'd already decided to have a band play at the festival. We'd reached out to the high school to see if the kids in the jazz band would like to play, but there'd been scheduling issues, so we'd planned to look for an alternative.

"It's her nephew's band."

"Which nephew?" Bess had many, and two of them were in bands. Very different bands.

"Not the one that plays country music." Which would have been acceptable.

"I see."

Johnny Tate called himself Jizzy these days and fronted a hard rock combo. He dyed his hair black and wore more jewelry jammed into various holes in his face than I owned. Still, I'd heard his band play at Cappy's, and they were pretty good. Maybe not right for the festival, but still not bad. Martha didn't need bail money. She and Bess needed a mediator.

"Let me talk to Bess and see what I can do."

"It won't help. I'm telling you. She's already cut the

check. Whatever will people think when they see a group of miscreants making a racket in the middle of town?"

Thumbing on the speaker option, I put a finger to my lips to keep the others from revealing their presence.

"If she paid them in good faith, I suppose we'll have to honor the deal. Why don't you let me talk to Johnny—see what I can work out." It would be cheaper than posting her bail.

"If you can fix this, you truly are a magician." There was a short pause before Martha changed gears. "Speaking of fixing things, I hear you've been spending time at the Wentworth. That house has a reputation, you know."

"As a party house? Sure. I know all about that." I deliberately misinterpreted her line of thought and then distracted her with a quick rundown of how the work was progressing. In Mooselick River, Martha Tipton was the equivalent of one of those recommendation websites. Knowing which contractors to use and which to avoid, she approved of Patrea's choices.

Now that she'd settled into gossip mode, I could picture Martha sitting behind her desk at the town office, fiddling with the bifocals hanging on a chain around her neck when they should be on her face. She'd put them on and take notes if I gave her anything juicy. With everyone in the car held hostage to the call, I didn't have time to give her anything juicy, but that wouldn't stop me from mining her for information.

"From what people have said, that last party was quite

a blowout. You weren't there by any chance, were you?" Her impressions would be worth gold if she had been. I should have thought to ask before.

"Good call," Patrea whispered low enough that Martha didn't hear.

"We made an appearance but didn't stay long. My Harvey wasn't much for parties and certainly not interested in attending them at what amounted to Peyton Place. And to think what happened to that poor young woman that very night. It gives me the chills all over."

I could hear her shudder over the phone and made a mental note to look up the reference as soon as possible.

"Did you know Vanessa?"

"Not really. I knew of her. Everyone did. You'd see the kids around when they were home. Gloria especially. She was more involved in town events than the rest. If we put on a benefit supper, Gloria came to help set up and serve the food."

"So the Wentworths weren't charitable people as a whole?"

Her tone turning sharp, Martha corrected, "That's not what I said. They always made a donation. Usually, a sizable one, but Gloria was the only one who came to help. I don't want you to think the wrong thing. I liked Gillie Wentworth quite a bit. She just wasn't one to pitch in and get her hands dirty."

"There's nothing wrong with charity from a distance. We relied on those types of contributors when I worked with the foundation."

Satisfied I wasn't casting aspersions, Martha settled back down and let me draw her back to anything she might remember from the night Vanessa died.

"I saw the girl. I don't like thinking of it now, I don't mind telling you. Gives me the shivers."

"Understandable. You didn't get an inkling there might be trouble?"

"None at all. I spent half the time avoiding Dolly Tibbets and the rest assuring Harvey we wouldn't stay long, but I've been going over and over that night since I heard the news."

"What about Ethan Middleton? Did you see him while you were there?"

"Ethan Middleton? Can't say I did. Why? Wasn't he Gloria's young man?"

"Former. Or so I'm told."

Jacy had pulled up the Wikipedia page for Peyton Place on her phone, and when she turned it so I could read what it said, I found myself having to swallow an exclamation. It seemed that The fictional Peyton Place was a small New England town like Mooselick River, but that's where the comparison stopped. In Peyton Place, scandal appeared to be the word of the day. Martha was the only person I'd spoken to who referred to the Wentworths in that light. Did she know something no one else did?

"From what I've been told, Ethan and Gloria had a troubled relationship, and this time, Gloria was finished. From what you know of him, was Ethan the type to retaliate?"

Martha sucked in a breath so hard it whistled over the phone. "You think Ethan Middleton might have killed Vanessa because Gloria came to her senses and gave him the boot?" I could almost hear the card catalog in her head, flipping back and forth while she put pieces of information together. The silence lasted a long moment.

Finally, she said, "Why Vanessa? Why would anyone in their right mind want to kill one woman because another didn't want him? It seems a bit convoluted, don't you think?"

Sighing, I wanted to disagree. "It could be argued that murderers are never in their right mind, but I suppose it does sound silly. Gloria admits she asked Vanessa to speak with Ethan at the party and make sure he understood that the relationship was over. I just thought that might have made him angry enough to lash out."

Someone came into the town office at that point. I heard Martha speak to them, and then she popped back on the line. "I've got to go. If you want to know more about Ethan Middleton, I'd suggest talking to Donald Kaminski or his son, Jerry."

"Why them?" I wasn't the only one in the car with a wrinkled forehead.

"Why not? Donald's oldest sister was Ethan's mother, after all." Distracted, Martha rang off, not realizing she'd left an entire carload of women dumbfounded.

Or maybe not the entire carload.

"What?" Neena looked from Patrea to me, trying to figure out why our mouths were open. "I don't get it."

"Jerry Kaminski is my plaster guy. He learned the trade from his father, Ethan's uncle Donald."

"Oh," Neena sat back in her seat as I pulled back onto the road. "I get it now. That gives him means even he doesn't seem to have a motive, which puts him back in play and us right where we started from this morning—with a suspect pool of one."

"I wouldn't say that," Jacy disagreed. "No one asked where Henry was at the time of the murder."

Because I was driving, I had to settle for mentally slapping my forehead.

"Still," Jacy continued, "we're no closer to establishing a motive than before. Everyone seems to have liked Vanessa, so why did someone kill her?"

"If I knew that, we'd have solved this case by now."

That thought rode home with me and stayed prominent even after I'd dropped everyone off.

"Vanessa! Are you here? We need to talk." I didn't expect her to show up, given how she'd left, but she did. Score one for me, I thought as I turned on the heater to counteract the chill she brought with her.

"I like your other friends. Well, all of them, really."

"Thanks, but I have a question. What was your opinion of Henry Ashton? Was he the man you'd have chosen for Gloria?"

To her credit, she took a moment to think. "To be honest, I didn't know Henry all that well. He seemed nice enough. The quiet type. I just figured he was shy. He kept to himself more than the rest our our little group. He wouldn't have been my first choice for Gloria."

She'd just given me the typical description of a serial killer.

"Who would have been your first choice, then? Did you have someone in mind?"

"Well, sure. There was a guy in one of my classes that seemed more her type. I planned to introduce them after Christmas break. Why?"

"Nothing. I was just wondering." He was the only person involved with the core group we hadn't talked to yet. "Did Henry know about your plans?"

Another moment passed while she tried to remember. "Maybe...probably...I'm not sure. I may have mentioned Fletcher in front of him. It's hard to remember because Henry faded into the woodwork, if you get my drift." Her hand covered her mouth. "You think he may have killed me to keep me from helping Gloria find someone else."

"It could be a motive, and that's been the problem all along. No one seemed to have a reason for wanting you dead."

"I don't believe it," she shook her head. "Not Henry. We hardly knew each other at all."

"You'd rather it was someone you were close to, then?"

The sudden increase in pressure made my fingers tingle as Vanessa drew herself up to respond.

"That's not what I said. You're just being mean."

My ears popped when she left. "Tell me how you really feel," I said to the empty car.

Passing by, I noticed Drew's car wasn't at the gym. Weird. He should have been at work. Maybe Riley needed to switch hours again. Or maybe no one showed up, and he closed, I thought when I pulled into the grocery store parking lot, and it was packed. I had to circle twice to find a space.

Inside, I quickly found out why. Eddie Mason's predicted storm was now national news. A good thing for the store owners but not for anyone who genuinely needed bread or milk. Neither was on my list, but the madness hadn't stopped there. The canned goods aisle was stripped to nothing but peas with mushrooms and a few cans of lima beans. The tinned soup section had been picked clean. Most of the pasta was gone, and the only cartons of eggs left on the shelf were the ones with cracked or dirty specimens. Looking at the sorry state of the meat cooler, I guessed we'd be having the last package of pork chops for supper.

I grabbed the sorry-looking chops along with a head of fennel—one of the few things left in the produce section—and the next to last bag of dog food in Molly's preferred brand, thinking it would have to be enough to tide her over for a few days.

At the counter, Robin Thackery ran my meager purchases through the scanner. "You're not stocking up?"

"On what?" I said. "There's not much left. You must have had a busy day." For once, she scanned every item correctly. That alone spoke to a possible apocalypse on the horizon.

"Storm's coming," she said as I swiped my debit card.

Sadly, that was the most coherent conversation I'd ever had with Robin Thackery.

I left with a feeling of mild unease and a firm plan to have Drew fill at least one of the bathtubs while I cooked up the chops. Except, when I got there, he wasn't home, and that was weird, too.

He showed up twenty minutes later, didn't offer an explanation, but wasn't acting odd, so I shrugged off any niggling doubt and settled for telling him about my day.

"The storm's not supposed to hit until Sunday," I said. "Mom's wedding schedule is clear, so I'm considering driving to Hackinaw tomorrow to talk with Henry Ashton. If he agrees, anyway. Do you want to go with me? I feel like we've hardly spent time together all week."

"We've both had full plates." Drew hesitated so briefly I could convince myself I imagined it. "Movie night tonight and a trip to Hackinaw tomorrow sounds great. We can take Molly for a—"

Hearing her name, Molly's head came up.

"Don't say the word." I laughed. "We'll never get her calmed down." Molly loved car rides almost as much as she loved chasing a ball.

"I almost put my foot in it. Clumsy me," he grinned.

"Okay. I'll call Gloria and make the arrangements."

Gloria didn't answer, so I texted her and set about fixing something to eat. Halfway through the movie we decided to watch, my text tone dinged. I hit pause on the remote and read her response.

"Looks like a change of plans. Gloria says she and Henry will come to us. No trip after all. Do you mind the change of plans? We can find something else to do."

"No worries, babe." Drew passed me the bowl of popcorn. "You'll want Patrea for this, and I'm a big boy. I have some errands I can do. Don't worry about a thing."

CHAPTER TWENTY-TWO

Two hours before it was time to meet Gloria and Henry, Dolly Tibbets walked through my front door. Literally. Well, not walked through so much as she stuck her head through. At least she rang the bell first.

"Everly! Can I come in?"

I didn't see why not since Drew had already gone off to run his errands, and I had the time. "Sure. I've got a little time before we have to leave to meet Gloria and Henry at Cappy's. Come on in. What can I do for you?"

"It's what I can do for you, I think. I have some news." She whizzed past me, leaving a chill across my skin, and headed for the living room, where she made herself comfortable. "I stopped out at Junior and Gillie's old place last night. I wanted to see the progress for myself and maybe invite that poor young girl to join in with the ghost alliance here in town."

Fireworks and rockets went off in my head. "The what now?"

"Well, it's not an official thing, you know. Nothing fancy. Just a bunch of us who get together now and then."

Color me intrigued. "And do what?"

"Like I said, nothing fancy. It's not like we can have

snacks and plan charity work or anything. Mostly, we talk about the living and lend support to those who haven't managed to fully pass on."

"Like a support group."

Dolly nodded. "Think of it more like a book club, but with gossip. That's the vibe."

"And how many of you attend these meetings?" I'd only met a couple of local ghosts during my time among them. Now that I wasn't confined to seeing only those ghosts who were stuck in the afterlife because of murder, I wondered how many more were floating around town.

Waving a dismissive hand, Dolly said, "It's just a handful of us now. You've seen to that."

"I was only trying to help."

Were the ghosts upset with me? Was that why I hadn't seen any besides Dolly?

"Pish," she waved that away, too. "You got rid of Abner for us. That makes you a paragon among women. He was an overblown buffoon in life *and* in death. There was a party in your honor."

While speaking ill of the dead is not nice, no one who met Abner would disagree. He hadn't been a nice ghost.

"Besides," she continued, "we wouldn't want to hold anyone back if it's their time to cross over. That's how it's meant to be. It's just that some of us take longer or have reasons to wait."

"Do you? Have a reason to wait, I mean."

"Just keeping an eye on my girl. When it's her time, we'll go into the light together. But that's not why I'm here. Like I said, I went out to invite Vanessa to our next get-together, and I have to tell you there's something strange going on at the Wentworth place." Her head bobbed as the temperature in the room dropped another degree or two. "Just plain weird."

I needed more information, and Dolly wasn't opposed to providing it. "Did you install some sort of barrier around the place?"

"Not me. Is that even possible?" If so, my house could use one.

Dolly shrugged. "How should I know? It was just that I couldn't get past the front steps. Every time I tried, something bumped me back."

Only one possibility came to mind. "My guess would be Charlotte. She's quite territorial."

"You mean the housekeeper? That Charlotte?"

"She's the only one I know."

Dolly's forehead wrinkled in puzzled surprise. "That poor thing," her tone turned to one of pity. "She's come to a few of our gatherings. Not lately, but in the past. I would have noticed if she had that much oomph, and this felt like dark energy."

"It probably was." Dolly listened with growing horror as I described the experiences Patrea and I had shared in that house.

"You're in over your head," she finally said. "This is bad. Really bad."

Now, she had me worried.

"What? Do you know what we're dealing with?"

But Dolly's body had begun to vibrate, and before she could clarify, she went poof.

"Why are they always doing that?" I sighed.

As usual, Molly failed to answer, but she did rest her head on my knee and gaze at me longingly until I gave in and got her leash. Halfway down the block, I realized the sweatshirt I'd grabbed wasn't nearly warm enough and confused the poor dog by returning home for a warmer jacket. With the temps dipping lower, it looked like the storm prediction was on track after all. Great. Just what we needed.

I wasn't the only one thinking about possible repercussions from the weather. Halfway home, I got a call from the prospective new farmhouse tenants asking if they could move in a few days early to get ahead of the storm.

"It's fine by me," I cautioned, "but you know that house doesn't have a generator installed. If we get what Eddie Mason's been predicting, you will likely be stranded and without power for a while."

"Not to worry," I was told. The new tenants had a portable generator and several gas tanks to keep it running. They were happy to add the prorated amount to the month's rent and had enough family ready to help with the move they thought they could manage in a day.

"I'll meet you with the keys, then."

Heading back to the house, I texted Drew to tell him I'd been called away. He responded with his usual contingent of hearts and kiss emojis.

"Wanna go for a ride, Molls?"

A full-body wiggle was all the answer I needed. Laughing at her antics, I put her in the car, went in for my purse, and grabbed the keys. Sliding back into the driver's seat, I shivered, and not from the pre-storm temperature change.

Charlotte sat in the passenger seat. Hiding a mild case of shock, I turned the key and backed out of the drive before saying hello.

"You've been talking to Dolly Tibbets." The disapproval in her voice was so strong I could almost touch it.

"I have. Well, she's been talking to me mostly. She only had nice things to say about you." A subtle rebuke.

"As if her opinion means anything." Charlotte sniffed.

Dolly had called Charlotte a poor thing. Now, I wondered why. "She seemed quite sympathetic toward you. Is there a reason she would be?"

Ghosts don't blush, but they do turn pale.

"She doesn't know anything about me, and neither do you. My life was mine to do with as I pleased. You and Dolly should both learn to mind your own. I've done my duty just as Miss Gillie would have wanted, and that's all you need to know. Stop talking about me behind my back if you know what's good for you."

Her ghostly finger poked through my arm just long enough to send the sensation of icy slime inhabited by skittering spiders across my skin, and then she was gone.

"Freaking ghosts," I muttered. Molly let out a gentle

woof of agreement. Later, on the way to Cappy's, I filled Drew in on my latest ghostly encounter.

"You know what it sounds like?"

"That Charlotte may have committed suicide? Yeah, I thought of that. Her obituary didn't list the cause of death, and I couldn't find anything on a quick web search, but I'll ask Gloria when we see her. Are you sure you and the guys don't mind having a drink at the bar while we talk?"

Taking his hand off the wheel, he patted my knee. "We have some man business to discuss, and eight of us at once might be too much."

"Man business?"

"Very serious stuff," he confirmed. "But if you need us, we'll be handy."

David, Patrea, and Chris were already sitting at our usual table, deep in discussion. She noticed us as we came through the door and waved me over.

"I saw Eddie Mason this morning. He says the storm won't wait until Monday like they're saying on the news," Chris said to bring us current on the topic of discussion.

Still skeptical, Patrea cocked an eyebrow. "Better have your tubs filled tomorrow."

"Laugh all you want," David said, "I've got guests who don't believe it'll be that bad. By Monday, they'll be comparing the inn to the Overlook and expecting creepy twins to appear in the hallways. You wait and see."

"Maybe it won't," I said. "But if Eddie says it'll be bad, my money's on him."

"I still blame you, Dupree. I never set out to become an innkeeper."

"Whatever, Barrington. Don't forget to put a share of the blame on Martha, but I'll remind you, neither of us was there when you signed on the dotted line." David's bluster didn't fool me. He'd settled into his new life well enough.

Jacy and Neena got the same weather warning when they arrived together. Brian wasn't far behind, and after a quick greeting, we banished the men to barstools until Gloria and Henry left. No sense in overwhelming them with too many of us at once.

"I had a visit from Dolly today and one from Charlotte. Dolly warned me against the dark spirit, and Charlotte warned me against Dolly. From what she said, I think Charlotte might have committed suicide. I'm planning to ask Gloria when she gets here."

"That's sad," Jacy said, her face matching the sentiment. "And speaking of, there's Gloria now."

Just inside the doorway, Gloria scanned the room. I waited until her gaze turned our way and waved her over. A smile lit her face when she saw us, and she grabbed her husband's arm to tug him in our direction.

During introductions, I got my first impression of Henry Ashton. Of medium height and build, nothing about him stood out in a bad way. Silvering at the temples, he wore his dark hair in nearly the same style as my dad. In fact, everything about him gave off a fatherly vibe, which made me realize we'd never asked if he and

Gloria had a family. Mental note to self, rectify that situation tonight.

"It's nice to meet you." Smiling blue eyes met mine without hesitation, and when he took my hand, his was warm. "Gloria told me all about her visit with you," he also included Patrea with a smile in her direction. "But I wanted a chance to thank you in person for the weight you've lifted off her heart. I'm only sorry you had to bear the brunt of such a gruesome discovery."

I could have told him I'd discovered worse, but I didn't.

Graciously, Patrea encouraged the couple to sit. Right on cue, Miranda appeared to offer drinks.

"You won't think less of me if I have a small sherry to calm my nerves, will you?" Gloria asked.

"Not at all. If you don't mind, I think I'll join you." Neena's slow southern style and warmth put Gloria at ease. Henry, too, though he stuck with soft drinks, as did the rest of us.

Once Miranda had gone, Patrea gave a quick rundown of what we'd learned from our various interviews, leaving out anything remotely ghost-related. Jacy filled them in for her when she missed a detail or two. Watching Gloria's face, I saw nothing but mild curiosity during the Derek and Evelyn section. Sober-faced, Henry gave nothing of his thoughts away.

Eventually, I got to ask him for his version of events the night of the party, which matched everything we'd heard up to and including pulling the wine-soaked rabbit out of the hat.

"I laugh about it now, but I would have been happy at the time if the earth opened up and swallowed me whole. Instead, I took refuge in the kitchen until Lottie gave me a stern talking-to and tossed me out." He sighed. "It's a good thing she did because not ten minutes later, Gloria found me hiding in the corner while Arthur beat the pants off Greg at a game of pool."

"You looked like a lost puppy. It nearly broke my heart." Gloria put a hand on her husband's arm, then grinned wide. "He'd tried to rinse the wine off of that foolish rabbit, which turned it mostly pink. It was still damp when he gave it to me."

"She kept it, you know. All this time."

"Aww." Always a sucker for romance, Jacy said, "That's so sweet, and you've been together ever since. Do you have kids?"

Saved me the trouble of asking.

Beaming with pride, Henry pulled out his phone to show off some photos. "Two fine sons and a daughter who looks just like her mother. I'm the luckiest man in the world."

Hating to spoil the mood, I had to ask, "When was the last time you saw Vanessa Morgan alive?"

The smile fell off his face. "It would have been when I decided to hide out in the kitchen after my failure with the rabbit. When I passed through, Vanessa was just going up the front staircase with Ethan Middleton. If I'd had an inkling of what was to be, I'd have done something to put a stop to it."

That set Gloria off on another bout of sniffles while I felt a mild tingle of something. Henry's information was important if only I could figure out why.

"What about Ethan? Did you see him again?"

"Well, sure. Right after Lottie kicked me out of the kitchen. She came in, caught me rinsing wine off the stuffed bunny, and gave me a hard time. Then she marched me out to make sure I didn't go hide in my room. 'Find Gloria and face your mistakes, boy. It'll make a man out of you', she said."

"Lottie worked in the kitchen? Was she one of the catering team?" Patrea needed clarification. She had her phone out and was taking notes on it.

"He means Charlotte, of course," Gloria spoke up, her voice husky with tears. "She always did have a soft spot for Henry. He's the only one who got away with calling her Lottie. I probably should have listened to her when she went on and on about how Ethan was a wastrel—her word, not mine—and wasn't nearly good enough for me."

"Now, darling," Henry said. "You know how thick your mother and Lottie were in those days. She was only repeating what Gillie said to her. Lottie thought your mother could do no wrong. She'd have done anything to protect her."

"Yes. I know. And I thought she just wanted to run my life. You know how it goes," Gloria appealed to the women at the table. "The more your mother tries to steer you away from a young man, the more you seem to want him."

All but Jacy responded with knowing nods or murmurs of agreement. Brian had been her first love and was anything but a bad boy.

The topic had veered off from Ethan, so I pulled it back.

"Tell me about Ethan."

Henry's eyes lost focus momentarily as he pulled the memory to the front of his mind. "He was in the great hall talking to Greg when Lottie and I walked in. I remember she had her hand on my arm, and when she saw him, she squeezed. Then she dragged me over there. Greg took one look at her and decided he had someplace better to be.

Thinking back on it, I can't say that I thought Ethan looked particularly guilty, but Lottie laid into him about how if he knew what was good for him, he'd leave and never come back. Gloria wasn't interested, and he had no business being there."

Having met Charlotte, I could picture the scene. "What happened next?"

"He tried to argue, but she didn't let up until he gave in and left. She followed him out to make sure he didn't sneak back in."

Eyes narrowed with annoyance, Gloria pinned her husband with a look. "You never told me anything about that."

Shrugging, Henry said, "Up until we learned differently, I thought maybe she'd had a similar conversation with Vanessa, and that's why she left. If I'd said anything, Lottie might have lost her job, and I didn't want to be the reason when I wasn't even sure she'd done anything."

Still miffed if her frosty tone was anything to go by, Gloria merely said. "I guess that's for the best since now we know she didn't. It wouldn't have changed anything."

"Can you run through it for me again?" Patrea asked, her fingers busily keying in notes on her phone. As Henry complied, she prodded him to estimate how much time passed between each significant event.

"Did you keep in touch with Charlotte after you left home?" I asked Gloria.

"I'm sorry to say I didn't. Mother was ill by then, and Charlotte didn't go with my folks when they moved to Arizona, so I confess I lost track of her. I think she passed away some time ago, but I can't remember how or when."

"It was after we lost Gillie," Henry reminded her gently. "I remember she sent a condolence card with a very touching message." To us, he said, "I took care of most of the funeral arrangements to spare Gloria more pain while she grieved."

I'd run out of questions, and since no one else had any, Henry mentioned it was time to leave if he and Gloria wanted to get to Bangor in time for their dinner reservations. When they'd gone, the men joined us."

"Find out anything new?" Drew leaned in and kissed me.

"Not a lot. Henry's probably not our killer, but..." Patrea broke off as Miranda came back to take our food order. "We did learn that he and Charlotte were buddies. Still, I don't see how that information helps us," she continued once the server had gone.

"I thought it did for a minute there. I got a tingle, but then it sort of fizzled out. He corroborated Derek's story. It's looking more and more like Ethan is our killer, and since he's dead—" I didn't get a chance to finish my sentence before a hand landed on my shoulder.

"If it isn't the lovely Everly Dupree. Must be my lucky night." The hand slid forward and down into uncomfortable territory as I turned to see a very drunk Jerry Kaminski at the other end of it. "How about a dance?"

"I don't think so, but thank you."

"C'mon. At least let me buy you a drink. Come sit with me at the bar. Make my night." His hand slid even lower.

My mouth opened, but nothing came out, and it didn't matter anyway because the creeping hand suddenly disappeared.

"I think you've had one too many already, Mr. Kaminski." In a blur of motion, Drew had Jerry by both arms. "Now, you'll want to apologize to my fiancé and say goodnight because it's time for you to leave. I'll just help you outside, shall I?"

I'll never know whether Jerry would have apologized because Drew didn't give him time for anything more. "Brian, if you could round up Jerry's buddy and tell him Jerry needs a ride home, that would be good. And tell Adam I'll pick up their bar tab."

"Sure thing," Brian headed toward the barstools at the

opposite end of the room, where earlier, he'd seen Jerry sitting with his friends and sucking down a pitcher of draft beer.

"Need any help, bud?" Chris drawled, but Drew shook his head.

"I'm good."

A hush fell, and nearly every eye in the place locked on to watch Drew march Jerry out of the bar. A few moments later, the guy Brian had tapped on the shoulder also went out. When Drew returned with a good-natured smile on his face, the whole place started buzzing.

"Looks like we're the pre-band entertainment for the night."

"You didn't hurt him, did you?" I asked.

"Not a bit. I merely explained what would happen if he put his hands on you again. He got the message, though I'll be surprised if he remembers it tomorrow. Not that I'm opposed to giving him a reminder if he needs one."

"That was entertaining." Miranda showed up at our table with a bottle of wine and a pitcher of beer. "These are on the house, by the way." To Drew, she said, "If you ever need extra work, we could use a good bouncer." She took our food order, but before she left, she leaned down and whispered in my ear, "You're a lucky woman."

I didn't disagree.

CHAPTER TWENTY-THREE

As Miranda walked away, the evening's entertainment arrived, and I remembered my promise to Martha that I would talk to Bess Tate's nephew about his part in the spring event.

Touching Drew's hand, I leaned over and said, "There's something I have to do. It won't take long. Go ahead and order for me, okay?"

With the jukebox pumping out tunes, a few people were up and dancing already. Including—to my utter shock, Vanessa and Dolly Tibbets, who wafted among the living. Dolly's exaggerated booty shaking went unseen by any eyes but my own. Frankly, I could have done without the show. She saw me, gave a little wave, and went back to her dancing.

"Hey, Everly," Johnny, who I refused to call Jizzy, even in my head—tilted his chin up just slightly in greeting. "We don't usually take requests, but I'd make an exception in your case."

If this was his version of flirting, he needn't have bothered. Even if I'd been single, on top of him being at least six years younger, the excessive piercings would have put me off. "I wasn't planning to make any, but I would like to talk to you for a minute if you don't mind. It's about the Spring Into Easter event."

"We already cashed the check and bought a new amp. You can't back out now."

"It's not about the money." And if it came to that, I'd make up the difference myself. "It's more about the music. We'd been planning on something a little lighter than…," the proper description eluded me.

"Goth rock," Johnny supplied with a smile. "No worries. Aunt Bess already laid down the law. No black clothing, no makeup, no visible tattoos or piercings, and only tunes that won't offend the delicate sensibilities of the elders and Generation X."

"Okay, then. Have a good night." Hoping he could pull all that off, I returned to my table. Dolly gave me another wave as I passed the dance floor.

It wasn't until we'd demolished two loaded sampler platters of appetizers and our entrées were half gone that the conversation circled back to Gloria and Henry.

We got to the point where Henry admitted he'd thought Charlotte drove Vanessa away. Jacy commented that Gloria hadn't been happy with him.

"I'm betting poor Henry's sleeping on the couch tonight." Brian dipped a chicken wing in Jacy's zesty onion ring sauce and ignored her arch look. "Wonder what he'll have to pull out of the hat to get back in her good graces. Probably his—"

"Don't finish that sentence, or Henry won't be the only one tossing and turning tonight," Jacy said, picking up her cup of sauce and dumping the rest over her onion rings. "Besides, she didn't seem that upset. Do we think Ethan came back after Lottie sent him off with his tail between his legs? Or do we put him on the innocent list for good this time?"

I pushed my plate back and rested my elbows on the table despite the fact that even from a mile away, my mother could probably sense the infraction.

"As much as I hate to admit it, he probably wasn't the killer. I think I wanted him to be because he was shady enough to give Gloria a fake engagement ring. Still, putting him on the innocent list leaves us with no suspects at all. We have to be missing something."

"Run us through the highlights," David said. "Maybe talking it out will help."

"I'll do it. I think I've worked out the basic timing of events." Patrea said and pulled out her phone to scan through her notes then, as if lecturing a jury, laid out the party's events in chronological order as described by our key witnesses.

"This is where it all falls apart," Jacy said, frowning. "I believed Derek when he said Vanessa was alive after Ethan went downstairs. Plus, we know Evelyn was downstairs, and she and Derek were together after that."

"Unless they were lying," Drew waved his fork with a cherry tomato on the end of it. "They've had years to perfect their story."

"I don't think they were," I said. "Besides, Greg

corroborated everything they said, and he'd have no reason to protect them."

"Someone's lying," Neena said. "They have to be, but who is trying to protect who, and why?"

"Whom," David corrected her and got a dirty look for his efforts. All of that registered with me before my mind kicked into overdrive and everything else faded away.

Only one person related to the household had mentioned being a protector, and hadn't Henry said Charlotte doted on Gillie Wentworth? Could she have murdered Vanessa and why?

"Go over the timeline again," I cut into the conversation that had continued around me. "Start at the beginning."

"You've figured it out." Patrea pointed at me. "Who was it?"

"Just go over everything again. I need to see if it all fits."

She did, and it did. The motive wasn't typical, but it all played for me. Now, I needed corroboration.

"I have to talk to Charlotte," I said. "Right now."

"You're not going without me," Jacy stood and tried to get Miranda's attention so we could settle the bill.

"If you're going, I'm going," Brian reached for his wallet.

"We're all going," Drew's tone suggested finality.

"Who's going where?" Dolly popped up beside me. Her timing couldn't be better.

To Drew, I said, "I'm good with a group outing so long

as you don't mind if Dolly rides along with us. You'll come, right?" That last was aimed at Dolly, who nodded and sent off waves of the scent of hairspray.

"Fine," he agreed without hesitation.

To Dolly, I said, "Tell Vanessa to give us a fifteen-minute head start and then meet us at the house. She shouldn't go in until we get there."

It took some time to get our things together, but soon enough, with Dolly in the back seat, we were driving along the lonely country road bathed in darkness.

"What's up, buttercup?" Dolly's energy was high enough to frost the windows. Drew turned the heater up full blast. "Why did you send the girl on ahead? Did you solve the crime?"

"Maybe." Ignoring the way the seatbelt scraped across my neck, I twisted in my seat to face her. "Do you happen to know where Ethan Middleton had his accident?"

"Sure do. Why?"

"I'd like you to go there and see if he's hanging around. Could you do that?"

Her eyes narrowed. "Are you trying to get rid of me?"

Mine rolled toward the ceiling. "Why would I want to get rid of you after I'd asked you to come along in the first place?"

"Oh," she said, "Right. Okay. I'll be right back. Don't go in without me."

Once she'd gone, the car turned stuffy in seconds. "Maybe we should hire Dolly to ride with us in the summer. Save on air conditioning," Drew said in a lame attempt to lighten my mood.

"Do not say that in front of her. She'll take you up on it."

She popped back into the car just as we turned into the driveway. "He's not there, and I took the liberty of checking with my network. As far as anyone knows, he went into the light. Nobody's seen him around, ever."

"Thanks." I leaned forward and cranked the heat back up. Her information clinched my theory. I only had to figure out how to handle what came next, but there wasn't much time to devise a plan. It wouldn't be the first time I'd had to wing it.

When we arrived, Vanessa waited on the front steps, but I didn't see Charlotte's face in any of the windows. That could be a good thing or a bad thing.

"Are you sure you wouldn't rather wait until tomorrow?" Patrea pulled out her keys but hesitated.

"Now's better. If my hunch is right, we're running out of time. It has to be now."

"If you say so." Patrea turned the key, and we all stepped inside.

If I'd thought the car was chilly before, it didn't begin to compare to the chill inside the house.

"I think the furnace is out." Her breath plumed into a cloud of mist when Neena spoke.

"I can hear it running." Chris walked over to the nearest vent and held his hand down to feel the meager warmth. "It's throwing heat."

Movement at the top of the grand staircase drew my attention to where Charlotte waited and watched. When Vanessa's body began to blur, Dolly moved closer to her, lending a supporting arm, and the young ghost became solid again.

"Come down, Charlotte. We need to talk," I said.

She made it halfway down before the black mist overtook her.

"Charlotte likes to tell secrets." The voice coming out of the vaguely human shape was knife-sharp. "It's better if she doesn't talk right now."

Every human in the room jumped half out of their skin when Dolly screeched, "Specter!"

"Yes, I know," I said.

"A what?" David's question came from somewhere behind me.

Turning, Jacy hissed out a reply. "Ghost of someone who did bad things and wasn't sorry. Powerful. Bad."

"And getting closer," Neena sounded nervous as the specter descended one more step.

I could barely hear myself speak over the sound of my heartbeat in my ears. "Why did you do it, Charlotte? Why did you kill Vanessa? It had to be you. I realized that earlier. You went upstairs with Derek, but he never mentioned seeing you go back down. So you had to have stayed behind, and you knew the house well enough to stash the body until you had more time to hide it."

I heard the shocked chorus of indrawn breaths from behind me as the dark figure descended one more step.

"You waited until Derek left, then you went down those stairs and put your hands around her neck. Didn't you, Charlotte? But why?" I was nearly certain I knew, but I kept repeating her name, hoping the more genial ghost would beat back the darkness and give Vanessa the closure she so richly deserved.

"Confession is good for the soul," Jacy stepped beside me, standing close enough to take my hand. "Tell us why you did it, Charlotte. Vanessa needs to hear the truth."

"Yes, Charlotte. Tell us why." Patrea took her place on my other side. Her hand locked itself to mine.

Dark Charlotte whizzed down three more steps, fury emanating from her form. My nose and the tips of my ears burned with cold. Neena stepped forward on Jacy's other side while the men ranged behind us.

"You know what you're doing, right?" Jacy shivered.

"Not a clue," my response slid between chattering teeth. "It doesn't matter. I already know why," I raised my voice. "You followed Derek upstairs and heard Vanessa say something to Ethan that sounded like she encouraged him to keep trying with Gloria. Something about second chances."

Charlotte's progress halted.

Shaking off Dolly's hand, Vanessa took a step forward. "I'm the one who encouraged Gloria to ditch that jerk, and you knew it. Besides, I wasn't talking about Gloria when I said that stuff about second chances."

For a heartbeat, Charlotte's human form shone through inky black.

"But you said—" The darkness rose to cut her off. "I heard what I heard."

"Really?" Vanessa's tone dripped sarcasm like bitter honey as she mounted the stairs. "Because if you'd heard everything, you'd have heard him say he didn't blame Gloria when his own mother turned him away. She was who I meant when I told him he could earn a second chance. You came down the stairs and put your hands on my throat. I remember it all now." Turning to us, Vanessa filled in the gaps. "There was a space behind the stairs that hadn't been closed off yet. She shoved me into that wardrobe they turned into a door, and locked it with the key. Later, when everyone else had gone to bed, she came back and sealed me up in the wall."

Like a dog shaking water off its coat, Charlotte shed the darkness, leaving it to swirl nearby. Her face reflecting the horror of her mistake, she took one more step down to meet her accuser.

"Gillie wanted Gloria to be with Henry, but Gloria paid more attention to your opinion than her mother's. I thought you'd taken Ethan's side. I had to do something."

"You could have asked me. Did you ever think of that? Was it really worth condemning your own soul?"

Focused on Vanessa, Charlotte failed to notice the swirling darkness rising behind her.

"Vanessa!" I shouted. "Look out!"

The roiling cloud enveloped Charlotte once again. Her voice rose in a scream of fury. "I am the protector." Dark hands rose toward Vanessa's throat.

"Don't let her touch you," Dolly shouted. "Don't you know specters can suck out your soul?"

"What do we do?" Patrea shouted in my ear.

"I don't know." All I could think was that I'd tried to bring Vanessa closure and doomed her soul instead.

That's when, operating on pure instinct, Drew flashed past us to put himself between Vanessa and the dark thing. "You know nothing of protecting. You won't touch her again."

"Drew, don't!" Screaming, I shrugged off the hands that would have held me back and raced up the stairs. Charlotte had him by the throat, and I knew well enough she could exert control over the physical world. If she wanted it badly enough, she could kill him, or suck out his soul. Or worse yet, she could do both.

After that, everything happened fast. I put myself between him and the specter, ignoring the utter absence of heat where her hands passed through me. "Let him go, Charlotte. I know there's a part of you that is decent and good. Come away from the darkness, Charlotte."

I felt her grip slacken for a moment and saw Charlotte's face swim up to the surface as Drew pulled in half a breath.

"The hell with that." Vanessa flashed past me to fling herself at Charlotte. "You're not protecting Gillie now, you witch. If you want my soul, you'll have to fight me for it, and this time, I won't go easy."

Vanessa's momentum took Charlotte over the side of the stairs and down. Drew dropped to his knees, whistled in deep breaths. "I'm okay," he said, his voice hoarse. "Finish it."

"We've got him," Chris said, appearing at my side as if by magic. I left my beloved to his friends and raced back down to join mine as they watched the ghost battle playing out on the great hall floor.

Physically, I was helpless to do anything, but maybe, I thought, I could talk reason into Charlotte.

"Do you remember the day we found Vanessa's bones? You told us to help her, Charlotte. Do you remember? There was part of you that wanted to be caught. Wanted to do the right thing. You said you came back to protect the house, but I think you came back to protect her because somewhere in there, you felt remorse. Let go of the darkness. Look for the light."

Through the cloud of whirling darkness, I caught glimpses of Vanessa and Charlotte as they battled.

"I think there was always darkness in you, but you kept it buried deep until that one moment when it took over. You didn't want to hurt Vanessa, but you couldn't help yourself, and when it was over, you buried the memory. But after you died, it came back as a specter. You're stronger than your worst mistake, Charlotte. Come back to the light!"

"You helped me, Charlotte," Patrea shouted. "And I'm grateful that you did. You saved this house so I could buy it and find Vanessa. You saved it so I could set her free. Come back to the light, Charlotte. I'll protect the house from now on, but you need to let Vanessa go now. You need to set yourself free. Only you have the power to do that."

We were getting through to her, I thought.

"Keep talking. It's working," Jacy said, then added her voice to ours. "Come back to the light, Charlotte."

"Gillie wouldn't have wanted this," Neena added her voice to ours. "Come back, Charlotte. Come back to the light. You need to shed the darkness if you ever want to see her again."

With each exhortation, Charlotte gained strength against the evil that had overtaken her. Finally, she shoved Vanessa clear, and in that moment, I thought she'd won. I thought we'd saved her.

"Go into the light, child," Charlotte spoke only to Vanessa. "Go now!"

"Come with me." Having stepped back far enough to be safe, Vanessa tried to bring Charlotte fully out of the depth of despair she'd created of and for herself. "We'll go together. Gillie's waiting for us."

"Not for me." With that, Charlotte dove toward the black cloud, gripping the seething mass in her arms. We'd never know whether the specter took Charlotte into the yawning pit that opened at her feet or it was the other way around. Either way, it closed over her head, and with the sound of a thousand zippers, it disappeared.

"What just happened?" Breathing as hard as if she'd just run a race, Jacy turned to me. "Did Charlotte just send herself to hell?"

For a moment, my mouth couldn't form words. I

turned to see Drew, livid, red marks marring his neck but standing on his own. I ran to him. "Are you all right?"

He nodded, then simply rested his forehead against mine and gathered me in.

"I won't be singing opera for a while," he joked.

Once I'd assured myself he was okay, I turned to answer Jacy's question. "I don't know if Charlotte went to hell or not. Only that she's gone."

"Good place for her if she did," Vanessa said without sympathy.

I'd forgotten she was still here. Why was she still here?

"Don't you start in with the vengeance stuff," I shook a finger at her. "You don't want to end up like Charlotte, do you?"

"No, of course not. She was sick, wasn't she? Like not right in the head."

"I think that's a given," Patrea answered for me. "Split personality disorder, maybe."

Vanessa nodded. "It won't be easy, but I think I can forgive her. I think I have to if I want to go into the light."

"Do you see the light?" I asked.

Tilting her head toward the stairs, Vanessa said, "It's over there. Only...before I go, do you think I could see Gloria one more time? I'd like to say goodbye."

"I suppose that could be arranged. Tomorrow. It's too late to call her now."

Cheered, Vanessa headed for the door. "Not here, though. I never want to see this place again."

"Can't say I blame you," Dolly spoke up. I'd forgotten

about her, too. "Come with me. I'll take care of her tonight." That last was aimed in my direction. Dolly took Vanessa's arm, and they winked out.

"Looks like you won't have to add haunted house to your sales pitch after all." I grinned at Patrea, who threw her head back and laughed.

"Guess not. Unless you can persuade Dolly to move in. She sure would liven up the space. Are we all ready to head out? I think I've had enough for one night."

CHAPTER TWENTY-FOUR

Gloria stood on my front porch, her arms wrapped around herself protectively.

"You don't have to do this if you don't want to," I said once I got a look at her pale features and felt the shudder that went through her when I put my hand on her arm to guide her inside. "Vanessa will understand." She'll be disappointed, but she'll understand.

"No." Head shaking, Gloria firmed her resolve and stepped forward. "I'm okay."

Gently, I led her inside. "Can I get you something? Tea? Coffee?"

Solemnly, she shook her head. "I'm not even sure I can swallow my own spit right now. If we could just—" Gloria circled a hand to indicate she was ready to get on with the reason for her visit.

"Okay." Instead of heading toward the kitchen, I led her to the living room and settled her on the sofa. Maybe settled was too strong a word since she sat right on the edge of the seat.

Trying to look around without actually looking around made Gloria twitch. "Is she here?"

"Not yet." Technically, Vanessa was waiting in my

bedroom to give Gloria time to adjust to everything and probably to get control of her nerves as well. "I'll get her."

"I feel like I swallowed a hornet's nest, and they're just circling inside me. I don't know how you can be so calm." That earned her a quick grin from me.

"It's not my first time, but if it helps. I'm nervous, too."

"It does. Maybe. A little."

Nodding, I left her waiting while I took the short trip to my bedroom to find Vanessa pacing from one side of the bed to the other. "She's here. I'm wigging. Like totally flipping. To the max, you know?"

Assuming she meant nervous, I said, "We all are."

"Glo, too?" Vanessa stopped pacing and waited for me to nod my answer. "Okay. I guess I feel better. I just need a second, and I'll be right out."

Her back ramrod straight, hands folded in her lap, face devoid of all color, Gloria watched me walk back into the living room with eyes big as an all-day sucker. "She'll be with us in a minute."

The minute dragged into two, but a pale, wispy figure finally materialized before us. I grasped Gloria's hand reassuringly as Vanessa's ghost took form, blurry at first, then sharpened into focus. She blinked in confusion, squinting at Gloria, then looking at me.

"Gloria got old."

That was one message I figured was better if I didn't pass along.

"Vanessa's here now."

Eyes wide, Gloria tried to speak, but what came out wasn't words. Only a series of squeaks.

"Tell her I'm sorry," Vanessa said.

The repeated apology put words back in Gloria's mouth. "What for? I'm the one who should apologize. She'd still be alive if I hadn't invited her to the house for the holidays. This was all my fault." Tears shimmered.

"Tell her not to be silly."

"Why don't you tell her yourself?"

"I'm trying, but I don't think I can. I'm too freaked out."

Against my better judgment, I held out my hand. As soon as Vanessa's ghostly essence came in contact with my physical presence, she slammed into view, startling Gloria into a four-letter exclamation.

"Van? Is that really you? You haven't changed a bit."

Without thinking, Vanessa lifted her hand from mine and remained visible. As the two friends talked, the soft glow that enveloped them intensified. I had to shade my eyes from the radiance.

Vanessa's spirit seemed more solid now, worry and grief falling away until she appeared as the carefree young woman she'd been in life. Gloria, too, was transformed, her expression peaceful and content in a way I hadn't seen before. At that moment, I realized their connection went beyond flesh and bone. What they shared transcended space and time. The wounds of the past had been healed, the friendship they'd thought lost restored.

I found myself holding my breath, unwilling to

disturb the sanctity of their reunion. This was a glimpse into the true nature of the soul, a reminder that our spirits endure long after our bodies fail us. Taking the peace as a sign to let them have time alone, I said, "I'll be in the kitchen if you need me."

Vanessa had maybe ten minutes before her energy began to flag. I could probably extend that time if I let her touch me again, and I would if necessary. Just call me the Energizer Bunny of ghostly activity.

Their voices low, the friends were still talking when I appeared in the doorway.

"It's time." An equal portion of joy and sorrow warred for space in Vanessa's eyes. "I need to go now," she said softly. "Or I might never want to leave."

Gloria nodded, tears glistening in her eyes even as she smiled. "I understand. You've been trapped here too long. Give your folks my best when you see them. And if you get the chance, can you tell my mom I love her?"

Vanessa reached over to touch Gloria's hand. Gloria shivered, her gaze flicking to me. I nodded that it would be okay. Then, with a grateful look at me, Vanessa turned toward the light. Her face glowed with strength and purity as it fell like a curtain. She only looked back once, her gaze resting on me for a long moment.

"Thank you," she mouthed, and then, at long last, Vanessa took her rest.

I stepped forward and placed a hand on Gloria's shoulder.

"I know it's hard to say goodbye," I said gently. "But

take heart—while her spirit may have moved on, the bond you share will never fade."

Gloria clasped my hand, blinking back tears even as she gave me a tremulous smile. "You're right. Do you have a best friend?"

"Three of them, actually. I'm one of the lucky ones."

"You hold them close, you hear me?"

"I will." It was a promise I'd die before breaking.

"Good." Gloria took a deep, steadying breath and straightened her shoulders. The vulnerability of the moment passed, replaced by her usual stoic strength. She rose to leave.

"Thank you, Everly," she said solemnly. "For giving us this chance to say goodbye. I can't tell you what it means to me."

I smiled, warmed by her gratitude. "Of course. I'm glad I could help bring you both some peace."

We stood in contemplative silence for a long moment, processing the experience. The room already felt emptier without Vanessa's spectral presence, though I knew her spirit still lingered in the friendship bonds.

I took a deep breath and followed Gloria onto the front porch, feeling the chilled evening air against my skin. Despite the bittersweet nature of Vanessa and Gloria's farewell, a sense of tranquility settled over me.

Charlotte had made her choices long before I'd walked into Wentworth house. It was a sobering reminder of the impact my abilities could have, not just on the living but on the dead as well.

Davina Benet had called her psychic ability a gift, while I'd considered mine more of a curse. Maybe neither of those extremes was right. My relationship with ghosts wasn't always easy. Connecting with the other side came with challenges few understood. But moments like these made moments like what happened to Charlotte worthwhile.

And if you ever tell anyone I said that, I'll send a ghost to your house. That's a promise.

The sound of boots crunching on gravel drew my attention back to Gloria. She pulled open her door and then turned to face me with a serene expression. She looked as if a weight had been lifted from her shoulders. Bringing two friends back together had been the right thing to do.

She nodded. I nodded back. Once she'd driven away, I stood for a long moment and let my mind clear.

The sun hadn't quite finished setting when a line of steel gray clouds loomed from the east and breathed the first snowflake over the town of Mooselick River. By eight o'clock, the power lines looked like they'd all been covered in white pool noodles. By eight-thirty, snow-weighted birch trees bent their backs into graceful bows, their tops touching the ground to be trapped there by the growing blanket of white.

Fir trees stood like cloaked sentinels or weird, folded umbrellas until those that couldn't handle the strain tipped and fell.

At seven minutes past nine, the power went out in

Mooselick River. It wouldn't come back on for nearly a week. This would go down as the storm of the decade, if not the century.

Before it was over, someone would die.

Thank you for joining Everly as she uncovered long-buried secrets in Mooselick River.

Up next is Wedding Presence, where wedding plans are complicated by a freak snowstorm, a collapsed venue, and, of course, another ghostly mystery.

~Also Available in Audiobook & Paperback Versions~

Quick Author's Note

Unwelcome Ghost gave us the opportunity to delve into the darker corners of Mooselick River's history. Introducing a more menacing spirit challenged Everly in new ways, and we enjoyed weaving this suspenseful tale. As always, Everly's resilience and determination shine through, and we hope you found this mystery as compelling as we did.

With ghosts showing up where they don't belong and the townspeople of Mooselick River growing increasingly suspicious, Everly's getting tired of pretending she's just quirky and not completely haunted. In Wedding Presence, she's got more than her own future on the line—because a certain someone is ready to say "I do"... assuming the spirit world doesn't crash the ceremony.

Anyway, if you've come this far with us and not decided we're complete and total whackadoodles...and especially if you have, we're offering a chance to sign up for our newsletters— the best place to get new release updates, sales notifications, and other fun content.

You can sign up for ReGina's newsletter and/or Erin's newsletter and as a thank-you gift for hanging out with us, you'll also get a FREE novella that isn't available anywhere else. And of course, we promise not to SPAM your inbox!

Love, hugs, and happy reading,
ReGina & Erin

P. S. If you enjoyed this book, it would be great if you could leave a review or recommendation on Amazon, GoodReads, or BookBub.

Your reviews help indie authors sell more books!

EXCERPT FROM
WEDDING PRESENCE

BOOK 12 OF THE HAUNTED
EVERLY AFTER MYSTERIES

At seven minutes past nine, the power went out in Mooselick River and wouldn't come back on for nearly a week. The house went dark and so silent we could hear the shush of wet snow slapping against the window panes. Next to me, Molly let out a quiet woof, then wiggled her butt into my side to get a bit closer.

"You don't realize how many appliances have lights on them until they all go out," Drew's voice came out of the darkness to my left. Unnerving when even though his body touched mine, I couldn't see him at all.

"Light pollution. It's a thing."

The two minutes before the generator kicked on seemed like they might stretch on forever. Maybe it wouldn't come on, that little annoying pessimist in my head insisted. Then it did. Lights flared, appliances beeped. Once again, I blessed Catherine Willowby, my ersatz benefactress, for sparing no expense when making her home something of a fortress. My parents had installed a similar system in the fall, and it cost, if not an arm and a leg, at least a finger and a toe.

Rising, Drew made the rounds to reset all the clocks that flashed the wrong time while I grabbed my phone and checked the Mooselick River community Facebook group. "At least my phone can get online. There are trees and lines down on just about every road in and out of town," I reported when he returned. "They've recalled the road crews because it's too dangerous to plow. I need to check in with all of the tenants."

My job as property manager for Leo Hansen paid better than it should, but then, Leo took good care of his properties, and so long as I kept the tenants off his back, considered the money well-spent. I'd had worse jobs, I decided, as the blanket text went out to those who used cell phones. Only two current tenants still had landlines, but both were in multi-units, so their neighbors could confirm that the generators were on.

One by one, the responses came back. Each taking a bit more worry off my mind.

"David's good," Drew reported. "He's making jokes about living in the Overlook."

"So long as no creepy twins show up, I guess he's safe." My phone dinged with another text notification. "Patrea just checked in. All's well at the farm. My parents are good, too. Just waiting for Jacy and Neena to give the all-clear." I got up and went to the front windows, hoping to see Neena's lights flicker on across the street—if I could even see that far with the amount of snow coming down.

Drew's phone signaled again.

"Brian," he announced. "They're fine. Jacy's checking in with her folks. Anything from Neena?"

"Not yet. Hush, girl. It's okay," I soothed as a muffled thump from outside set Molly barking and sent my heart rate speeding. "Was that a tree?"

"Could be. I'll check." Drew headed toward the coat closet.

"No," I grabbed his arm. "It might not be safe."

Chuckling, he grabbed what he'd gone in there for. His high-powered flashlight. "I was planning to stay on the porch."

Even so, I watched out the window and when the light popped on, got a glimpse at the changes wrought since a wall of unrelenting gray clouds sent the first snowflakes drifting over town. The power wires coming in from the pole bowed under the weight of the snow-formed tubes coating them. It would be a wonder if they didn't break.

Unable to help myself, I stepped outside with Drew to listen to the creak and pop of branches sagging under the growing blanket of white. One of the birches on that side of the house stooped until its lower branches caught in the wrought iron of the backyard gate. It was silly, but the urge rose in me to shake off the snow so the tree could find the sky again before it toppled.

"It'll hold, I think." Drew must have known something of my thoughts because his tone reassured me almost as much as the arm he slung around my shoulders. Turning, he aimed the light across the lawn and driveway to play it over the garage roof where a large fir bough lay half-buried in a furrow of snow. "That must have been the noise we heard. If we're lucky, that branch will be the only thing that falls." He angled the light higher. The pine towered over the garage, its top higher than the light could shine.

"There's nothing we can do about it now except maybe stay away from that side of the house in case it falls."

Shrugging, he followed me back inside. "It'll hit the garage first."

Somehow, with both our vehicles parked inside, that thought failed to offer a basic level of comfort. I'd hardly had my new car long enough to break it in. Still, better to lose a vehicle than part of the house.

Since Neena hadn't answered my text and even from the porch, I couldn't make out whether or not her generator was running, I called. When it rang until her voicemail picked up, worry crawled up and wrapped its icy hands around my throat.

"That's it." I headed back toward the coat closet. "I'm going over there. She's probably hanging off the dining room light again."

Drew stepped in front of me to block my way while he looked at me with puzzlement. "Why would she do a thing like that?"

"Never mind. I can't just sit here if she needs help."

"Why don't you call Dolly? Ask her to go over and check on Neena. Snow shouldn't bother a ghost."

"If I do that, she'll stay. For hours. Or at least as long

as it takes to give me a rundown of the top ten snowstorms in Mooselick River history. Do you want that? Do you? Because I certainly don't."

"I'll go." He shoved past me to grab his boots and coat.

"And leave me here alone to imagine both of you in trouble. Nope. Not happening." I darted around him and snatched up my own boots. "Besides, the visibility sucks. You could get lost and end up wandering around until you freeze to death. I've read Little House on the Prairie. I know things like that happen."

That earned me a quirked grin. "This isn't the prairie. I think I'll be fine."

"If you're going, I'm going with you. We'll tie a rope around the post on the front steps so we can find our way back."

Later, I'd have to give him credit for not laughing in my face as he indulged my latest flight of fancy. "If that makes you feel better. I'll grab a coil of climbing line, and we'll go see if Neena's okay."

Ten minutes later, regret weighing nearly as heavy as the wet coat on my back, we wallowed through sixteen inches of ever-deepening snow on our way to Neena's front door.

"See, I wouldn't have lost my way. It's a straight shot." Her house loomed before us while the rope I'd insisted on using trailed behind.

"Fine. Be right about that if you want, but I don't hear her generator, and I don't see any lights, do you?"

Maybe some of my worry translated to him because

his negative response came in a subdued tone. Once we'd fought our way up the front steps, he banged on the door and called her name loudly. I should have brought her key.

After a minute passed with no response, he didn't bother hiding his concern. "I'll go around and check the other door."

"Not by yourself, you won't. Where you go, I go."

Why we hadn't strapped on snowshoes was one question I barely had the breath to ask myself as I tried to follow his footprints down Neena's driveway. When I slammed into Drew's back, even that one went right out of my head.

"What's wrong?"

"I heard noises in the garage." He changed direction abruptly, and I followed. When we got closer, ours weren't the only footprints through the snow. A set led from the direction of Neena's back door. Relief replaced worry.

"Stupid contraption." Neena's voice, raised in anger, sounded like angels singing to me just before Drew yelled to announce our presence.

"Need some help?"

It wasn't any warmer in the garage, but at least snow wasn't blowing in my face.

Neena stood in the pool of light created by a battery-operated camping lantern, her face a mask of fury tinged with despair.

"I'm glad you're here," she said to Drew. "And annoyed that I need you."

"Thanks," he said. "I think. What's the problem?"

"How should I know? Hudson and his dad set this thing up. They bragged for weeks about routing the exhaust, adding a smart panel to the system, and how it's just the right size for the house and uses far less fuel than one of those on-demand types. You'd think it was a contest or something, the way he went on about it. I followed the instructions, which he painted on the door, even. Switch the power from house to generator, make sure it's full of gas, set the choke, and push the button to start."

So saying, she jabbed the start button. Nothing happened. "So why doesn't it start? Hm? Why? And don't you dare say it's a man thing. I shouldn't have to have a penis to push a button." Turning, Neena kicked the door that gave her access to the lean-to enclosure.

"No. Of course not." Drew held back any comment that might put him in danger. Couldn't say I blamed him. "When was the last time you started it?"

She looked at him like he'd asked the most obvious question in the world. "The last time the power went out."

"That would be last winter? More than a year ago."

"Yes. That's right. Why?"

"Well, I hate to say it, but I suspect your battery is dead. Want me to pull-start it for you? I promise not to use my penis."

His attempt at humor was ill-timed, but after glaring at him for a moment, Neena stepped back and let him do what needed to be done. The engine roared to life, and the lights came on in the house. After a moment, he set the choke and closed the door. "All set."

"Thanks." Calmer now, Neena pushed a dark curl off her forehead. "Sorry. I didn't mean to cause offense to your manhood."

"None taken," Drew smiled. "Once the storm is over, we'll see about replacing the battery."

"No, really. I'm sorry I snapped at you. You guys took the time to check on me, and I acted like a shrew."

Because she seemed to need it, I hugged her. "We're here for you. But if you feel the need, you could repay our kindness by making those amazing wings the next time we have game night."

"You're so easy. I can always buy you with food," she joked. We'd been through a lot since we'd met right after I moved back to town, and there was a time not so long ago when I wasn't sure if our friendship would survive.

"They're really spectacular wings. Call if you need anything."

"Have you heard from everyone else? Jacy?"

"Brian checked in. They were waiting to hear from Jacy's folks. Patrea and Chris are good. David's hunkered down at the inn. All the tenants and my parents reported back."

"Good," Neena nodded. "Eddie Mason nailed it when he predicted this storm, didn't he?"

"They should put him on the news."

With that, we headed back out into the weather. An inch of new snow had already begun to fill in our tracks, and it took Drew a minute or two to find the coil of rope he'd left just outside because visibility was worse than it had been.

Back at home, Molly danced through the snow we tracked inside, then ran out and sailed off the front steps when Drew held the door open. The look of doggy surprise she shot back over her shoulder spoke volumes.

"I'll shovel a spot for her while you check in with Jacy. Then, I'm thinking hot cocoa and a DVD."

"You're on." But I took a few minutes to sweep snow out of the hallway and shed my wet clothes first. Finally beginning to warm up, I stood near the heat vent and read through the texts that had come in while we were gone.

We're fine, Jacy had written. *One of the birch trees crushed Wade's swing set.* A photo in shades of blue and black accompanied the text. *And there's another one on the back deck. Brian says it took out two sections of railings, but he thinks that's the worst of it.*

—Tell Wade Auntie will get him a new swing. We have a branch on the garage roof and just got back from Neena's. Drew had to pull-start her generator. Otherwise, we're good. Your folks okay?

—Mom's worried about her garden, but Dad's taking it all in stride. As usual, they've got all the unprepared neighbors over there. The house is full.

—That should keep her too busy to worry. I answered, thankful that everyone I loved most was okay.

News reports called it the worst spring storm in fifty years. Grammy Dupree would have rated it at a solid three-bathtubs on her scale of how much water it would take to get through the storm.

Wedding Presence is available now. Keep reading for a preview of the free novella you'll get for joining our newsletters.

Excerpt from A Snowball's Chance in Spell

*L*ightning flirted in shadows of the dark clouds hovering over my house when I came home from work the afternoon before my twenty-second Christmas Eve. Nothing unusual there. With three elemental faeries living in the house, weird weather happened all the time. Or rather, every time my temperamental godmothers mounted some sort of snit.

The godmothers idled at snit.

Going back to work wasn't an option. I'd cleared the last match of the year—a lovely couple with a shared affection for online gaming—and I was no coward. When it came to diffusing faerie fights, I consider myself an expert, and this one didn't look like it rated more than a two on the volcano scale.

Yes, you heard right. I measure faerie fights on the scale of whether or not a volcano might erupt in my backyard. Living with faeries is never boring. Occasionally dangerous—especially because I have yet to come into the magic that is my birthright, but never boring.

A quick check proved they'd contained the madness to the inside and/or the backyard. The two feet of snow on the front lawn was still there and still white—you try explaining black snow to your neighbors sometime. I didn't see any winged denizens—fae or otherwise— dotting the roof ridge, or hear any ominous sounds. If not for the fact that lightning is rare in Maine during the winter, and rarer still when confined to a single area, I'd have thought it was a quiet day in the household.

In my head, I downgraded the threat to a level one, and went inside.

For the most part, my place looks like an ordinary, New England style home. Built by my great grandparents, it's the oldest house in a neighborhood that grew up around it when the suburbs expanded into what was once a rural area. Because, I think, the faeries wanted to give me a normal upbringing, they left the house in mostly the same condition it was in when they came to take care of me and only added on a wing for their own use.

I stepped into the front hall expecting...well, just about anything. Did I mention the faeries love holidays? Maybe they don't have them in the faelands, or maybe they do and go overboard there, too. I can't say since I've never been, but I could tell at a glance there were more decorations than there had been when I left.

"Terra!" I yelled, but got no answer. Terra, faerie of earth, held sway over all the flora and fauna found on dry land. She would be the one responsible for the pine boughs twining over anything that held still long enough. Fire faerie, Soleil, contributed by setting sparks of faerie light to twinkle inside the delicate ice bubbles crafted by her sister, Evian, mistress of water. The effect was lovely, but not as lovely as the three women could be when their faces weren't twisted, as they were now, with rage.

I came upon them in their favorite fighting grounds: the kitchen. It looked like I'd caught this one early since there was relatively little damage done so far. Steam rose from a puddle of water at Soleil's feet which I assumed had come from Evian. Vines snaked from between the kitchen tiles to twine around Evian's ankles, and there were a few smoking embers dotting Terra's hair. Nothing more than a minor spat.

Keeping it casual, I asked, "What's going on?" There's no rhyme or reason to what will settle a fight or send one into the red zone.

Terra turned one granite pink eye in my direction. "This doesn't concern you." The fingers of her left hand twitched and the vines slithered from Evian's ankles to her knees.

Retaliating, Evian conjured a gush of water from thin air, and doused the smoking embers. The scent of pine boughs couldn't compete with the stench of burnt hair, or the pungent funk erupting from the flowers that burst into bloom near her feet.

"Now look," I pointed out to Terra before she conjured something worse. "Evian is trying to help."

"Was not." Evian snapped her fingers and turned Terra's wet hair white with frost, except because the vines were now questing higher, she overshot the mark and doused a few of Soleil's decorative sparkles.

That was the moment I lost control.

Oh, who am I kidding? I never had control.

Soleil let out a screech and lobbed a fireball at Evian, who encased it in a ball of water and batted it toward Terra. I felt scoured clean when Terra called all the dirt and dust in the house to form a layer over the bobbing ball of doom which now resembled a small planet whizzing back toward Soleil.

It might have ended better if I'd have kept my mouth shut, but I didn't.

"You're going to put an eye out with that thing."

The ire of three faeries is a potent thing, but not as potent as a flaming mudball. I ducked, rolled, and hit the latch on the patio door in what I'd like to think was a graceful move. Probably looked like a seal rolling off a rock.

The flaming fireball arced over my head, its warm breeze tossing my hair, and rocketed off into the sky.

Crisis averted. Except, it wasn't. I should have known.

A Snowball's Chance in Spell is only available by signing up for one of our newsletters here:
https://reginawelling.com
https://erinlynnwrites.com

OTHER BOOKS

I f you'd like to meet more people who live rent-free in our heads, here's a list of other series we've written. Our books are all set in fictional towns in Maine, and some characters like to flit back and forth between series. The cast of Psychic Seasons hangs out with Everly and also with Lexi Balefire from the Fate Weaver series. Mag and Clara Balefire are Lexi's grandmother and aunt!

Psychic Seasons
Four women, four love stories, and a whole lot of supernatural surprises. In the quaint town of Oakville, Maine, psychic visions, ghostly whispers, and fate itself conspire to change lives—and hearts—forever

Haunted Everly After
Everly Dupree came home for a fresh start—not a full-time gig solving ghostly murders. But when the dearly departed start demanding justice, what's a reluctant medium to do?

Ponderosa Pines Mysteries

Nothing bad ever happens in the weird little town of Ponderosa Pines...until someone dies. Now it's up to best friends Chloe and EV to solve the mystery—before the town's secrets bury them too.

Fate Weaver

Lexi Balefire—matchmaker, witch, and accidental fate-weaver—must balance love, magic, and a family legacy of chaos before destiny decides for her!

Mag and Clara Balefire Mysteries

Sister witches Mag and Clara Balefire move to a sleepy Maine town for a fresh start—only to find themselves conjuring up trouble, solving murders, and keeping their magic under wraps in this charmingly witchy cozy mystery series

Laurel Haven Witches

Four witches, destined by blood and magic, must embrace their power, battle a dark legacy, and surrender to the love that could break the curse—or bind them to it forever.

Nell Page: Accidental Investigator

Nell Page owns a bookstore, drinks too much coffee, and has a habit of noticing things she probably shouldn't. With warmth, wit, and an accidental talent for investigating, Nell tackles mysteries that don't always involve murder—but always matter.

www.ingramcontent.com/pod-product-compliance
Lightning Source LLC
Chambersburg PA
CBHW061642190726
48289CB00006B/1705